Hania Allen was born in Liverp... longer than anywhere else, having ... the country (despite nine months ... ...d three months of bad weather). Of Polish descent, her father was stationed in St Andrews during the war, and spoke so fondly of the town that she applied to study at the university.

She has worked as a researcher, a mathematics teacher, an IT officer and finally in senior management, a post she left to write full time. She is the author of the Von Valenti novels and now lives in a village in Fife.

Also by Hania Allen

DI Dania Gorska Series

THE
MAZE

Hania Allen

CONSTABLE

CONSTABLE

First published in Great Britain in 2024 by Constable

1 3 5 7 9 10 8 6 4 2

Copyright © Hania Allen, 2024

The moral right of the author has been asserted.

A CIP catalogue record for this book
is available from the British Library.

ISBN: 978-1-40871-787-5

Typeset in Bembo by Photoprint, Torquay
Printed and bound in Great Britain by Clays Ltd, Elcograf S.p.A.

Papers used by Constable are from well-managed forests and other
responsible sources.

Constable
An imprint of
Little, Brown Book Group
Carmelite House
50 Victoria Embankment
London EC4Y 0DZ

An Hachette UK Company
www.hachette.co.uk

www.littlebrown.co.uk

CHAPTER 1

'Ach, you're rubbish at this. Here, give them to me.' Ailsa reached across and tugged off the headphones. Before her younger sister could react, she put them on, then, none too gently, snatched the metal detector from the girl's reluctant hand. Since she was taller, she had to adjust its length.

Chloe, who was holding the shovel, watched Ailsa swing the search coil left and right as she walked slowly along the furrow. 'You're not much better at it yourself,' she muttered.

The teenagers had decided to give the field a good going-over, and had been systematically searching for the past two hours. It had been top of their list ever since Ailsa had overheard a guy at school talking to his mates about the vast cache of Roman coins buried around here. She and Chloe had had to wait until school broke for summer and their dad was busy on the combine harvester before they could 'borrow' his metal detector. Fortunately, at this time of year their mum was too busy on the farm to notice her daughters sneaking away.

The headphones, which were sitting loosely on Ailsa's head, had a habit of sliding off. She paused to rearrange them, catching her long, fair hair in the speakers. Although the LCD screen display flashed when anything was detected, she preferred the distinctive tones of the audio. As she adjusted the headband's grip, she became aware of the early chorus of birds, making her wonder why there seemed to be so many crows. She'd been here before on a field trip, but hadn't seen nearly as many.

This area north of Dundee was fields and woodland and little else. But over the gentle rise of the hill lay Alderwood Manor and the surrounding estate. And in the estate was the famous Victorian Maze, which, according to what Ailsa had also overheard, had reopened in May after a long period of renovation. When she'd heard that there was to be a competition to see who could pass through the Maze in the fastest time and – more importantly – discovered how much the prize money was, she and Chloe had decided to make it a priority to learn its secrets, especially as this was no ordinary maze. And for people who knew this part of Dundee well, it was child's play to find a way into the back of the estate and sneak into the Maze without paying.

'Well, are you going to get on with it or what?' Chloe said. 'We haven't much time left.'

Ailsa made a point of ignoring her. She squinted into the July sunshine, then lifted the detector and resumed the search, swinging the coil rhythmically. So far, their hoard consisted of several beer-bottle tops, an old pre-decimal penny and a metal button.

She'd reached the edge of the field and had moved on to the grassy border when a change in tone came from the detector.

'I've got something,' she called.

Chloe, who'd been playing with her mobile, hurried over. 'Where?'

'Just here.' Ailsa moved the device slowly. The sound waxed and waned, allowing her to pinpoint the location.

Without waiting, Chloe thrust the tip of the shovel into the grass. After several goes, she succeeded in pulling back the turf.

The ground underneath was dry, thanks to the recent lack of rain. She dropped to her knees and, ignoring the curls falling into her eyes, dug deeper, stopping now and then to run her hands through the dark earth.

'Keep going,' Ailsa commanded.

'No, wait, I've got it.' She lifted something out of the soil.

Ailsa bent over, trying to make out what her sister was holding.

'Aye, I think it's a coin,' Chloe said excitedly.

'Hold on.' Ailsa fished in her rucksack and removed a water bottle. She poured the water over the coin, getting much of it over her sister's hands.

Chloe ran the object down the side of her jeans, then held it up. 'There's a man's head. He's wearing a crown.'

'What's on the other side?'

She flipped it over. 'Looks like a lion standing on something.' She brought it close to her eyes. 'It says 1939. And 1945 underneath.'

'It's a war medal,' Ailsa said, straightening. 'See that bar at the top? There'd be a ribbon attached to it, ken.'

'So, where is it?'

'Must have rotted away.'

'Do you think it's worth anything?'

Ailsa tilted her head. 'Aye, well, it will be to the person who lost it.'

'What do we do with it, eh?'

'We should hand it in to the polis.'

'Won't they ask how we got it?'

'We'll say we found it lying somewhere.' Ailsa looked around. 'In those woods.'

Chloe looked unconvinced. She followed the direction of her sister's gaze. 'I vote we have a keek in there.'

'Why?'

'Whoever told you there are Roman coins here seems to have got his facts wrong. There's nothing in this field. But maybe there's something in the woodland.'

Ailsa studied her sister. For once, she might be on to something. The guy at school had prattled on about the area west of Emmock Road, and given a reasonably clear description of how far north to drive before the turn-off, but the more she thought about it the more she was starting to question whether this really was the right place. When it came to burying treasure, woodland was a better bet than a field, which would be ploughed regularly.

Chloe wiped her muddy fingers on the grass, and pulled back the sleeve of her sweatshirt. She peered at her watch. 'We've got time. Let's just go in a wee way.'

'Ach, fine. But if we find anything, you do the digging.'

'Don't I always?' Chloe said sulkily.

They made for the trees.

The previous autumn had carpeted the ground, and the damp winter had turned the leaves into a rotting mulch. The absence of footprints or disturbance in the leaves made it clear that few people came here. Did that mean that no one had yet poked around? And found the treasure? Ailsa felt her spirits rise.

The girls ventured further into the wood, Ailsa skimming the detector over the ground. A sudden loud cawing made her pause. The crows rose into the air, flapping their ragged wings. As she turned her head to the left, gazing between the column-like tree trunks, she spotted something that looked out of place. Everywhere the ground was flat. But a short distance away, in front of a line of closely packed trees, it curved into a long mound.

'You think that's it?' Chloe said, glancing at Ailsa.

'No, that's not it.'

'How do you know?' Chloe said, a note of defiance in her voice.

'Treasure would be buried deeper than that.'

But the instant she said it, she knew she'd have to go and investigate.

Chloe was chewing her thumb. 'I think there's a body under there. It's the right length for a Roman soldier.'

'Aye, and when was the last time you saw a Roman soldier?' Ailsa said, not bothering to keep the sarcasm out of her voice.

Yet she had to admit that the mound would easily accommodate a man. Could it be one of these burial barrows she'd learnt about in school? She made her way through the trees, mentally ticking off the possibilities. One was that someone had indeed found the treasure but, rather than take it home, he'd reburied it, giving him time to decide what to do with it. He was probably scouring sites online where he could sell it.

The mound was covered with leaves. Ailsa was tempted simply to kick them away, but something made her hesitate. She lifted the detector and ran it over the barrow. The sudden noise in the headphones was so loud that even Chloe couldn't have failed to hear it. Before she could stop her, Chloe had dropped to her knees and was pushing away the leaves.

It was the gleam of metal that made Ailsa grab her sister's arm and drag her away. Chloe tumbled on to her back.

'Hey, what the hell did you do that for?' she yelled. 'You told me to dig.'

But Ailsa had stopped listening. She was staring at what was clearly a pistol. And the hand that was holding it, the fingers reduced almost to bone. Slowly, she became aware of the crows, sitting not far from the barrow, watching. And waiting . . .

5

'So, don't you want me to keep digging?' Chloe asked petulantly. She hauled herself to her feet and brushed soil off her clothes.

'We're getting out of here,' Ailsa said, her voice sounding strange.

'Why?'

'There's a body under there.'

'A Roman soldier?'

'Did the Romans carry pistols?' Ailsa snapped.

Chloe stared at the mound. Her expression changed. She brought a trembling hand to her mouth. 'We need to call the polis.'

'We're leaving, and we're not telling anyone we were here.' Seeing the doubt on her sister's face, Ailsa gripped her arm and added, 'You know fine well what will happen if we do. We'll be up to our necks in the brown stuff.'

'Because we took Dad's metal detector without his permission?'

'No, you numpty. Because we took Dad's *car* without his permission.' She closed her eyes briefly. 'Neither of us has a driving licence. Remember?'

CHAPTER 2

'I take it you've not been here before, boss.'

'Alderwood Manor?' Dania shook her head. 'My first time. You?'

'Same.' Honor steered the car smoothly on to Strathmartine Road.

Dania had been along Strathmartine on a previous case that took her way up north to Balkello. On her return, she'd marvelled at the view, a dizzyingly vast sky that stretched from horizon to horizon over Dundee's spires and old jute chimneys. As fine views of Dundee went – and there were many – it was one of the best.

DI Dania Gorska and DS Honor Randall were off shift, and had decided to spend the afternoon at Alderwood Manor estate. It had been the article written by Dania's brother, coinciding with the reopening of the Victorian Maze two months earlier, that had prompted them to visit Alderwood. The Maze had been closed for several years for a major refurbishment, and the good citizens of Dundee had been pawing the ground to see what it looked like now.

'And how is your brother liking the new job?' Honor said.

'Marek? He seems to be enjoying his promotion.'

'Principal investigative journalist. That must come with a hefty increase in salary.'

Dania smiled. 'With Marek, it's never the money.'

'I did wonder why he'd left DC Thomson to take a position with a new newspaper.'

'He told me he has more freedom. He can start an investigation without needing permission from the top brass. And he's managed to negotiate some time for himself.'

'How does that work?'

'He might take on an assignment that wouldn't necessarily lead to an article. He gets those now and again.'

'Does he have people working for him?'

'A few.'

'If he's as good a boss as you are, boss, he'll have no difficulty getting them to follow orders.'

'Are you trying to butter me up, Honor?'

'Yep. I'm hoping you'll pay my entrance fee.'

Dania laughed. 'It's done.'

'Already?'

'I bought the tickets online. Numbers are restricted, so I applied early.'

'Do you think the place will be heaving?'

'Friday afternoon? I expect so.'

They turned on to the A90. 'So, when's the Maze competition?' Honor said, pressing down on the accelerator.

'I think it's the end of August.'

'You know, when I heard what the prize money was, I nearly fainted.'

'I'm betting you have to pay to enter, and the fee will be almost as much,' Dania said cynically. 'Are you thinking of giving it a go?'

'I'll reserve judgement till I've seen what the Maze is like.'

But Dania knew that Honor would almost certainly enter. There was something about competitions that she couldn't resist.

But whether it was to prove herself to others, or only to herself, Dania had never been able to establish.

They'd reached Old Glamis Road. Minutes later, the sat-nav directed them on to Emmock. The road narrowed considerably. Or appeared to. It was the stone walls and overhanging branches with their canopy of leaves that gave the impression they were hemmed in.

'And how is Marek coping with having a woman for a boss?' Honor said suddenly.

'Probably as well as you are.'

'Have you met her?'

'Not yet. Okay, watch out for the entrance.'

'On it.'

Honor slowed almost to a crawl. She must have spotted the ornamental gates on the right because she took the turn-off in good time. They followed a road surfaced with tarmac. On either side were pyramidal hedges trimmed to perfection, a task that must have required an army of gardeners. Dania was relieved there were no potholes as they'd taken her Fiat 500. Honor had insisted on driving, not because Dania's rank had its privileges, but because she claimed to know this area of Dundee well. By that, Dania concluded that her latest man lived somewhere around here.

A minute or so later, they passed a small stone building set back from the road. A sign told passers-by that this was Alderwood Manor Lodge. It looked deserted. Perhaps, in the past, visitors to the Manor had had to stop here and wait while the estate keeper checked a register, then phoned through that they had arrived. Or lifted his shotgun and told them to clear off. Peering between the hedges gave visitors a glimpse of manicured lawns. The marble statues dotted about were of scantily clad women draped with garlands of flowers.

At the end of the short drive, there was a huge house with honey-stone walls, its wings capped with steep, tiled roofs. Ornamental planters, their flowers spilling colour on to the ground, stood either side of the entrance. Dania's first thought was that she hoped the sash windows were double-glazed as she'd been in such houses before. When the wind blew, the windows rattled alarmingly and the draught was sometimes strong enough to disturb the curtains.

A man was standing watching the car approach. He checked their tickets, then smilingly but firmly directed them to the right.

At least he didn't have a shotgun, Dania thought, putting away her phone.

They followed the arrows to a field that had been converted into a car park. From the number of vehicles, it was clear everywhere would be crowded.

'Do you think it's the Maze they've all come to see, boss?' Honor said, pulling into the nearest free space.

'I'm not sure. There are other activities on offer. Mind you, the Maze might be the big attraction. Everyone seems to know about the murders that took place there.'

Honor switched off the ignition. 'That's news to me,' she said, looking curiously at Dania.

'You didn't read my brother's article carefully enough.'

'I have to confess that I didn't read it at all. Who was murdered, then?'

'Several members of the McGarry family. All siblings.'

'Crikey. When was this?'

'Sometime during the Victorian era. Not long after the Maze was built, in fact.'

'What happened? Why were they murdered?'

'The oldest was in line to inherit. He was the first McGarry found dead in the Maze.'

'Don't tell me. One by one, the others were killed, too.'

'And in order of age, until there was only the youngest left.'

'Surely he was the prime suspect.'

'And he was able to prove that he'd been nowhere near the estate each time a body was found.'

'But I bet forensics then wasn't what it is now.'

'I'm sure our scientists would have shredded his evidence. Anyway, he inherited. The husband of the present owner, Glenna McGarry, is a direct descendant. But they're divorced, and I understand he no longer has a claim to the estate.'

Honor was frowning. 'I had no idea the place has such a rich history.'

'Marek did some digging in the archives. It was all about dynastic power.'

'Like *Game of Thrones*.'

Dania smiled. 'But without the nudity and the dragons.'

They left the car. The air was sticky with humidity. 'Do you think it's going to rain?' Dania said, studying the sky.

'If it does, it'll rain for forty days. And if it doesn't, it'll be fine weather for forty days.'

'How do you make that out?'

'It's July the fifteenth. St Swithin's Day.' Honor looked cheekily at Dania. 'Are you superstitious, boss?'

Dania threw her a warning look. 'It's unlucky to be superstitious.'

They followed the signs to the Maze, passing the Manor. A peek through the conservatory windows revealed a red-tiled floor, cream rattan furniture and tubs planted with small orange trees. There was even a tiny fountain. As Dania turned away, she thought

11

she saw a shadow move near the door into the house. Someone had been sitting in the conservatory. Glenna McGarry, perhaps?

As if echoing her thoughts, Honor said, 'So, this Glenna McGarry is the book publisher, right?'

'She bought up the company, which was running at a loss, and turned it round. It's made her extremely wealthy. Mind you, she was wealthy before.'

'Yep, I remember now. She was interviewed on the radio. There's also a newspaper arm to the company, isn't there?'

'*Dundee Today.*'

'Which is the newspaper Marek now works for,' Honor said triumphantly. 'I've finally joined the dots.'

'I've heard that *Dundee Today* is selling better than either the *Courier* or the *Evening Telegraph*.'

'I'm sure that's largely down to your brother.'

'*He* says it's largely down to his boss. She's always ahead of the game when it comes to publishing what Dundonians want to read.' They'd stopped under a tree alive with sparrows. 'Which way now?' Dania said, studying the warning on the adjacent post: it was forbidden to allow unaccompanied children into the Maze, children had to be supervised at all times, and the owners of the estate would take no responsibility if these rules were not followed and visitors came to harm.

'Hang on, there's a QR code.' Honor whipped out her mobile and held it over the image. 'Great, here's a map of the estate.'

'Can you download it?'

'Done. So, which do we try first, boss? We have a choice: zipwire through the trees, although it's a bit of a trek to get there. And there's a treetop walk. Then there's the Maze. It's behind that wall.'

Before Honor could continue, Dania said quickly, 'I don't fancy the zipwire. Or the treetop walk.'

'That's what I reckoned. The Maze it is, then,' Honor added eagerly. She sounded as keen to try it as Dania was.

Behind the wall was hedging, which disappeared in both directions. Next to the gap in the hedge was a sign declaring that this was the entrance to Alderwood Manor Maze.

Honor ran a hand over the bright green leaves. 'Hey, this is artificial.'

'That's right. The whole Maze is like this.'

'I should have read Marek's article.'

'You know what makes this Maze unique?' Dania asked, realising that, if Honor hadn't heard about the main feature, she was in for a surprise.

'I don't, boss. I assume that if you keep one hand on the wall, you'll be home in time for cocktails.'

'I think that might be a labyrinth rather than a maze.' She felt a smile creep on to her lips. 'Tell you what, let's just go in and see what happens.'

'Lead on.'

A short distance beyond the entrance, a hedge barred their way.

'Where now, Honor? Left or right. You choose.'

'Let's go left.'

Dania had been in mazes that would have finished off anyone suffering from claustrophobia. But although the hedges were tall, the paths between them were wide enough that she didn't feel hemmed in.

They stopped in front of a dark statue standing on a plinth.

'This is the famous Minotaur,' Dania said.

'What's famous about it?'

'It was made especially for the Maze, which means it's unique. Mind you, this statue looks too new. Either it's had a makeover, or it's a copy.'

Honor was staring at the bulge under the Minotaur's skirt. Her gaze drifted to the bull's head with its horns and ring through the nose. And its fierce expression. The creature was brandishing an axe in each hand. 'He doesn't do it for me,' she said. 'I'm not sure I'd even like to get acquainted.' She moved away, playing with her phone. 'There doesn't seem to be a map of the Maze, boss. Do you happen to know if there's only one way out?'

'I remember reading that there are several.'

At the end of the path, they turned right, seeing another statue at the far end. They were partway along when, with no prior warning, a grinding sound shattered the calm. Dania felt a tremor under her feet.

Honor wheeled round. The Minotaur had followed them, taking up position at the corner of the path. It glared menacingly at Honor.

'Boss,' she murmured. 'Am I seeing things?'

Dania laughed. 'You're not. Or, rather, you are. The statues in this maze can move. For that matter, so can some of the hedges.' She indicated the ground, which was criss-crossed with what looked like tram lines. 'There are wheels under some of the objects, and they roll along these tracks. According to Marek's article, the Victorians were famous for building automatons, and the designer of this maze decided to use a similar mechanism here.'

'What about health and safety?' Honor said primly. 'Or did the Victorians not care about that?'

'Nothing moved while people were in the Maze. The owners shifted things around after everyone had left, so the Maze was different the next time it opened. Now, though, objects move with visitors still inside.' Dania peered up towards the top of the hedge. 'Marek said there are cameras everywhere. Someone, somewhere, can see everything that's going on. They'll be careful not to do anything that might cause an accident. But the cameras seem well hidden.'

'How did Marek come by this intel?' Honor said. She'd dropped to her knees and was running her fingers over the tram lines.

'He interviewed Glenna McGarry for his article. She has the blueprints for the old Maze. There were underground tunnels everywhere. She even had the diagrams showing how the objects were moved. So, for example, with the Minotaur, someone would open a trapdoor under the pedestal, wind up the mechanism, and then flick a switch to get the statue going. And then close off the trapdoor.'

'Is that how it's done now?' Honor said. She was back on her feet, brushing the dust off her jeans.

'The tunnels are no longer in use. In fact, I suspect they've been filled in. Nowadays, it's all done electronically. The operator sits in front of a large screen, getting feeds from the cameras, and seeing who is standing where. He or she then works the controls and, hey presto, something moves.'

'Hardware *and* software, then.'

'It's taken years to get the Maze rebuilt so it can be operated this way,' Dania said, standing back to let a group of people pass.

'And what happens during the competition?' Honor asked, as they wandered on, running into people coming from the opposite direction.

'I've no idea. I once took part in a maze competition in Poland, where you had to collect items as you went along. I suspect that here it's whoever reaches one of the exits first.'

'I didn't know there were mazes in Poland.'

'There's a famous one in Zakopane, although I think it's a labyrinth. It's made of snow. There's a castle and ice statues, and so on.'

'Whoa! It's made of snow? You know, boss, the more you tell me about your country, the more I want to visit.'

They rounded a corner. At the end of the long path, a statue of a knight in full armour turned slowly towards them. With his left hand, he lifted his visor. His glowing eyes stared in their direction.

'Now, *that* is creepy,' Honor muttered, slowing down.

'I'm inclined to agree. It means that someone is following our every move.'

Honor was looking distinctly spooked. 'Let's go back and find another route,' she said. Without waiting for a response, she turned round. But at that moment, the hedge on one side swung through ninety degrees, blocking her way.

'Looks as if we'll have to keep going,' Dania said.

They could now take only one path, so they pressed on until they came to a choice of direction. Hearing voices, Dania steered Honor towards them.

'Look, Chloe, I'm telling you it moved,' a girl's voice said.

'The trouble with you, Ailsa, is that you can never accept you're wrong.'

Two teenagers were staring upwards, shielding their eyes from the sun. Perched in a row at the top of the hedge were several huge birds that Dania couldn't identify. They stared down without expression. Now and again, one of them moved its head, or fluffed out its wings.

'Cripes. It's like something out of *The Birds*,' Honor murmured.

One of the creatures had black feathers tipped with red, and a huge curved beak. As Dania stepped away, it moved its head so that it had her in its sights. She half expected it to swoop down and attack her. In some ways, she found this more disconcerting than the moving Minotaur, or the knight lifting his visor.

Honor seemed to have regained her composure. 'There must be a hidden camera inside one of those things. Look at the way they're moving their heads.'

'See that one right at the end?' Dania said loudly. 'I wonder how far it can extend its wings.'

As if the bird could hear – and understand – her, it spread its wings, flapping them slowly before folding them again.

The experiment had told Dania what she'd wanted to know: there were hidden microphones as well as cameras. She'd need to ask Marek about them.

The teenagers had slipped away. Dania wondered how old they were, given that unaccompanied children were expressly forbidden. The fair-haired girl had thrown her an insolent look as if to say: *I'm old enough to be here, so mind your own business.* The one with the wild curls had avoided Dania's gaze, making her suspect that they were indeed underage.

She and Honor continued through the Maze, coming across visitors who were either trying to find their way back to the main entrance, or wandering aimlessly, simply enjoying the experience. From time to time, they heard the grinding noise as something moved behind them. But whoever was operating the Maze seemed to have lost interest in them, because all the hedges and statues on their route remained in position. Dania, who had a good sense of direction, pressed forward, as she suspected that some exits were to be found on the side opposite the entrance.

Honor was keeping a hand on the hedging. 'What do you think happens when it's closing time and there are people still in here?'

17

'I think the Minotaur is released and chases people out. What does it say on your download?'

She peered at the phone. 'Okay, so there are arrow-shaped lights in the ground. They're illuminated when it's near closing time.'

More grinding behind them, followed by peals of laughter as people found themselves trapped. Or released.

It took roughly an hour before they finally reached a gap in the hedge. Dania spotted a field with dense woodland beyond. She wondered how far the estate stretched.

They left the Maze and made their way back to the main entrance. Dania counted three more exits, and those were just on one side. There would doubtless be exits elsewhere. But given that there were also tram lines on the outer path, it was likely that the hedges that formed the perimeter could move in such a way as to close off one or more exits, and open them up elsewhere. It all depended on the whim of the operator. She wondered where the controls were. Inside the Manor, perhaps? But who worked them? Maybe the person whose shadow she'd glimpsed in the conservatory had been away to the control room to start the operation. Yet surely this wasn't Glenna McGarry, the publishing magnate. Working the Maze looked like a full-time job.

Honor broke into her thoughts. 'Are you thinking of entering the competition, boss?'

'I'm thinking that we have time to try the zipwire. Or we could get coffee and cake in town. But we can't do both, as I have to be somewhere later.'

Honor ran a hand down her skinny red jeans. 'Right. So, it's another activity. Or it's a café in town.' She made a weighing motion with her hands. 'Zipwire. Or coffee and cake.' She smiled slyly. 'Tough choice.'

CHAPTER 3

Marek Gorski was in the kitchen, checking that everything bubbling away was under control. He had one of those stoves with six rings instead of the usual four and, if he didn't keep an eye on what was going on, mayhem could ensue. He opened the bottle of Australian Shiraz to let it breathe. Nothing but the best for his sister. She was coming for dinner, and he wanted to hear how she'd got on with the Maze.

He was setting the plates to warm when he heard the buzzer. He hurried into the corridor and threw open the door. 'Come in, Danka. You're exactly on time.'

'Why do you sound so surprised?'

'Because I *am* surprised. You're usually late. But that's because something's come up at the last minute,' he added hastily, seeing her expression.

'It's a detective's life,' his sister said, slipping off her jacket. 'It must be the same with you.'

'Ah, but I can delegate now.'

In the kitchen, he handed Danka a glass of Shiraz. 'Now tell me,' he said, pouring one for himself, 'how did you like the Maze? It was this afternoon, right?'

'Right. Honor and I were off shift at the same time. That

19

doesn't happen often.' She sipped the wine. He was relieved by the appreciative look on her face. When it came to red wine, his sister had standards. Mind you, he was like that with vodka.

'She was a bit unnerved by the moving statues,' Danka went on.

'That's not like her. She strikes me as someone who's never fazed by anything.'

'Well, everyone has something that spooks them. With you, it's spiders, I seem to remember. That smells wonderful, by the way.'

'It's *bigos*. We're having it with dill potatoes.'

'What's in all the other pots? You've got six on the go.'

'Five have *bigos*. I've decided to make it in bulk and freeze most of it.' He threw her a crooked smile. 'I have less time to cook now.'

'The perils of promotion. Have you tried making it in a slow cooker?'

'I haven't, no. That'll be my next experiment. Right, I'm ready to serve up. Why don't you go through, and I'll bring it in?'

Over dinner, they discussed their work, as far as they were able to. Marek knew there were things that Danka couldn't go into, and the same was true of him and his investigations.

'And have you signed off on your last?' he said. 'The corpse in the bedroom?'

It was a case that had fascinated Dundee. A woman's body had been found in a Lochee apartment just after New Year. She'd been lying on her back in bed. The press had run with the story, calling it the 'Sleeping Beauty Murder'. Solving the case rested on establishing the time of death, which becomes notoriously harder to calculate the longer the post-mortem interval. The woman had been asphyxiated, but the husband had an alibi, which the police were able to verify. It was when one of the forensics officers examined the ice-cube tray in the freezer that their suspicions were raised. The couple had taken to setting a penny on top of one of the ice cubes. If the electricity was off for any length of time, which seemed to happen frequently where they lived, the ice melted and the penny sank to the bottom, where it stayed when the water refroze. The forensics officer – who did this herself ever since she'd had a nasty bout of food poisoning when her freezer contents had thawed and refrozen after a power outage – saw the coin at the bottom of the tray and contacted the power company. They confirmed that the electricity had been off for the best part of a week, which explained why the freezer's contents had defrosted. But with the electricity off, and the apartment badly insulated against the plummeting outside temperature, the time of death had to be adjusted accordingly. And when it was, the husband's alibi no longer stacked up. After persistent questioning, he confessed to his wife's murder.

Marek listened attentively. 'You know, Danka, that would make a great plot for a crime novel. You should consider changing jobs.'

'Talking of which, how are you getting on at *Dundee Today*?'

'I'm loving it. It was a good move.'

'When am I going to meet your boss?'

'Clare?' He refilled his sister's glass. 'I'll have to have you both over for dinner.'

'She could have come this evening.'

'She's away at the moment. Back on Sunday.'

'Is she married?'

'She was. But they divorced soon after.'

'What is she like as a boss?'

Marek puffed out his cheeks. 'Calm, thinks before she speaks, is willing to listen to my ideas. It makes a welcome change. My boss at DC Thomson was always on a short fuse.'

'And you said that she gives you plenty of rein.'

'That's the best of it. I can follow my instincts. She encourages it, in fact.' He gathered up the plates. 'I'll fetch the *sernik*.'

He returned with the cheesecake.

'There was something I wanted to ask you about the Maze,' Danka said.

'Fire away.' He cut through the soft creamy dessert, savouring the smell of vanilla. Baked cheesecakes were the best. Fortunately, his sister agreed with him.

'I know there are hidden cameras everywhere,' she said, 'but I wasn't aware of the microphones.'

He passed her a plate. 'How did you work that out? Most people don't know about them.'

'There was a huge bird on top of one of the hedges. I said to Honor that I wondered how far it could extend its wings. And the bird immediately obliged by showing me.'

'The microphones were installed with the cameras.'

'Why?'

'It's all part of the fun. Someone says something, and the operator tries to find a way of responding. So, for example, if you suggest going in a particular direction, the operator can immediately bar your way by moving a hedge. Or not.'

'Where does the operator sit?'

'At the side of the Maze, there's what looks like a shed. It's the control centre.'

'Must be a full-time job.'

'Not necessarily. Sometimes nothing in the Maze moves because there's no operator.'

'This cheesecake is delicious, Marek.'

He smiled, feeling self-conscious all of a sudden. 'I'm glad you think so. I baked it myself.'

'I thought you no longer had time for that,' she said playfully.

'When it comes to dessert, I make an exception.'

'Your own recipe?'

'It's our grandmother's.'

Danka smiled, and lifted her fork. 'Well, if it doesn't work out at *Dundee Today*, you've another career lined up. You can supply baked cheesecake to the *Polski Sklep*.'

They ate in silence, always a good sign. He'd been anxious that the pastry wouldn't come out properly, as it was the first time he'd made it. To him, it was on the heavy side, but it had received the seal of approval from his sister, which was what counted. He cut them another slice each, then left to make the coffee.

He returned to find that Danka had finished the cheesecake, and was eyeing up his second slice.

'I wonder what it must have been like operating the original Maze,' she said, as he set the mug in front of her. 'The place is huge, so those tunnels would have been like a rabbit warren. I expect it was a massive operation to fill them in.'

'From something Glenna told me, they're still there.'

Danka stared at him. 'How do you get into them?'

'I've no idea. It can't be from the control room, as that's a fairly recent construction. Maybe there's no one left who knows. After all, the Maze was out of use for as long as anyone can remember.'

'Didn't you see anything in the blueprints?'

'I didn't look too closely, to be honest.' He sat back, studying her. 'Are you asking me these questions because you're going to enter the competition?'

'I've decided against it,' she said, playing with the mug. 'With everything moving around, the odds are stacked against the competitors.' She tilted her head. 'What are the rules?'

He lifted his hands. 'No one knows. It's a well-kept secret, from what I understand.'

She was watching him in silent concentration. He could tell that she didn't believe him. She thought he was intending to use his friendship with Glenna McGarry to wheedle everything out of her and win the competition himself. But that was the furthest from his mind. His claustrophobia would ensure that he went nowhere near that Maze.

'Play something for me, Danka.'

She rose promptly and strolled over to the piano. He smiled. He never did have to persuade her. She lived for music. Once again, he asked himself why his sister hadn't pursued a career as a concert pianist. She'd have made far more than she did as a detective. She pulled out the stool and settled herself. After a glance over her shoulder, she brought her hands down on the keys.

'What the heck was that?' Marek said, when she'd finished.

'It's "The Teddy Bears' Picnic" in the style of Chopin.'

'The poor man will be rolling in his grave. What on earth possessed you?'

'I heard "Happy Birthday" played in the same manner, and it got me thinking. I've been adapting well-known pieces.' She grinned. 'Do you want to hear "Chattanooga Choo Choo"?'

'Not particularly. Let me hear something Chopin actually wrote.'

She turned to the keyboard and played one of the composer's livelier waltzes, which Marek recognised immediately. He loved the way it set itself up for the mad sprint towards the end.

'Fabulous,' he said dreamily.

She gazed at him, frowning.

'What are you thinking, Danka?'

'I'm wondering if it's going to rain before the day is over.'

'Why?'

'Today's St Swithin's Day.'

'Ah.'

24

CHAPTER 4

Marek Gorski backed his black Audi Avant into the parking spot. One of the disadvantages of his new post was that the premises on East Dock Street, which were the headquarters of *Dundee Today*, were just a tad too far for him to walk. But this was compensated for to some extent by having his own designated parking space.

He locked the vehicle, and sauntered across the car park. It was hard to believe that this area had once been full of alehouses frequented by sailors fresh off the three-masted ships docking here. Now, there were garages and retail parks. And the old gasworks further along. But the converted warehouse where he worked was not too far from Gallagher Retail Park, so he could get his lunch from M&S Simply Food.

Inside the building, he nodded to the receptionist, who rewarded him with her usual relaxing smile, and made for the huge open-plan area. As always, it was thrumming with activity.

Clare Conlee was leaning over someone's shoulder, peering at his computer screen. She said something to the man, which caused him to laugh. Seeing Marek, she smiled and indicated with a nod that he should come to her office.

'Take a seat, Marek,' she said, when they were inside. She had a soft, unhurried voice, and an unwavering smile. And a beautifully formed mouth. But it was her brown eyes that held everyone who spoke to her. They were wide, as though constantly astonished by what they saw.

He pulled out a chair at the table used for meetings, wondering if today would be the day when the long, blonde hair piled on top of Clare's head would come tumbling down. He'd never been close enough to see how it was fastened, but it looked too loose to stay up for long. And yet it always did.

'I loved your recent article about the upmarket cocaine dealer who handed out business cards at student parties,' Clare said, taking the chair opposite. 'We're going to run with that in tomorrow's edition.'

It had been a stroke of luck on Marek's part to be slipped this piece of intel by one of his informants. The dealer, concluding that he had a huge market in the student community, had decided to turn up at their regular raves. It hadn't taken Marek long to infiltrate the community and pose as a student, albeit a mature one. His bodycam had captured the dealer in the act of handing out his cards. Marek, pretending to want some sniff, had had a card thrust into his hand. He'd followed it up the next day, phoning the man, and was taken through the protocol: he was directed to an address in the West End, where he was to push the money through the letterbox, and a small bag would be pushed out. Marek had been accompanied by the Drugs Squad, who'd watched with interest as he'd shoved in the tenners. When the bag of white powder that appeared promptly was confirmed to contain cocaine, the squad had broken down the door and arrested the dealer. The huge stash found in his elegant Edwardian home would be enough to have him locked away for a considerable time.

'Who'd have thought that such a pillar of the community would turn out to be a cocaine dealer?' Clare said, gazing at Marek.

'It makes a change from buying the stuff on the street. And it's safer for the buyer.'

'I understand that the head of the Drugs Squad has been speaking to the students.' She inclined her head. 'Do you think it will have any effect?'

'I doubt it,' Marek said, remembering the overheard conversations. One of the students had talked about his daily routine of sniffing, and how he couldn't wait for that kick and flash. 'Locking up a dealer is like cutting off a hydra's head, Clare. Two more spring up. But I understand that the Drugs Squad's informants will be attending the student parties incognito from now on.'

She laughed. 'That'll be fun for everyone.' She made a silent clapping motion. 'Anyway, well done.'

He smiled his acknowledgement, and got to his feet.

As he was leaving the room, his phone rang.

'Marek Gorski speaking,' he said, pulling the door shut behind him.

'Mr Gorski? My name is Luca Terranova. You don't know me, but I need your help.'

'I'm listening.'

'Can we meet this afternoon? I'm staying at the Hampton by Hilton.'

'I know it. What time would suit you?'

'Shall we say two thirty?'

'Downstairs in the lounge?'

A pause. 'Would you mind meeting me in my room? I wouldn't want our conversation to be overheard.'

'I understand. That won't be a problem.'

'Thank you.'

Before Marek could ask for the room number, the man rang off.

At 2.30 p.m., Marek strolled into the Hampton. At this time of afternoon, the lounge was empty, which meant that he could have met Terranova there without fear of being overheard. But still, it wasn't up to him to set the rules for meetings.

'Hi, Marek,' the receptionist said, grinning. He was a keen-eyed man in his thirties, and had a husky, smoker's voice because he breakfasted daily on a packet of cigarettes. He and Marek went back a long way to the time a drunken customer had thrown a punch, which might have landed on the receptionist's face had Marek not stepped in and wrestled the man to the ground. Since then, he'd shared the odd drink with the receptionist, and the receptionist had shared with him anything he'd overheard that might interest an investigative journalist.

'Can I get you a wee bevvy, Marek?'

'I'm afraid I'm working.'

'What about a glass of something without alcohol? Can you get alcohol-free vodka?'

'Yes, it's called water.' Marek leant on the counter. 'I had a call from a Luca Terranova asking me to meet him in his room.'

'Aye, he mentioned it earlier. Interesting name. Wasn't *Terra Nova* Amundsen's ship?'

'I believe it was Scott's. Can you give me the room number?'

The receptionist peered at the screen. 'It's room twenty-three.'

'Thanks. And will you call him and let him know I'm coming?'

'Sure. So, when are we going out on the town again?' the man called after Marek.

Marek smiled over his shoulder. 'I'll text you when I'm free.'

There was a queue at the lift. He needed the exercise, so he took the stairs two at a time.

Room 23 was partway down the corridor. He knocked loudly. The door opened so quickly that he suspected the occupant had been standing waiting for him. With those dark eyes and black hair smoothed back over his head, he reminded Marek of a Sicilian gangster. His next impression was that the face looked familiar. Yes, he'd definitely seen it before.

'I'm Luca Terranova,' the man said, smiling. He had a quiet, silky voice, and spoke with an English accent. 'Thank you for coming at such short notice, Mr Gorski.'

Terranova. Of course, he should have known. 'You must be related to *Piero* Terranova,' he said.

'He's my twin brother.'

As Luca ushered him into the large room, Marek caught the musky scent of expensive cologne.

'Please do take a seat,' Luca said, indicating the blue-fabric sofa. 'I've had coffee sent up.' A coffee pot and crockery stood on the table, but Marek's gaze was drawn to the plate of multicoloured macaroons. 'Unless you'd prefer tea?' Luca added.

'Coffee will be fine.'

Their coffees poured, Luca settled himself in the chair opposite, and unbuttoned the jacket of his tailored grey suit. Marek half expected to see a gun holster, but the Italian was simply making himself comfortable. 'Mr Gorski, you're probably wondering why I've contacted you. It's to do with my brother, Piero.'

'Go on.'

'You know, of course, that he's a fashion designer.'

'I think most of Dundee has been to the V&A to see his exhibition. Some have been more than once.'

29

The clothes, all women's, were – as Clare Conlee had informed him – fabulously designed and fabulously expensive. She had been quick off the mark in getting an exclusive with Piero, sending one of her more experienced journalists to the V&A to interview him. She herself had unfortunately been called out of town, so had asked Marek to attend the opening reception as her representative. He'd hoped for a brief chat with Piero Terranova, but the designer, instantly recognisable by his flamboyant clothes, was constantly under siege from the guests, and Marek had to resign himself to traipsing around the exhibition. The mirrors surrounding the display area gave the impression that there were more dresses than there actually were, but he'd very much enjoyed gazing at the floaty, gauzy evening gowns on the headless mannequins. It was more the fall of the cloth than the dusty, pastel shades that had gripped his imagination. The dresses seemed to be designed for tall women. He could see Danka wearing any of these. Where she would wear them was the question, as her life revolved round her work. That trip to the Maze with Honor had been an exception.

'I think Dundee is extremely lucky to have a New York fashion designer bring his exhibition here, Mr Terranova,' Marek said, raising an eyebrow.

'Piero has wanted to exhibit at your V&A for some time.' Luca swallowed noisily. 'I'll come to the point, Mr Gorski. My brother is missing. And I'd like you to find him.'

Marek was taken aback by the abrupt shift in conversation. Before he could reply, Luca added, 'I've asked around, and your name has come up as someone with a track record of finding missing people.'

'Have you reported this to the police?' Marek said, setting his empty coffee cup on the table.

Luca waved a dismissive hand. 'I've been led to believe that the Dundee police have more important things to occupy themselves with than missing persons. If it's anything like London, the name will be registered in a database and little will be done.' He hesitated. 'Rest assured that I will, of course, accept your fee and meet any obligations towards your expenses.'

It was the catch in his voice, and the anxiety in his eyes that settled it. Marek took out his notebook. 'When were you last in touch with him?'

'I have it on my phone.' Luca pulled his mobile out of his jacket pocket, and scrolled through. 'I texted him on June the eleventh.'

'That was a week after June the fourth, the day the exhibition started.' Marek glanced up. 'It's now July the nineteenth, roughly five weeks later.'

Luca must have heard the question in Marek's voice because he said, 'Unlike young people, my brother and I don't message each other every day. Piero was busy with the exhibition – there's always much to do, especially at the start – and I had my own work to attend to.'

'And what is that, if I may ask?'

'I have work as a voice coach at Covent Garden.'

'The Royal Opera House?'

'That's right. And June and July are extremely busy. It's a demanding position, timewise.'

'But a fulfilling one, I'm sure.' Marek gestured to the phone. 'And what was the nature of your text?'

Luca smiled. 'Simply that I wished him every success with the exhibition, and that I was sorry I hadn't been able to make it to Dundee for the opening.' The smile faltered. 'It was on a Saturday, and I'm always tied up at weekends.'

'Did Piero message you back?'

'He replied, thanking me, and said he'd call me when he had some free time.'

Marek sat back. 'What makes you think Piero is missing?'

'I tried to ring him a few times over the weekend.'

'This past weekend?'

Luca nodded. 'Each time, my call went to voicemail.'

'And that's unusual? He might have been particularly busy. It was the weekend, after all.'

'I asked him to call me as a matter of urgency. And he didn't.'

Marek hesitated with the next question. 'And are you able to tell me what was so urgent?' Seeing Luca stiffen, he added quickly, 'It may have a bearing on his disappearance.'

'It was a personal matter. I'm organising a joint birthday celebration. It's next month, and we're holding it in Italy. I needed to consult with him about it.' He smoothed back his already smooth hair. 'These things are better done face to face or, failing that, over the phone.'

'I understand.'

'I couldn't get it out of my mind that something must have happened to him, so I decided to take a flight up this morning. I knew he'd been here at the Hampton, and thought he might still be, but I was told he'd checked out.'

'Checked out when?'

'On June the ninth. He hadn't left a forwarding address. I expect that's no longer done these days.' Luca ran a hand over his forehead, a tense expression on his face.

'Mr Terranova, do you think Piero is still in Dundee?'

'Why would he leave? His exhibition doesn't finish until the end of the month.'

'True, but from what I understand of these things, all the setting up and publicity and so on takes place at the start. Piero would then have had time on his hands until he had to oversee the packing up, which could be done relatively quickly. Could he have taken a trip around Scotland? Or even returned to New York?'

Luca looked mystified. 'I suppose so. But knowing my brother, I doubt it. He wouldn't have moved far from his creations. No artist does.'

And leaving Dundee didn't explain why he hadn't answered his phone. 'What is your brother like?' Marek said. 'I mean, what sort of a person is he?'

'Impetuous, impatient. Quick-tempered, but warm-hearted.' A smile touched Luca's lips. 'Aren't all artists like that?'

'Has he ever gone missing before?'

'Not that I know of. I can't be sure, of course. I mean, we haven't always kept in touch.'

'If he checked out of the hotel, could he have moved into rented accommodation?'

'He did talk about viewing a few places. He might well have moved, and it slipped his mind that he hadn't given me his new address. As I said, we were both extremely busy at the time.'

Marek closed the notebook. 'I'll make some enquiries, Mr Terranova.'

'Does this mean you'll take this on?' he said eagerly.

'It does. Will you be staying in Dundee long?'

'I have to return to London this evening. Here are my contact details.' He gave Marek his card, then got to his feet and extended his hand.

Marek shook it firmly. 'I'll call you as soon as I have anything.'

'I'm grateful to you,' Luca said, the catch back in his voice. 'I'm worried sick that something bad has happened to him.'

As Marek left the room, his first thought was that twins have a special connection, which makes them sense when something is wrong. He and Danka were twins, and he sometimes had that chill in his bones when he believed her to be in trouble, which seemed to happen often. So Luca's misgivings might well prove to have foundation.

His second thought was that he hadn't been offered a single macaroon.

CHAPTER 5

Luca Terranova watched the door close behind Marek Gorski. He picked out a yellow macaroon, and flopped on to the sofa, munching slowly. The meeting had gone better than expected, and he would have to thank the receptionist for giving him the Pole's name and number. Had he had more time, he might have started the search himself, not that he was trained in that area, but his Edinburgh flight was later the same evening. He'd reassured the new soprano from Stockholm that he would be at the piano first thing the following morning, ready to start her training, and he didn't intend to miss the appointment. Her reputation as someone who liked to belittle men was well deserved, and he'd quickly appreciated why she'd earned the nickname, the Nutcracker Swede. He would have to summon all his resources to keep his mind on his work, as he was deeply disturbed by his brother's disappearance. Not only because Piero was his brother, but because this joint venture in which they were engaged would then have to be completed by himself alone, and he wasn't sure if he had the stones to carry it out.

He threw the rest of the macaroon into the bin.

* * *

Marek left the Hampton and crossed at the roundabout, reaching West Marketgait without incident. Given the traffic in the city and the fact that the West Port circle was particularly busy, it wasn't always a sure bet that he'd get across. He followed the Marketgait until it curved east, and then swung south towards the V&A. He was glad he was wearing his blue summer suit, as the temperature was expected to touch the mid-twenties. The soft wind that usually freshened the Riverside Esplanade at this time of year had taken itself elsewhere, and he found himself sweating into his shirt. He loosened his tie, and unbuttoned his collar.

Remembering that he hadn't had lunch, Marek stopped outside the V&A Doughnut Hut and grabbed a cinnamon bun and coffee. He sat on the bench in front of the building, and pulled out his notebook. What he'd learnt was that 9 June was when Piero Terranova had checked out of the Hampton, and 11 June was the last time he and Luca had been in touch. A police officer would have had access to phone-mast data that would have pinpointed Piero's location, but that was denied to a mere investigative journalist. He was tempted to try Piero's number until he realised that he hadn't asked Luca for it. He was losing his touch, he thought, sipping the coffee. No matter. It was likely that Piero had left a record of it at the Hampton. If all else failed, he could ask Luca.

Marek finished the doughnut, and thought about buying another, but time was slipping away. And where a missing person was concerned, time was everything. Dawdling on the Esplanade was something he couldn't afford to do.

Inside the V&A, the girl at reception glanced up as he approached. She had deep, dark eyes and glossy hair the colour of wheat. Always a winning combination. He was relieved to discover that he knew her.

'Hi, Marek, you here again? So, what can I do for you, eh?'

'I'm looking for Piero Terranova. Is he around?'

'I've no idea. I haven't seen him the day.'

Marek was tempted to ask whether she'd seen him the day before when she said, by way of explanation, 'I've been on holiday the last couple of weeks. Are you after an interview?'

'I am, as a matter of fact. You wouldn't happen to have his address, would you? I could come in tomorrow, but my boss is giving me a hard time over this.'

'Okay, hold on, let me see what he's given us by way of contact details. Right, here's the address. I'll write it down for you.' She scribbled on a pad, tore off the sheet and handed it to Marek. 'I've put his mobile number there, too.'

'Whatever they're paying you, it's not enough,' he said, injecting a note of gratitude into his voice.

'Ach, I ken that,' she replied dismissively.

He smiled his thanks, then turned and left.

It was as easy as that.

He'd reached the car park at *Dundee Today*, and was getting into his Audi when he remembered that he had a meeting at 4 p.m. And this was not one to miss. Glenna McGarry would be attending and, as the newspaper's principal investigative journalist, he would be presenting a progress report. He buttoned his collar, and straightened his tie.

CHAPTER 6

Marek was making good progress along Drumsturdy Road. He was thinking about the previous afternoon's meeting with the matriarchal Glenna McGarry, who owned *Dundee Today*. She and Clare Conlee were no-nonsense types, but where Clare was charming when she felt the need to criticise, Glenna was the polar opposite. Fortunately, Marek had never been on the receiving end, but had concluded that if it ever happened and he disagreed with her, he would give as good as he got. He'd learnt from experience that tough women didn't appreciate wimpy men. Yesterday, however, Glenna was there to listen, and he had the feeling that his report had left her with a favourable impression. The meeting had gone on into the early evening, and he'd decided to leave his visit to Piero's until the following day. If the designer was at home, then getting there first thing meant that he was likely to catch him in. Possibly even having breakfast. Which he might offer to Marek.

Drumsturdy was one of those country roads with fields on either side punctuated by farms and homesteads. It meandered north-east of the city all the way to Panmure, but the cottage Marek was after wasn't far from the turn-off. That is, if he'd found the right place on Google Maps. He slowed down, locating the building easily enough. It was set back from the road, skulking behind a dense screen of trees, which were shedding their blossom. Mind you, Google Maps could sometimes be wrong, and so could sat-navs. He'd once found himself attacked by a German shepherd after arriving at the wrong location. He eased into the drive, following the curve until he came to a large, white-walled bungalow with a rim of bricks bordering the front door. A black Mercedes stood in the gravel courtyard.

Marek turned off the ignition. Before he'd left his flat, he'd tried Piero's mobile but the call had gone to voicemail. That meant nothing. The man might be one of those who switched off his phone at night and didn't switch it back on until after he'd showered and shaved. Perhaps he was in the shower right now.

Marek strolled across the courtyard. A glance through the Mercedes's passenger window told him that Piero had left his jacket inside. Maybe he'd been for a drive the evening before. It had been muggy and warm, and he could have taken off the jacket and forgotten it. Easily done. Marek had done it himself. He pressed the buzzer and waited, hearing the sound echo through the house. A while later, he tried again. Could Piero be out for an early-morning run? Difficult to see where, as the cottage was encircled by trees. Marek stood listening to the sweet sound of a blackbird, uncertain as to what to do next.

He peered through the window on the left, seeing an oak-floored room scattered with kilim rugs, and several plump, maroon-leather chairs. On the wall was a huge television screen. A pile of split logs stood in the corner by the wood-burning stove. The room on the right was smaller, and appeared to be a study: what he could see of the opposite wall was covered with books. A rolltop desk and chair stood in front of the window, presumably to get the best of the light.

Marek decided to try round the back. The long window gave on to a modern kitchen with the kind of appliances that come with detailed manuals. He glimpsed a number of objects on the wooden table, including a vase of dead yellow tulips and a white mug decorated with Scotland's blue saltire.

The back door was fitted with a small frosted-glass panel. If he was going to find a way in, he'd need to do it without leaving a trace. He pulled on the latex gloves, a gift from Danka, gripped the metal handle and turned it. To his surprise, the door opened smoothly. He had a sudden presentiment that something wasn't right. It was that tickle at the back of his neck that did it every time. Something made him hurry to the Mercedes and try the driver's door. It was locked.

You lock the car, Piero, but not the cottage. Why?

Marek returned to the back, pushed the door open and called loudly, 'Mr Terranova? Are you at home?' Silence. He'd been in similar situations before but this felt different. The tightness in his chest made him want to turn and run.

His tension mounting, he stepped into the kitchen. The stale, cheesy smell told him that no one had been here for some time. He traced it to the jug of curdled milk on the table.

The door at the end led to a corridor with rooms leading off. There was no mail on the mat, but that wasn't unusual for rented accommodation. Marek checked out the living room and study. No papers, or anything to confirm that Piero was renting the place. The rolltop desk was unlocked, but there was nothing inside. That was the problem with technology, he thought glumly. Everything you needed could be stored on your phone, or accessed from it. And the phone would be with Piero, wherever he was. For that matter, so were the car keys. Marek hadn't found them either.

The bedroom contained a double bed and side tables, an inbuilt wardrobe and a couple of chairs. The bed had been made, and a pair of cream silk pyjamas lay folded neatly on the pillow. Inside the wardrobe were men's clothes, although Marek had to look closely to be certain. There were floral shirts, and suits in jewel colours. Even a cape in a cheery pink. The pockets in the jackets and trousers were empty. As was the red wheelie underneath. He pulled open the drawers of the bedside cabinet, but there was nothing there.

He was beginning to wonder if he was in the wrong cottage, and the owner was about to come thundering in. With his phone, he took pictures of some of the clothes. Maybe Luca could identify them as Piero's. He'd spotted a sticker on the window of the Mercedes, and recognised the name of the car-hire company, but they might understandably be unwilling to open up to an investigator, citing Data Protection.

The en-suite bathroom was tiled in primrose yellow, and contained a shower, wash-basin and toilet. On the shelf under the mirror were the usual objects: toothbrush and paste, dental floss, soap, electric shaver. And a bottle of Missoni cologne. Marek removed the cap. The same musky scent he'd smelt on Luca nudged him into believing that this was indeed Piero's rental. If he was right, the brothers had the same taste in men's perfume.

He left the cottage, and made his way to the front. He leant against the wall, studying the Mercedes. If it hadn't been for the dead tulips and sour milk, he'd have suspected that Piero had gone for a ramble in the countryside, and had simply forgotten to lock the back. And he'd left his phone switched off, as he'd wanted to enjoy the delights of rural Dundee in peace and quiet.

I asked him to call me as a matter of urgency. And he didn't.

Luca's words. He was referring to the calls he'd made during the weekend. And it was now Wednesday. No, if Piero was missing, as Luca had thought, he'd been missing for some time. Marek straightened, and returned to the kitchen.

Inside the fridge was a half-full pint of milk, a packet of butter and some sorry-looking croissants. He examined the sell-by date on the milk carton: 15 June. The butter's date was 18 June. Today was 20 July.

He closed the fridge door, his thoughts swirling. Piero hadn't been in this cottage for over a month. His clothes and the car he'd rented were still here, so it was unlikely that he'd gone away for a holiday. Then where the hell was he?

As Marek turned away, his gaze fell on the cardboard box lying on the table. The writing on the label was too faded and smudged for him to read. Carefully, so as not to damage the box, he teased off the lid. Shock surged through him. It was crammed with cartridges. And then he saw what he had missed earlier. Half hidden under a napkin was a pistol. He lifted back the cloth carefully, as though the very act of exposing the firearm would make it come to life.

On the bottom of the grip, enclosed in a circle, were the letters 'PB'.

CHAPTER 7

Marek had finished the rounds of his contacts, and it was now after five. He'd emailed Luca at midday and suggested a time to call. That time was rapidly approaching.

He trudged past the statue of Desperate Dan, then turned into the wide square in front of the Caird Hall. A few smudged clouds hung in the east, but otherwise there was nothing to spoil the unblemished blue of the sky. He flopped down on one of the benches, and loosened his tie. For once, he wished it would rain and freshen the air. What had Danka said about St Swithin's Day?

He was mopping the back of his neck with his handkerchief when his phone rang.

'Marek Gorski,' he said.

'Mr Gorski? It's Luca Terranova. Is this a good time?'

'It is. Did you get the photographs I emailed?'

'And I can confirm that those clothes do indeed belong to my brother. I particularly remember the cape. He wore it at the Cannes Film Festival.' A pause. 'How did you find the address, may I ask?'

'The receptionist at the V&A is a friend. She passed it on.'

A soft laugh. 'You're well connected, Mr Gorski. Now, you

43

said in your email that the back door was unlocked. Did you find a key?'

'I'm afraid not, neither in the back door nor the front.'

'What else did you find in the house?'

'Milk that was well past its sell-by date. I think your brother hasn't been in the place for some time.'

The pause was so long that Marek thought the connection had been lost. 'Hello? Mr Terranova?'

'Yes, I'm here. Were there any documents?'

'Nothing. And no phone.' A thought struck him. 'Unless it's in the jacket in the Mercedes. It wasn't easy to tell. Unfortunately, the car was locked, too.'

'I don't suppose you've ever picked the lock on a Mercedes, Mr Gorski.'

'It's not something I'd like to try. There'll be a loud, shrieking alarm, the kind that wakes the dead. But if it's our last resort, I suppose I could do it, although I might be arrested.'

'I wouldn't want that. Do you have any other leads you could follow?'

'I've asked around my contacts. So far, no one's seen Piero, but they'll keep a watchful eye out. They all know who he is, as his image has been in the local media. I've still to check again at the V&A, but I can't do that until tomorrow, as it closes at five.' Marek hesitated. 'There's something I need to talk to you about, Mr Terranova. In the kitchen, I found a pistol and a packet of cartridges.'

The alarm in the man's voice was unmistakable. 'Good Lord!'

'Did you know that your brother owned a firearm?'

'If he did, it's news to me.'

'I'm not an expert, but the pistol had the letters "PB" on the grip.'

Luca spoke slowly. 'I'm at a loss as to what to say. Do you think he'd bought the pistol with the intention of shooting rabbits or pheasants, or something? I looked up the cottage from the address you sent me. It's surrounded by woodland.'

'It's possible, but unlikely. Shotguns are usually used for that. Look, Mr Terranova, I think we need to call the police.'

'No, don't do that.'

'But owning a firearm without—'

'Let's give it till the end of the week. What's today? Wednesday. I can be back in Dundee on Saturday. Sunday at the latest.'

Marek was about to ask how that would help when Luca said, 'I know what you're thinking, Mr Gorski. That possession of this firearm might be illegal, and I'm trying to preserve my brother's reputation. Be assured that that is not at the forefront of my mind. It's my brother's welfare I'm more concerned about.'

'I don't understand. The police have access to resources I don't. They might be able to find him quickly.'

'Be that as it may, I still think it best we wait until the weekend. There may be a simple explanation for all this.' He must have taken Marek's silence for disapproval because he added, 'I know how uneasy you must feel, but a couple of days is hardly going to make any difference.'

It was on the tip of Marek's tongue to point out that, where a missing person was concerned, a couple of days might make the difference between life and death.

'Very well, Mr Terranova. There are some avenues I have still to explore.'

'I'll be in touch as soon as I know my travel plans.'

He disconnected, leaving Marek with an uneasy feeling that this was going to end badly.

CHAPTER 8

'So, that's your plan, Chloe? We're going to map out the Maze?' Ailsa sneered. 'I think you're havering.'

Chloe glared defiantly at her sister. 'You can think what you like. And if you're not prepared to help me, I'll do it myself.'

Ailsa nodded slowly. This was one of her sister's dafter ideas. 'You do know that the Maze can move, don't you?' she said.

'Aye, but it won't move for the competition. It would be unfair on the competitors, as some would benefit and others wouldn't. I've studied the rules. They're online.'

'*I've studied the rules. They're online,*' Ailsa said, mimicking her sister's whiny voice. 'Listen, you little numpty, if you map out the Maze as it looks today, how do you ken that that's how it will be set up for the competition?'

'Ach, I've *thought* of that. I'm also going to map out the rail lines in the ground.' Chloe was shouting now. 'The ones the hedges move around on.'

'Okay, okay, keep the heid.' Ailsa narrowed her eyes. 'So, what will you do once you've finished all that?'

'I'll draw the diagrams. One for every combination.'

She's away with the wee men, Ailsa thought. There's no way

she could pull this off. There were simply too many possibilities. 'And then what, Chloe?'

'I'll keep studying them until I know them off by heart. That way, I reckon I'll have the best chance of winning.'

Ailsa noticed that Chloe had switched to 'I' instead of 'we'. But she was beginning to come round to thinking that her sister's plan wasn't all bad. She had a good memory, right enough, if her winning the Robert Burns recital competition every year was anything to go by. Not everyone could recite 'Tam o' Shanter' from beginning to end.

'I've a better idea,' Ailsa said suddenly. 'We could use my tablet and put all the diagrams on that.'

Chloe's gaze sharpened. 'Only one of us can enter, ken. We haven't enough cash for two entrance fees. We've talked about this, remember.'

'Aye, we have, and that arrangement hasn't changed. All I'm saying is that if I lend you the tablet and you win the competition, we stick to our deal of splitting the prize money down the middle.' She paused. 'And I'll help you with this mapping thing.' She nodded at the pencil and notepad in her sister's hands. 'While you make the sketches, I can use my phone to take photos of the hedges and the rails.'

It would be better than sitting on her bahookie all day. And her sister was likely to make a mess of this. They'd look at the drawings afterwards and not make head nor tail of where anything was.

'Okay,' Chloe said, drawing out the word.

They were sitting on the crest of the hill, with the Maze below them and woodland behind. Ailsa was conscious that it was just over a week since they'd found the body under the leaves. She'd crept back there once or twice without her sister, who was acting as though she'd forgotten the entire incident, which Ailsa knew she hadn't. Today, their parents were at a cattle show somewhere in the Highlands and had taken the four by four, leaving the family car. Which had given the girls the opportunity they needed. They'd left the vehicle in the small parking place by the gate that marked the entrance to one of the many rambling paths. It was then a short walk to the hill, and the Maze.

Ailsa had done her homework and knew that the Maze was closed today so, provided they were careful, they could sneak in without being seen. Once inside, they'd have the place to themselves.

'Are we going in, then?' she said, pulling out her phone.

'I suppose so.'

They got to their feet and sneaked down to the back of the Maze.

Chloe was about to slip through the gap in the hedging when Ailsa said, 'Better if we enter the way we will for the competition.'

'Aye, that's a good idea.'

They inched round the side, passing the shed, which they'd read housed the controls for the moving objects, then made their way to the front and into the Maze. Chloe started drawing furiously, labelling the turn-offs with letters and numbers. She instructed Ailsa to label her photos the same way. They should then be able to put everything together.

It was a scorcher of a day, and Ailsa was glad that the high hedges kept the sun off their faces. Most of the time, anyway. But as they moved deeper into the Maze, she started to doubt whether anything would come of this. They'd been at it for only an hour, and Chloe was already halfway through her drawing pad. Maybe a drone would have been better. Pity they didn't have one.

A statue of a dark-green frog wearing a white ruff and golden crown greeted them as they rounded a corner. It was sitting on a stone in a yoga position, legs crossed and arms extended. There was a knowing expression on its face, which reminded Ailsa of their dad.

A while later, Chloe said, 'I've run out of paper.'

'Turn the pad over and use the backs of the sheets,' Ailsa said, taking a gulp from her water bottle.

'I've already done that.' She leant against the hedge, gazing at the statue of Mary, Queen of Scots. The woman was dressed in black, and was holding a crucifix in her right hand. 'Do you think those pearls in her hair are real?'

'Nah. They'll be made out of paste.'

'Pity they didn't put a real dress on her.'

Ailsa saw that Chloe was without water. She handed her the bottle. 'We can come back tomorrow and finish it. The Maze is closed then, too.'

'I suppose so.'

She sounded so downhearted that Ailsa said, 'We'll take up where we left off, eh.' She jerked her head at the statue. 'If we spend the rest of the day transferring everything to the tablet, we should be able to find Queen Mary in no time at all.'

They made their way to the entrance, Chloe using her diagrams to direct them. As they approached the shed, it came to Ailsa that whoever worked the controls must have a comprehensive map of the Maze on their computer. Not only that, the layout for the competition was probably there, too. Now, who did she know who could pick a lock? But on reaching the shed, she saw that there was no padlock. The way in was via a keypad. Bummer.

They trudged up to the top of the ridge. After a pause to get their breath back, Chloe started towards the field where they'd searched for coins the previous week.

Ailsa gripped her arm. 'It would be quicker to go through the wood.'

'We'll get lost.'

'We won't.'

'I know why you want to go in there. You want a keek at that body again.'

'It might have disappeared by now.'

'Aye, right.' Chloe glared at her. 'Why didn't we report what we found to the polis, eh? I wanted to, but you stopped me.'

'Ach, you know why. They'd have questioned us for days, like they do on telly. And we were driving without a licence. That would have been bound to come out. There'd have been a hefty fine, and no mistake. Dad would have had to pay it. He'd have grounded us for the rest of the summer. Maybe next summer, too.' Ailsa kicked at the fallen leaves. 'But I know what we did was wrong. We should have reported it.' She lifted her head and gazed at Chloe. 'Okay, if the body's still there, we'll go to the polis. Agreed?'

Without waiting for a reply, she turned and made for the trees. Chloe followed silently.

They tramped through the woodland, shielded from the climbing sun by the overhanging branches, and were approaching the area where they'd found the body when they heard the barking.

'Let's go back,' Chloe murmured.

Ailsa peered through the bushes. An evil-looking Alsatian was pawing at the leaves piled up on the barrow, flinging them in all directions. Its owner, a man in jeans and a light-green shirt, was bent over, hands on knees, vomiting violently.

Chloe had grabbed Ailsa's arm, and was tugging it fiercely. Ailsa let herself be pulled away. Her last image was of the dog, on top of the barrow now, its muzzle buried deep into whatever was under the soil.

CHAPTER 9

DI Dania Gorska was at her desk in the incident room when the call came in. She listened carefully, gazing at Honor who was sitting across from her. Given the look on the sergeant's face, it was clear that she'd guessed something had come up. She didn't wait for Dania to finish the call before springing to her feet.

'Where are we going, boss?' she said, grabbing her jacket.

'The other side of Alderwood Manor. Someone walking his dog found a body in the woodland. The uniforms are already out there. I've got the directions.'

They hurried to the station's car park, and scrambled into the only squad car available. Dania relayed the location to Honor, then called Professor Milo Slaughter at the University of Dundee. She was put through to his secretary, a woman used to urgent calls from the police. Dania explained the situation, knowing that the secretary would pass everything on to Milo.

Unfortunately for the officers, there'd been an incident on the southern stretch of Old Glamis Road, necessitating a detour, which even the sat-nav struggled with. The consequence was that Dania and Honor arrived just after Milo and his team. Dania recognised his van, parked next to a red Renault Clio. The Scenes of Crime Officers were zipping up their over-suits, ready for action.

Milo was talking to Lisa, a young photographer with long, dark hair swept up into a ponytail. He glanced across as the squad car came to a halt near the five-barred gate. Dania and Honor climbed out.

'Ah, ladies, we meet again,' he said, in his bass voice.

'And it's always in unfavourable circumstances,' Dania replied. 'How are you, Milo?'

'Never better.'

Dania looked around. 'Who found the body?'

A uniformed police officer stepped forward. She could have been mistaken for a teenager, but her firm, unwavering gaze made it clear that she was more than capable of putting down anyone who questioned whether she could do her job. 'It was this gentleman here,' she said, turning to a man in a green shirt, whose complexion was almost the same colour. At his feet sat a huge Alsatian. It was panting heavily, saliva dripping from its open mouth.

'I'm DI Dania Gorska,' Dania said to the man. 'And this is DS Honor Randall.'

He stared at them, a glazed expression on his face.

'We've taken his statement, ma'am,' the uniform said. She glanced at him, then indicated with her eyes that they should move out of earshot. 'He's in a state of shock, I'm afraid,' she murmured to Dania. 'I really need to get him home. My colleague can take you to the scene,' she added, indicating the male uniform scuffing the ground and trying to avoid her eyes. 'It's not far. Another officer is guarding the area.'

Dania nodded her agreement.

Milo handed the detectives their over-suits. As soon as they were gowned up, Dania signalled to the uniform. He opened the gate and led them and the SOCOs along a path that meandered through the wood. The air was thick with the grassy smell of earth, and the trees grew so close that the branches formed a meshed canopy, allowing only slivers of light to penetrate.

After a few minutes, the uniform stopped and pointed. 'It's just beyond that line of conifers. You can't miss it,' he added quickly. It was clear that he didn't want to venture further.

Dania glanced at Honor. The expression on her face suggested that she was thinking the same. Dania steeled herself to expect the worst.

As they skirted the trees, she became aware of the smell, recognising it immediately. Milo said something to Lisa, indicating that she should pull up her mask.

Behind the trees was a long mound, with leaves and soil scattered about. A uniform was flapping his arms to discourage the crows making various attempts to land. Their companions were lurking in the branches, seemingly waiting their turn and cawing in apparent indignation.

Seeing the group arrive, the uniform said, in a rush, 'The man who stumbled across this couldn't stop his dog from messing up the leaves and soil. He said he reckoned the animal had taken a mouthful, right enough.' He gestured further along. 'He threw up over there, by that bush,' adding unnecessarily, 'The man, not the dog.'

Dania tightened her mask and approached slowly, her overshoes sliding over the rotting leaves. The stink grew ever stronger. She felt Milo's hand on her arm, holding her back. He moved close to the mound and bent over it, but it took only moments for him to pronounce the victim dead. He straightened quickly. 'Lisa,' he said.

Lisa was standing with the SOCOs. Hearing her name called, she came forward and adjusted the camera.

Dania watched her go to work, her thoughts in a whirl. The fierce stench told her that putrefaction was under way. As far as she could tell from the glimpse she'd had, the body was buried in a shallow grave, but deep enough to have slowed the process of decomposition. She would need to read the statement by the dog walker to learn what condition the grave had been in before the Alsatian had had a go at it, as that would have a bearing on the time of death. And it all rested on that – the time of death. She hoped that Milo would be able to narrow it down.

They waited for Lisa to finish. She worked with her usual meticulousness, bending low over the grave for the close-ups, then taking photos of the surrounding area. Dania wondered how she could do her job, until it struck her that Lisa was probably wondering how Dania could do hers.

'That's me done for the moment, Prof,' Lisa said, straightening and fiddling with the camera.

Milo walked over and said something Dania didn't catch, but the gratitude in Lisa's sky-blue eyes suggested that he was complimenting her.

He nodded briefly at Dania, the signal that she could now approach.

The scattered soil left her in no doubt that the grave had been disturbed. Apart from one or two bare patches around the chest area, it was from over the head and shoulders that the soil had been flung off. Dania stared at the face. What was left of the skin was marbled. Fluid had seeped from the mouth and nose, leaving a dirty, crusty trail. The swollen tongue protruded from between the lips, and where there should have been eyes, there were gaping reddish-brown holes. Her gaze drifted back to the chest. Muddy yellow material, torn in places, was visible through the soil.

Milo was examining the corpse's head, and speaking into his recorder. But Dania wasn't listening. Her attention was drawn to something poking through the leaves. It reminded her of a scene from a horror film: the fingers of a hand, the flesh torn off, were curled round a pistol.

She became suddenly aware of Honor standing next to her. The woman was breathing heavily, although whether it was from the heat or the shock of what they were seeing wasn't clear.

Honor gestured to the pistol. 'I'd say it was suicide, boss . . .'

'. . . if it weren't for the fact that whoever it is has been buried,' Dania said.

Milo stepped back, shaking his head. Perhaps he'd come to the same conclusion.

The SOCOs began the unenviable task of gathering evidence, starting with the soil. Milo would have to wait until this was done before he could take the body to the mortuary. At each stage, Lisa was summoned to take photographs. Dania would normally have left them to it, as the painstaking nature of the process meant that it would take several hours, but she wanted a better look at the corpse. Or, rather, what was left of it.

The uniforms were erecting a wide cordon round the scene. 'What did the dog walker tell you?' she asked them. 'I'll read the statement later, but I wondered if there's anything you can tell me now.'

The men stopped what they were doing. The one who'd been chasing away the crows looked doubtfully at his companion. 'All he told us was that he was walking his dog, and it suddenly went berserk and leapt on to that mound, where it started digging like there was no tomorrow.' He paused to wipe his brow. 'He called it back, right enough, but the dog didn't respond, so he ran over to see what the fuss was all about. The animal was tearing at something, and he reckoned it might have dug out a wee piece and swallowed it. That was when he saw the face with those dark, staring eyes. He threw up, and then he got the dog under control. He went back to his car, called 999 and waited for us there.'

'The Renault Clio is his?'

'Aye, ma'am. We'll arrange to get it back to him.' The uniform shook his head. 'He was in a right state, and no mistake. Greetin' like a bairn, he was.'

'Okay, thanks,' Dania said, with a faint smile.

He nodded, and continued with his work.

Dania returned to Honor, and relayed what she'd just learnt. 'So, some time between the dog walker seeing the corpse's face, and the uniforms arriving, those crows picked out the eyes,' she finished.

'At least we now know what colour they were,' Honor said grimly.

They continued to watch the SOCOs as they worked tirelessly, dropping samples into evidence bags and labelling them. Dania knew that this was just the start. They would then have to comb the area for clues. The pistol in the hand meant that they'd be looking for a cartridge casing, after which a test fire would be conducted to confirm a match. One of the early cases Dania had worked on at the Met involved a murder where the perpetrator had thrust a pistol into a dead woman's hand to make it look like suicide. For some reason, this wasn't done until hours after the killing. It said something about how little the killer knew about ballistic forensics that he'd placed the wrong pistol in the victim's hand. It immediately promoted the killing from suicide to murder.

Time crawled by, and then the SOCOs struggled to their feet. The soil covering the corpse had been removed, and would soon be on its way to the lab for analysis.

After Lisa had taken another round of photographs, Milo beckoned to Dania.

Now that the body lay exposed, the first thing she noticed was the shirt. It wasn't the shade of yellow you'd describe as lemon-yellow, or even canary-yellow – an expression she'd heard in a play – but darker, more of a nicotine-yellow.

'I'm guessing from the build that it's a man,' she said to Milo.

'I'd say so. The wide shoulders and narrow hips are the indicators here.'

'But I can't see anything that might identify him. He's not wearing rings. And where's the watch?'

'Many people take their time from their phone, these days.'

'Have you checked his pockets?'

'Not yet.'

She knelt beside the body and, trying not to breathe too deeply, slipped her hand first into the right trouser pocket, then the left. There was nothing in the right pocket, but in the left she found two keys on a ring. One was a Yale, and the other a key for a mortice lock.

'A front-door and a back-door key,' the professor said.

'Now you're thinking like a detective, Milo.' Dania indicated to Lisa to take a photo, then handed the keys to a SOCO, who slid them into an evidence bag. 'They were in the left-hand pocket of his trousers,' Dania said. 'But there's no phone. And no wallet.'

Milo had unrolled a sheet, and was smoothing it out. 'We need to turn him over,' he said to the SOCOs.

Two officers came forward and, under the professor's directions, carefully lifted the corpse and placed it face down on the sheet.

Soil and dead leaves were stuck to the back of the head, and would have to be picked off before the post-mortem. Dania didn't envy whoever would be tasked with this. Milo had several assistants, and she wondered idly how he assigned the more unpleasant duties. Did they draw straws? Between the leaves, she glimpsed black hair, cut short.

More photos, and then the gathering of the soil from under the corpse began. Milo, meanwhile, was supervising the loading of the body into the mortuary van.

Dania turned to Honor. 'I think we've learnt all we can here,' she said.

'Does that mean we can go?' Honor said eagerly.

'Are the flies bothering you?'

'It's not the flies, boss. It's those bloody birds. They're the kind that can attack.'

'They're only crows.'

'That's what I mean. The kind that can attack.'

'I thought those were seagulls.'

Honor gripped the front of her over-suit and pulled it out, as though it had stuck. 'And this heat is something else.'

'I'll just have a word with Milo, and then we'll go.'

Dania returned quickly, having been given a rough estimate of when the autopsy might take place. Back in the car park, they struggled out of their over-suits.

'So, no ID on the guy,' Honor said, as they climbed into the car.

'Nothing. I'm waiting for the day when everyone on Planet Earth has to be fitted with an RFID chip.'

'But he had his house keys. That's something, I suppose. I mean, once we have his identity, we'll be able to check it by using the keys to gain access to his house.'

'I'm wondering why the killer took everything else but not the keys.'

'You think he was murdered, then.'

'I do,' Dania said emphatically. 'Murder made to look like suicide.'

'Here's a theory, boss. I saw it in a film – suicide made to look like murder. A man killed himself because he wanted his family to get a payout. He made it look like murder, because suicide can invalidate life insurance.'

Dania smiled. She knew which film Honor was referring to. 'I'm open to ideas. But how would that work in this case?'

'Okay, so we know that this guy was buried in a shallow grave. It's not impossible to dig one, get in and cover yourself almost up to your head. I mean, kids are always doing it in the sand, right? Then just before you pull the trigger, you take a deep breath, and scoop the earth you've piled up on either side over your head. Then you shoot yourself.'

'Okay as far as it goes, but why go to all that trouble?'

'Like I said, it's to fool the police into thinking it was murder made to look like suicide.'

'Wouldn't he at least have arranged to leave behind some clues to point to a murderer? He might have wanted to frame someone.'

'Not necessarily, boss. He might simply have wanted a payout.'

'And yet he has absolutely no ID on him. It might be some time before his identity is established,' Dania added, her heart sinking as she appreciated the implication of her words.

'Yep. That's the weakness in the theory.'

'But it's not a bad theory.'

They reached the A90. Dania was relieved to see that the diversion signs had disappeared, which meant they could continue down Old Glamis Road. But as they made their way south towards the city centre, Dania kept returning to the 'suicide made to look like murder' theory. The remote location would lend itself to that hypothesis. Yet the very remoteness of the place also worked against it. She couldn't help wondering exactly how the man had got himself out there. He couldn't have walked: there was no habitation for miles.

Until she remembered that, according to Google Maps, Alderwood Manor lay just beyond the woodland.

CHAPTER 10

'I've been checking MisPers, boss,' Honor said. 'There's no one with cropped black hair and dark eyes reported missing.'

Dania was scrolling through the images Lisa had uploaded, while simultaneously stuffing sandwiches into her mouth. It had been nearly five in the afternoon before they'd returned from the woodland, and they'd been lucky that the canteen still had anything left. There'd been a run on the food, the manager had said with an embarrassed smile, making Dania wonder what it was about hot weather that made her colleagues ravenous. When Honor had pointed out that neither she nor the DI had had lunch, the manager had sprung to attention and said he'd personally make them something to eat.

'How far back did you check?' Dania said.

'Three months.'

'I'd go back further. We don't yet know how long he's been buried. Another three months should be enough.'

'On it.'

Dania enlarged the photos of the firearm in the corpse's right hand. Lisa had done an excellent job with the close-ups, which were so good that the markings were clearly visible. Along the short barrel were the words: P BERETTA-CAL.9 CORTO

The rest of the line was scratched and indecipherable, but underneath she made out the words GARDONE V.T.1942-XX. At the bottom of the grip were the letters 'PB', enclosed in a circle.

Dania twirled a lock of hair. Then she reached for the phone and called Cosmo Denison. Since Kimmie's death in a motorcycle accident the previous winter, Cosmo had been appointed chief forensics officer, leaving a similar post in London.

'Cosmo Denison speaking,' came the reply.

'Hi, Cosmo. It's DI Dania Gorska. Have you got a moment?'

'Sure. How can I help?'

'I'd like to come over and chat about what we found in the woods today.'

'Please do. See you soon.'

A short while later, she'd reached the building housing the Forensic Science Laboratory. She felt a rush of sorrow as she remembered the many interactions she'd had there with Kimmie. The woman had died while Dania was in Warsaw, and she'd been unable to attend the funeral. Marek, on learning of Kimmie's death, had been particularly affected, as the two had got to know each other well through Kimmie's Edith Piaf Singing Society.

Cosmo glanced up from his long table as Dania entered.

'DI Gorska,' he said, with his usual enigmatic smile.

He was tall and lanky, with a shock of dark, wiry hair. But it was his eyes that held her, as they did every time. They were those of a dreamer, which seemed particularly incongruous, as Cosmo Denison was anything but. He had the same unrelenting determination that Kimmie had had, and worked the same long hours to aid the police. Dania had concluded early on in their relationship that London's loss was Dundee's gain.

'How are you, Cosmo?' she said, taking the seat next to his. He must have guessed the reason for her visit because one of Lisa's photos of the Beretta was up on his screen.

'Raring to go with this case, Inspector,' he said. He gestured to the image. 'I take it you've come about this.'

'It's not a firearm I'm familiar with.'

He scratched his head, messing his hair. 'What can I tell you? It's a Beretta Model 1934. Semi-automatic. Made in Gardone Val Trompia.' He ran a finger under the lettering on the barrel. 'This "CAL.9 CORTO" means it takes a nine-millimetre Corto cartridge, otherwise known as a .380 ACP.'

'Nine-millimetre? Like a Parabellum, then?'

'Not as powerful.'

'Would you call this a collector's item? Is it much sought after?'

'This one was made in nineteen forty-two, which means that it doesn't qualify as an antique. Although some collectors would certainly value it. Unfortunately, whoever owned it didn't apply for a firearms certificate.'

'If I wanted to get hold of a working model, how would I go about it? You see, I'm wondering how someone in the UK would have one, legally or otherwise.'

'Smuggled in, I expect, or bought on a US online site. I've not had time to do much research on the history, as I've been concentrating on the forensics, but I understand that they're popular with American gun enthusiasts. The GIs serving in Italy would bring them home as trophies, so they're widely available in the US.'

'And have you dusted it for prints?' Dania said hopefully.

Cosmo threw her a pained look. 'I'm afraid we're out of luck there. Come and have a butcher's at this.'

The Beretta and magazine had been laid out on a tray at the end of the table. Six cartridges were lined up neatly.

'There isn't a single usable fingerprint anywhere,' Cosmo said. 'Not even on the cartridges. Killers who wipe away prints from the pistol and grip often forget about the shells and the magazine. But not here. Whoever loaded this mag and snapped it into the pistol wore gloves.'

'That's significant in itself.' She studied the Beretta. 'The victim wasn't wearing gloves, though. No prints from him, either?'

Cosmo gave his head a slight shake. 'All useless. They were smudged due to the body fluids seeping from the hand.'

Dania shifted her gaze to the cartridges. 'Six bullets. It means you'll be able to do a test fire. Although it may not tell us much more.' She tried a smile. 'But you never know. So, how many rounds does a Beretta magazine hold?'

'Seven. I've yet to hear from SOCO as to whether they found the cartridge. They're still sifting through everything.'

'That's the trouble with a woodland killing. It's all so messy. So, what's your next task?'

'The clothing.'

'I'll leave you to it. Are you still on shift?'

'It finished two hours ago. I'm guessing it's the same with you.'

Hers had finished three hours earlier. But she just nodded.

As she left the building, her phone rang.

'DI Gorska,' she said.

'Dania? It's Milo. I'm just giving you a heads-up. We've scheduled the PM for tomorrow afternoon. Two o'clock.'

'I'll be there.'

'I wanted to let you know that there'll be two of us conducting the autopsy. We're in luck here. One of my associates spent the last year studying at the Anthropology Research Facility at the University of Tennessee. Also known as "The Body Farm". She's come back with a wealth of knowledge about body decomposition that I don't possess.'

'Excellent. Have I met this person?'

'Indeed you have.' A pause. 'Her name's Jenn McLaughlin.'

CHAPTER 11

It was Thursday afternoon before Marek had a chance to drop in at the V&A. He'd had an article to finish, and had been putting it off for too long. Clare had said nothing, but her silence had told him better than words what he needed to know: that she expected it on her desk by lunchtime, which was well past the deadline. He worked furiously and produced what he concluded to be one of his best pieces. The growing smile on her face as she read it suggested that she felt the same. He left the office buzzing inside. Job done.

He strolled into the V&A, expecting to see the same girl on reception, but today a young man was on duty.

'Hi, I'm Marek Gorski,' he said, without preamble.

The receptionist grinned. 'Aye, I ken who you are. I've read your articles in *Dundee Today*.'

Marek smiled what he hoped was a smile of appreciation. 'That's good to hear.'

'How can I help you?' the man said, with an earnest expression.

'I'm looking for Piero Terranova.'

'To interview him? I can give you his address.'

'Actually,' Marek said quickly, 'I'm not sure you're allowed to do that.' If he had the address, there'd be no reason for him to stay, and what he wanted was to speak to the staff who'd worked closely with Piero.

The receptionist nodded solemnly. 'You're absolutely right.'

'Does he happen to be in today?'

'I haven't seen him. To be honest, I haven't seen him for ages.'

'Is that unusual?'

'Ach, not really. There's a huge flurry at the start of an exhibition, publicity and parties and the like, but then it dies down. The designers usually drop in from time to time, although not always. Look, why don't you go round to the display? Some of the staff there might know when he's coming in.'

'Thanks,' Marek said.

He ambled round the corner to the display area. The only person there was a young woman who was adjusting the mannequins. Her wavy blonde hair was clipped back on one side, and fell loosely to the waist on the other. She was dressed in jeggings and a boyfriend shirt, which did her no favours. Perhaps it really did belong to her boyfriend, Marek thought.

She finished repositioning a mannequin that was draped in a coffee-coloured chiffon gown. Slowly, she pulled out the skirt and stood behind it, gazing at her reflection in the mirror.

'I think this would suit you better,' he said, indicating a rose-pink satin dress with a fishtail hem.

She studied him in the mirror, then looked directly at him. 'Pink for girls, blue for boys,' she chirped, nodding at his blue suit. She had what some would describe as a 'posh English accent'.

Marek laughed and, noticing the heels on her shoes, held out a hand to help her down from the platform.

'Are you here to look at the gowns?' she said, angling her head enquiringly. She had enormous green eyes and a pale, oval face.

In another life, she'd have been the model for a Botticelli Madonna.

'Actually, I saw them when I came for the opening reception,' he said.

'And you are?'

'Marek Gorski.' He smiled. 'At your service.'

'Oh, yes, you write for *Dundee Today*, don't you? My name's Sylvia. So, are you wanting Piero?'

'I am, as a matter of fact. Do you know where he might be?'

'I couldn't say.' She shrugged. 'Probably at home.'

'When did you see him last?' he asked, realising as soon as the words were out that the question had been clumsily put.

She stroked her hair. 'It was sometime in June. I can't remember when, exactly. He'd just found a place to rent, and told us he was moving. You'd think he'd be happy, but he was in a right mood.'

'What sort of a mood?'

'Hard to describe. As though he was a rubber band and someone had pulled it tight. Everything kept getting up his nose, and he wasn't usually like that. He was a dream to work with, actually.'

'Do you know why he became like this?'

'No, but it happened when he went to look round the Maze. You know, the one at Alderwood Manor. It had opened in May, and a group of us were talking about going. When Piero heard about it, he was really keen to see it, so we set a date.'

'Can you remember when this was? This trip to the Maze?'

'I've got it all on my phone.' She pulled out her mobile and scrolled through. 'Here it is. June the seventh. We bought tickets for two o'clock. I didn't go in the end. I had a burst pipe in my flat and had to wait in for the plumber.'

'But your colleagues went, didn't they?' Marek pressed. 'Did something happen to Piero there?'

'It must have done, but no one saw what. From what they told me afterwards, they all took separate routes, and met up in the car park once they'd found their way out. Which wasn't easy. Do you know that parts of the Maze can move?' She rolled her eyes, and smiled. 'Course you do. You wrote that article. Anyway, all I know is that Piero went into that Maze as his usual happy self, and when he came out, he was a changed man.'

CHAPTER 12

Dania was standing with the procurator fiscal, watching proceedings in the main dissection room at Ninewells Hospital. Jenn McLaughlin, wearing scrubs, cap and plastic apron, was bent over the corpse lying on the steel table. Of those assembled, she was the only one whose face wasn't covered. Where everyone else was gagging at the stench leaching through their masks, she seemed almost to relish the odour of putrefaction.

Jenn had been seventeen when Dania had encountered her during her first case in Dundee. After leaving school, the girl had started working with Milo Slaughter as a trainee assistant. Since then, her path had crossed with Dania's a number of times, usually at Ninewells. She was softly spoken, but the determination in her eyes made it clear to anyone who met her that she was in complete control of every situation she found herself in. Honor had referred to Jenn as 'creepy', saying that she lived in her own little bubble, and was inexplicably happy to.

Milo had begun the autopsy by announcing the date and time, speaking clearly into the microphone above his head. He'd stated that the body was that of a white male in his thirties, and then handed over to Jenn. Now that the corpse had been cleaned and dried, what was clear was that the left and right hands and wrists showed markedly different levels of decomposition. The left hand, which had been buried, had its flesh more or less intact, and was the same marbled yellow-green as the torso and legs, whereas the exposed right hand was missing almost all its flesh. Consequently, it was the part of the body that had been in the ground that would provide them with an estimate of the time of death.

Jenn had studied the chest area, which was undamaged, indicating that the dog walker had been wrong in his assumption that the Alsatian had ripped out a piece of flesh and swallowed it. She was now concentrating on the left arm. 'There are signs of wet decomposition consistent with burial in soil,' she said. 'And there is considerable skin slippage.'

Dania heard the fiscal's sharp intake of breath, a mistake as he then started to gag and cough. Jenn ignored him and continued to scrutinise the rest of the body. After she seemed satisfied that she'd covered everything, she straightened and said to no one in particular, 'The fact that the corpse was buried has resulted in a slower rate of decomposition, due to the temperature below ground being more stable.'

She sounded as though she was quoting from a textbook. And maybe she was, Dania thought.

Jenn gazed directly at her. 'Before I can provide a time-of-death estimation, I need to wait for the results of the soil analysis, particularly the pH value.'

'Can you give us anything at all?' the fiscal said, in a hoarse voice.

Dania glanced at him. What she could see of his face suggested that he badly wanted this to be over.

The expression in Jenn's eyes was unreadable, and one that Dania remembered from their previous interactions. 'My best estimate from the condition of the body, and assuming that the victim was buried not long after he died, is that the post-mortem interval is four to eight weeks.'

Dania knew that Jenn was using the rule of thumb: one week exposed above ground equals eight weeks below. The bloating and the skin colour, as well as the odour of putrefaction, would have informed her assessment.

'Four to eight weeks?' the fiscal said, with contempt. 'Can't you do better than that, lass?' He was a steely-eyed man with a whiny voice, attributes that somehow didn't go together.

Dania stared at him, conscious that he'd be unable to see her expression under the mask. Given the circumstances, and without the results of the soil and other analysis, four to eight weeks was all they could expect. But when it came to dealing with scientists, the fiscal was famous for demanding the impossible. The man had a tendency to pick on the professor's female staff, giving them a hard time as if testing their competence. Of all the fiscals Dania had worked with, he was the worst by a country mile.

It was Milo who came to Jenn's defence, as he always did when he felt that his staff were being unfairly treated. 'My associate has given you the benefit of her experience, gained from her studies at the world-leading Anthropology Research Facility at the University of Tennessee,' he said coldly. 'We should respect her opinion.'

For a moment, Dania thought there was going to be what Scots referred to as 'a wee stooshie'. The fiscal had crossed swords with Milo before, and Dania was curious to see how the scenario would play out. She hoped the fiscal would continue the attack, as she relished the thought of seeing him brought down with one of Milo's well-placed verbal blows.

The fiscal shrugged, saying nothing. But Dania could see his resentment simmering. There was still time for it to boil over.

'When should we expect the results of the soil analysis?' she said calmly, directing the question at Jenn.

Jenn seemed unfazed by the exchange. She nodded thoughtfully. 'I'd say by the end of next week.' As if to stave off the next salvo from the fiscal, she added, 'We need to test the soil over, under and around the corpse.'

'I understand,' Dania said encouragingly. She thought she saw Jenn's expression soften.

'Have you anything else to add?' Milo said to Jenn.

'Only that I've examined the bones of the right hand. There are marks caused by bird and animal predation, consistent with the hand not being buried.'

'And do we know why that hand was exposed?' the fiscal growled.

'That's a question for the police,' Dania said firmly, 'not for a pathologist.'

He threw her one of his looks, but said nothing.

'I think that finishes the preliminaries, Jenn,' Milo said. 'You're welcome to stay, of course.'

'Thank you, but I think I'll leave you to it. You know where I am if you need me.' With a brief nod and smile at Dania, she left the room, ignoring the fiscal.

Milo approached the corpse, and studied the head carefully. 'The CT scan indicates that the right side of the frontal bone has been forced in and splintered, consistent with a single entry wound. The much larger exit wound is on the left of the parietal bone at the back of the head.'

Before the autopsy, Milo had shown them the results of the scan, confirming that there were no bullets in the body. What had grabbed Dania's attention, however, was the path that the projectile had taken through the brain. She'd seen scans from suicides who'd shot themselves. Either they fired into the temple, or they shot themselves through the mouth. One or two had placed the weapon against their chest. The bullet track and the entry and exit wounds made it clear which method had been used. Yet this was something she'd not seen before – the bullet had entered the right side of the forehead and exited the back of the head, but on the left.

'There are faint muzzle burns around the entry wound,' Milo was saying, 'consistent with a contact shot.' He let his gaze drift down the face. 'The eyes are missing.'

'Well, that was bloody obvious,' the fiscal muttered, so that only Dania could hear.

Milo pulled the corpse's lips apart gently. 'The teeth are intact.' He glanced up at Dania as if to say, *You might get an ID from that.*

She nodded her acknowledgement. Given the bloating of the face and the missing eyes, a visual identification would be impossible.

'There is no evidence of a struggle, or defence wounds on the arms or the left hand,' Milo continued.

'Are there any tattoos?' Dania asked.

'None. In fact, no identifying marks that I can see.'

'Scars suggesting needle use?' the fiscal said grumpily.

'It's impossible to tell with this level of decomposition. The toxicology report might reveal the presence of opiates in the blood stream.'

Milo continued his examination, speaking clearly through the mask. The drone of his deep voice might have lulled Dania to sleep were it not for the fact that she had to take in everything he said, as the clue to the deceased's identity might be in there somewhere.

'Nothing under the fingernails,' Milo said, examining the left hand. 'And the CT scan shows that no bones have been broken.'

'Fingerprints?' the fiscal said.

'Decomposition has rendered them useless.' He straightened. 'I'm about to open him up. You may want to move further away.'

Dania and the fiscal didn't need telling twice. They took the chairs at the back. From a distance, they watched Milo get to work with the Stryker saw. He talked continuously about what he was doing, and what he was seeing. Dania was familiar with the procedure: the order in which the internal organs would be removed from the body and taken away by the young male assistant, the weighing, the examination away from the table. The stench grew stronger until it seemed to seep through her every pore. How Milo and the assistant could keep going was beyond her.

The fiscal inclined his head. 'What do you think, Inspector? Suicide?'

'I doubt it. The bullet going in at an angle is strange, to say the least. And the right hand exposed like that? No, I don't think he buried himself and then put the gun to his head.'

'So, what's your theory?'

'I think someone shot him, buried him, then at the last minute hit on the idea of putting the gun into the victim's hand to make it look like suicide. He had to pull the arm out of the soil in order to do it, and he didn't bother reburying it.'

'It's a theory, I suppose,' the fiscal admitted reluctantly. 'How do you intend to proceed?'

'We'll check the teeth for a match. My DS has been looking through MisPers.'

'And failing that?'

'We can't put out a photograph of that face. Not with the eyes missing. We may be able to do a facial reconstruction and get that into the media.'

The fiscal was nodding his approval.

'But we might learn something if we put an image of his shirt in the papers. It's an unusual colour, a sort of yellow-brown. Not one I've seen many people wear.'

'And where is it now?'

'It's with Forensics. I think we could get a photo out quickly.'

Milo had lifted his head and was staring at them to get their attention. Dania got to her feet and approached the table so that he didn't have to shout through the mask. The fiscal followed reluctantly.

'Regarding his internal organs,' Milo said, 'there's nothing out of the ordinary. He was a healthy individual. The pathology report will be sent to you in due course. But the cause of death is a single gunshot to the head.'

The fiscal sighed, as if to say, *I could have told you that.*

CHAPTER 13

Saturday afternoon saw Dania at West Bell Street police station, taking over from Honor, who'd been on the early shift. Her sergeant's parting statement – delivered over a loud yawn – had been that she'd gone back a further three months in MisPers, but no one of the deceased's description had been reported missing. Given that Jenn's estimate of the post-mortem interval was four to eight weeks, Honor's announcement came as no surprise.

Dania connected to the station's server and checked through the reports uploaded so far. The statement by the dog walker told her nothing new – he'd seen a long mound covered with leaves and before he could stop him, his Alsatian had made a dash for it. He'd moved closer to call the dog off, but when he'd seen what the animal was doing, he'd nearly passed out. His horror was made worse by glimpsing the face with the dark eyes staring at him. When asked if he'd noticed anyone nearby, he said he hadn't. He didn't normally take his dog to that area, but he'd fancied a change. And, no sir, he wouldn't be going back.

Dania suspected he might not shrug off his experience. One thing she'd need to check was whether he'd been assigned a family liaison officer.

She pulled down the report from SOCO. The first piece of positive news was that they'd uncovered the cartridge casing. *And* they'd found the bullet. Dania sat up as she read on. The bullet had lodged in the trunk of a nearby tree. Photos had been taken, not only of the surroundings, but of the trunk, in close-up, after the projectile had been removed.

Dania made a quick call to the Forensic Science Laboratory to check that Cosmo was in. Then she grabbed her bag and left the station.

As she reached the lab, she wondered how long it would be before she could enter the building without thinking of Kimmie. When would she not experience that feeling of sadness as she thought of their many forensics experiences? Probably never.

Cosmo was slouching at his table, gazing into the screen. 'Inspector,' he said, in his faraway voice. 'Nice to see you.' He indicated the chair next to his. 'Please take a seat.'

There was a faint, acrid odour in the room, which Dania assumed was down to the combination of chemicals that Cosmo used in his investigations. Either that or he was wearing an unusual brand of aftershave.

'Just to get the preliminaries over with,' he said, when Dania was settled, 'I can confirm that the cartridge casing, the bullet extracted from the tree, and the Beretta in the victim's hand all match.'

'You've done a test fire already?'

'I try not to let the grass grow under my feet. Now, there's something I want to show you.'

He tapped the screen, and an image appeared. It was an artist's impression of the area of woodland where they'd found the body. Dania recognised the line of trees and the burial mound. A dark-haired figure was standing away from the grave, his back to them.

The artist had given him a yellow-brown shirt and black trousers. In other words, the clothes the dead man had been wearing.

'This is a representation of the victim,' Cosmo said. 'And this tree here,' he added, indicating a large pine some distance behind the man, 'is where we found the bullet. Knowing the muzzle velocity of a Beretta M1934, and how far into the trunk the bullet was lodged, and given the man's height and the bullet's parabolic trajectory, we can say with a fair degree of accuracy that this is where he was standing when he shot himself. Or when someone did it for him.'

'And which do you think it was?' Dania asked, knowing the answer.

'If he shot himself, then someone had to be on hand to bury him. All that talk about the man burying himself in a shallow grave, then shooting himself, is a load of baloney, pardon my French.'

'Let's suppose someone shot him. Were there any footprints nearby?'

'Nothing, I'm afraid. It's notoriously difficult with leaves, and time isn't on our side with this case.'

Dania studied the image. 'The thing that puzzles me is the bullet trajectory through the brain.'

'About that, I've had access to the scans from Ninewells. Have a butcher's at this.' Cosmo tapped the screen again, and a red line appeared. 'This shows the path the bullet took. The victim would have been facing in the direction shown.'

'Why would the killer do it like that? At an angle. Why not shoot straight through the centre of the forehead? If you're looking at the mark, that's how you usually do it.'

Cosmo's smile was more enigmatic than usual. 'Maybe something distracted him. Or the victim gripped his hand at the last minute. That would be my guess. After all, if he knew he was about to be shot, he'd have had nothing to lose.'

'And it was only keys that were found on him?'

'Nothing else.'

'No secret pockets?'

A previous case of theirs concerned a victim who'd had a specially made jacket with a number of pockets sewn into the lining. Each had contained a packet of cannabis.

'No secret pockets, Inspector. So, shall we look at his clothes?'

Cosmo led her to the back of the lab, where the victim's clothes were laid out under glass. Dania was struck by the shape of the shirt, which looked more like a smock. Given the length, she'd have expected it to have been worn loose, yet it had been tucked inside the trousers. It was muddy and torn around the chest, and the stench of putrefaction seemed to seep through the glass, taking her back to the autopsy of the previous day. Or maybe she was simply imagining it.

Cosmo must have seen the direction of her gaze because he said, 'Not the kind of shirt I'd wear myself.'

Dania turned away so that he couldn't catch her smile. Cosmo's clothes were always tight-fitting: his T-shirts looked as though they'd been sprayed on, and his skinny-fit stretch jeans left nothing to the imagination. She'd often wondered why he wore clothes that only emphasised his thin frame.

'What does that shirt say about him, Cosmo?'

He angled his head. 'A Shakespearean actor, perhaps?'

'Wouldn't a Shakespearean actor only dress like that on stage?'

'Possibly. But maybe he was living the part? Dunno.'

'There doesn't seem to be a label.'

'Which suggests that it was made especially. Maybe he *was* an actor.'

'And the trousers?'

'Oscar de la Renta. They're quite baggy. Pleated in the front.'

Dania said it for him. 'Definitely not the kind *you'd* wear. *I* wouldn't either,' she added quickly. 'So, was there anything on his clothes that could help us?'

'I found different types of pollen. Mainly oak and pine. In these parts, they peak in June.'

'We've been given a post-mortem interval of four to eight weeks, so it fits.' She nodded at the shirt. 'It would be good to get that into the local media. Although we can't do it in that condition.'

'Why not leave it with me, Inspector? I can come up with an artist's impression, complete with an accurate colour.'

'An artist's impression?'

Cosmo inclined his head modestly. 'I used to be an artist in a previous life.'

'What made you leave that life and go into forensics?' she said, genuinely curious.

'Alas, there was no money in the type of art I created.'

She was tempted to ask what that was, but decided against it. There was something she needed to do that afternoon, and Cosmo was likely to regale her with his artist's life history. 'Let me know when the image is ready, Cosmo.'

'Will do, Inspector.'

As Dania left the building, she hoped that he was indeed able to produce something they could give to the press. The shirt was distinctive enough that anyone seeing it would remember it, no question. That was assuming, of course, that someone *had* seen it. It could have been new on, and only the killer had had the privilege.

CHAPTER 14

Dania started the car, and headed north. She made good time, reaching the ornamental gates to the Alderwood estate without mishap. After passing Alderwood Manor Lodge, which looked as deserted as it had the week before, she sailed past the hedges and lawns towards the Manor.

As she neared the end of the drive, a man waved her down. 'You'll need to go to the car park,' he said.

'I'm here to see Glenna McGarry. I'll leave the car in front of the building.'

'Do you have an appointment?' he asked, in a manner that could best be described as challenging.

Dania held up her warrant, saying nothing.

The man stiffened. He looked about to protest, then seemed to think better of it. 'Why do you wish to see her?' he said gruffly.

'That's a matter for myself and Mrs McGarry.'

Without waiting for a response, Dania pulled away. In the rear-view mirror, she could see the man glowering after her. She drew up in front of the house, and left the car. The flowers in the ornamental planters looked as though they hadn't been watered, something she might mention to the man if he was still there when she left. She rang the bell, hearing the thunderous echo through the house.

She was on the point of giving up and trying round the back when the door opened. She recognised the tall woman, her brown hair cut in a short, elegant style, because she'd seen her picture in the papers. The woman was wearing a low-cut crimson dress that hugged her figure, and seemed more suited to the evening. Her breasts were so huge that her pendant was lost in the cleavage. Dania put her in her fifties.

'Mrs McGarry?' she said, holding up her warrant. 'My name's DI Dania Gorska. Could I have a word?'

The woman hardly glanced at the card. In Dania's experience, most people either went into a flap, bending over backwards to accommodate the police and their enquiries, or grew sullen and behaved rudely. Glenna McGarry did neither.

'Of course. Please come in,' she said, standing back to let Dania pass. She had a clipped English accent.

The man Dania knew was watching some distance away couldn't fail to have seen Glenna's response. She resisted the urge to look back at him.

'Shall we go into the conservatory?' Glenna said, making it sound like a statement rather than a question. She had a voice deep enough to be a man's.

Dania followed her along the dark corridors until they came to a glass-panelled door. She recognised the red-tiled floor and cream rattan furniture from her peek through the window the time she'd visited the Maze. As they entered, the tinkling from the fountain reached her ears.

'Please take a seat, Inspector,' Glenna said, motioning to the chairs.

When they were settled, she asked, 'Are you related to Marek Gorski, by any chance?'

'He's my brother.'

'Ah yes, he mentioned that he had a sister when I interviewed him. I can see the family resemblance. So, how can I help you?'

'I'm here about the body found on your estate.'

It had been a stroke of luck that one of Dania's team had searched the Land Register of Scotland, and discovered that the area of woodland where the body had been buried lay within the Alderwood boundary.

'On my estate?' Glenna's expression hardly changed. It was as if she'd been expecting the question. But then, the press had been quick off the mark, although the details and precise location of the corpse had been kept from them. All they'd been told was that a man's body had been found in woodland somewhere north of the city centre. 'Where, exactly, Inspector?' she said.

'Behind your Maze, the land rises and then falls down to woodland.'

'I know the area you mean.'

'On Thursday, a man walking his dog stumbled across a shallow grave in those woods.'

'And as this is my estate, you need to ask me some questions.' She sat back, gazing calmly at Dania.

'My first question is: have any of your workers gone missing in the last few weeks? Either handed in their notice, or simply disappeared.'

'That's one for my daughter-in-law, Hayley. She manages everything to do with the house and gardens, including the Maze and the other outdoor activities. She does it very efficiently, I have to say. It leaves me and my son, Arron, free to concentrate on the publishing business.'

85

'And where might I find Hayley?'

'At the moment, she'll be in the control room, operating the Maze. If you've no further questions for me, I can take you to her.'

'I don't want to disturb her while she's working.'

'We're due to close up in ten minutes.'

Glenna took Dania outside, then led the way past the conservatory towards the Maze. She ignored the man trying to attract her attention, and turned right, following the path to a small, single-storey brick building.

'Hayley operates the Maze from this control room,' Glenna said. She entered a six-figure code and opened the door.

The windowless room was brightly lit and smelt of floral air freshener. The faint hum of the air conditioning accounted for the pleasant temperature, but the absence of radiators made Dania wonder how the room could be heated in winter. At the far end, on a long table, was the largest screen she had ever seen, larger even than those used by the police. It was divided into a number of sections, each showing a different area of the Maze. A woman with orange-red hair dragged back into a ponytail was sitting facing the screen and working the controls at the bottom. She was wearing headphones, which Dania assumed allowed her to listen in to the various conversations, such as the one between Honor and herself.

Glenna approached the table and laid a gentle hand on the woman's arm. The woman looked up, then removed her headphones, leaving them lying round her neck. 'Hayley, let me introduce Inspector Dania Gorska,' Glenna said calmly. 'Inspector, this is my daughter-in-law, Hayley McGarry.'

The woman wheeled round and stared at Dania. The skin of her face was tight with fear. Dania couldn't help noticing that her right leg had started to tremble.

Glenna must have seen Hayley's reaction, but acted as though she hadn't. 'The Inspector has some questions for you. I'll leave the two of you together.' Without waiting for a reply, she made for the door, where she paused, adding, 'And could you show the Inspector the way to her car when you've finished? It's at the front door.' She nodded politely to Dania, and left.

Hayley got slowly to her feet. She was wearing a white T-shirt, baggy distressed jeans and dark trainers. The startling blue eyes in the freckled face made Dania think of a schoolgirl who's been caught by her teacher, and knows she's in trouble. It was a strange reaction, and Dania's immediate thought was that the woman had something to hide.

'What would you like to talk to me about?' Hayley said, her words faltering. She had a soft English voice.

'It's about the body found in the woodland near here. You may have read about it?'

She was trembling all over now. 'I can't say that I have,' she said finally.

'Shall we sit down?' Dania was afraid that the longer they remained standing, the more likely it was that the woman would keel over.

For a second, she thought Hayley would say no, but then her shoulders drooped. She indicated the chair next to hers.

Dania pulled out her notebook. Hayley stared at it as if it might jump out of the detective's hand and bite her.

'Mrs McGarry, we're trying to establish the identity of the man in the woods. There was no ID on him, or anything that could identify him.' She paused, seeing Hayley's eyes widen. 'Your mother-in-law told me that you manage the estate, and might therefore be in a position to help us.'

'Help you in what way? Isn't this just one of the drugs-related deaths that we're always reading about?'

'We don't yet know why the man died,' Dania said, choosing her words. 'It's early days, I'm afraid, so we're keeping all options open. I'm wondering if he might have been someone who worked for you. Have any of your employees left recently?'

Hayley's expression cleared. She relaxed visibly, her confidence returning. 'They come and go. The work we offer here is seasonal.'

'What do they do?'

'They manage the various outdoor activities.'

'Such as?'

'We have a zipwire, a treasure hunt – that's always very popular with the children – and there's a nine-hole golf course. Oh, and we have a tree walk. So, let me see, what else?' She rubbed her cheek. 'And the Maze, of course,' she added, glancing at the screen.

Dania could see people making their way towards the various exits. 'I think I get the picture,' she said. 'So, how many people do you employ?'

'At the height of the season, it's about fifty.'

'And the height of the season is now, right?'

'Right.'

'When does the season start? I mean, when do your workers arrive?'

'We open in May,' Hayley said brightly. 'The workers arrive a week earlier to make sure that everything is operating properly.'

'You said they come and go. Would you be able to supply me with a list of those who left your employ between four and eight weeks ago?'

She hesitated. 'It might take some time.'

'You surely keep electronic records.'

'Of course.'

Dania glanced at the laptop. 'Could you check now?'

'Yes, I can do that.'

While she tapped at the keyboard, Dania studied the large screen. All the visitors had gone. And nothing was moving, which wasn't surprising, as Hayley wasn't working the controls. Dania had to resist the temptation to tap at the icons to see what happened.

A moment later, Hayley turned to her and said, 'Two men left about six weeks ago.'

'And do you know why?'

She picked at her lip. 'I had to let them go. They were always squabbling with each other. It had reached the stage where I thought they'd start fighting. It was affecting the other workers, and I couldn't have that. For one thing, it's dangerous. Managing the outdoor activities has to be done with care and attention, and requires team effort in some cases.'

'Were the men local?'

She glanced at the laptop screen. 'They had addresses in Dundee.'

'Have you got their photographs?'

'I'll put them up.' She sat back so that Dania could see.

One of the men had fair hair. But the other had short, dark hair. And dark eyes.

'And do you know where they went?' Dania said slowly. 'Did any of the other workers keep in touch with them, to your knowledge?'

'I really couldn't say.'

'I'll need you to send me what you have on these two.' Dania handed Hayley a card. 'If you could email it to my address, it would be very helpful.'

'Shall I do it now?'

'If you would. I'll need their addresses, the dates their employment started and terminated, their photos and anything else you have on them.'

'Okay. Give me a second.'

As Hayley gathered the data, Dania's attention was drawn to a movement in the Maze. Two girls had slipped inside. Judging by their location, they'd found a way in on the side opposite the main entrance. She recognised them as the teenagers – Ailsa and Chloe – that she'd seen on her visit. She watched, fascinated, as they moved from one on-screen section to the next without pausing. It was almost as if they knew exactly where to go. It was the girl with the curly hair who was in the lead. Before long, they'd reached an exit, and disappeared from view.

'Right, Inspector, that's everything sent on.'

'Thank you. If anything else about these men comes to mind, please don't hesitate to get in touch.'

Hayley chewed her lip, nodding. 'Okay, I will.'

Dania looked encouragingly at her. 'It must be something of a challenge running everything. I understand you manage it on your own.'

'I'm afraid I have to. My husband, Arron, works with his mother in her firm.'

'And what does he do exactly?'

'He's the new-business manager.'

'Looking for new writers?'

'Not just that. His role is to seek out other publishing opportunities.'

'And you operate the Maze.'

'Not every day. Sometimes people arrive to find that nothing moves.'

'Well, thank you for your help, Mrs McGarry.' Dania got to her feet. 'I need to be going. I think I can find my way out.'

'Great. It'll give me a chance to close down the Maze before I check on the other activities.'

'What does closing down the Maze entail exactly?'

'During the day, I move the hedging and some of the statues. But after we close, I return them all to their original positions. We call that the "base state". It then allows me to go into the Maze and double-check that no one is still in there.'

'But can't you tell that from this big screen?'

'Actually, no. There are some blind spots that aren't covered by the cameras. Health and safety requires us to check physically.'

'And it's always you who checks? None of the workers does it?'

'Sometimes it's Glenna, or Arron. We all know the base state like the backs of our hands. Even Clare. She's been known to help out.'

'Clare?'

'Clare Conlee. She lives in the grounds. In the Manor Lodge. You'll have passed it on your way here.'

'She runs *Dundee Today*, doesn't she? Marek mentioned her.'

Hayley slapped her forehead. 'Of course. Marek Gorski is your brother.'

'It must be convenient for Glenna having Clare living nearby.'

'Yes, they often have meetings in the conservatory.'

'Well, goodbye, Mrs McGarry,' Dania said. 'Thank you again for your time.'

But as she left the control room, she made a mental note to run a background check on Hayley McGarry. Because a mental flag had been raised. The level of fear on the woman's face when she'd learnt that Dania was a police officer was one she'd rarely seen before. Hayley was hiding something. It might or might not have any bearing on the case of the man buried in the woods, but something told Dania that she would be wise not to ignore it. In fact, a background check on all three McGarrys would be advisable.

CHAPTER 15

Marek had spent part of Sunday morning at home checking social media. But other than Piero Terranova's website, which showcased his creations and gave details of his upcoming fashion shows, all Marek could find were online articles about, and interviews with, the designer. There seemed to be no shortage of people clamouring for an audience. A quick read through the text told him that everything Piero wanted to say about himself was there, which explained why he had neither a Facebook nor a Twitter account.

But these interviews had taken place mainly in the US. Here in the UK, Piero was less of a name, which was presumably why he had brought his creations to Dundee's famous V&A, intending to use the venue to kickstart a season of shows. And his star was in the ascendant, given the growing interest in his fashions.

Marek ran a hand over his face. He'd tried Luca's number several times but without success. The voicemail message was starting to irritate him. The man had said he'd be returning at the weekend, Sunday at the latest, but Marek had heard nothing. He was on the point of giving up when his phone pinged. It was a message from Luca – he'd be taking the train up to Dundee the following day. It gave Marek the impetus he needed. He left the flat, and scrambled into the car.

He knew that, at this time of morning, Hayley would be operating the Maze, but Arron should be around, and might be in a position to help. It was weeks since Marek had seen him. Arron worked mostly at the Manor, whereas his own meetings with Glenna and Clare were usually conducted at the East Dock Street premises. It was when there was a social at Alderwood that Marek and Arron got together. The two had hit it off brilliantly that first time when they'd quickly established they were both fans of Dundee United. If anything was likely to start a bromance, it was supporting the same football team.

Sunlight was pouring from the sky, and Marek guessed that Arron would be working outside. He drove past the lawns towards the building, ignoring the man trying to direct him to the car park. A sharp right turn, followed by a left, and he reached the back of the building, where a parking area had been reserved for the Manor's guests.

Marek pulled up in one of the many free spaces, and cut the engine. The other car there was the black Maserati, which told him that only Arron was at home. Marek peered through the windscreen towards the patio, seeing a figure sitting under a huge yellow parasol. There was a laptop on the table, a coffee pot and a jug of what could have been Pimms. And a plate of something brightly coloured.

Arron must have recognised him because he lifted an arm and waved him over. Marek strolled across and up the steps.

'Hey, Marek,' Arron said, getting to his feet. 'It's been too long.' He was wearing shorts and a Hawaiian shirt, which made Marek, who was in a light-grey linen suit, feel overdressed. At least Arron wasn't in his usual black-and-tangerine T-shirt. Whoever had come up with those colours for Dundee United needed his head examined.

The men gripped hands, then Arron said, 'Are you here to see Glenna? She's out, I'm afraid.'

'No, it's you I've come to talk to.'

'Me? I'm honoured, and no mistake. Take a seat, man. How about a wee swallie?' he added, lifting the jug. 'It's whisky sour.'

'I'm afraid I'm working,' Marek said, with a grin.

'So am I. But it doesn't stop me having a drink.'

Marek stared at the plate of macaroons.

Arron must have seen him looking because he said, with a laugh, 'Help yourself. And there's coffee in the pot.'

Marek's gaze hadn't travelled that far. He poured himself a mug, savouring the rich aroma. Alderwood seemed to offer the best coffee in town, something he attributed to Glenna's taste rather than her son's. He flopped into the chair Arron had pushed towards him, glad of the parasol's shade. 'So, what are you working on just now, Arron?' he said, picking out a lemon macaroon.

'Have you heard about these papers that were found in the archives at St Andrews?'

'The university?'

'That's right. They date back to the seventeenth century. Some professor is working on a transcription. We're hoping to publish them, ken.'

'Anything interesting there?'

'Lots of juicy stuff, apparently.' He winked. 'Amazing what academics get up to. Anyway, what about you? You've come all the way out here to see me. Must be something important, eh.'

Marek hesitated. He didn't want to give away Piero's name, not until he had something solid. 'I'm looking for someone. A drug dealer.' It was the only thing he could think up on the spur of the moment, and totally plausible. He'd been on the trail of drugs men before, and had written extensively about Dundee's drugs problem. But he was now convinced that Piero's disappearance had to do with what happened in the Maze. Sylvia's words at the V&A were still ringing in his ears:

All I know is that Piero went into that Maze as his usual happy self, and when he came out, he was a changed man.

'A drug dealer?' Arron ran a hand through his thatch of fair hair. 'So, how can I help?'

'I have intel that he came here to meet someone.'

'Here? At Alderwood Manor?'

'In the Maze.' Marek picked out another macaroon. 'I really need to know who this man is.'

'When was this?'

'June the seventh. In the afternoon.'

Arron's gaze sharpened. 'Are you saying that drug pushing is going on here, pal?' he said softly. 'And you've not thought to tell us?'

'I've only just found out,' Marek said, in a hurried voice.

'Aye, well, I guess the Maze would be the ideal place for a bit of dealing if it weren't for all the cameras. Mind you, few people know about them.'

'That's what I wanted to ask you. How long do you keep the camera footage?'

Arron took a sip of whisky sour, and smacked his lips. 'To be honest, I don't think Hayley's thought about that yet. It all goes on to a hard drive. It must still be there.'

Marek couldn't believe his luck. He'd expected the footage to have been wiped. In fact, he was surprised that it had been stored at all. But then, the new system hadn't been in operation long. 'So, you've kept all the recordings from when you opened in May?'

'I presume so. Do you know what this drugs guy looks like?'

'I've seen a photo of him.' Marek wished now that he'd told the truth, but it was too late to backtrack. He wolfed the macaroon, and took a couple more.

Arron grinned. 'That's the fifth you've had. I was beginning to think you weren't hungry.'

'I haven't eaten anything today. I went to early Mass.'

'I can make you a bacon butty.'

'Maybe another time.'

'Aye, I get it.' He laughed softly. 'You want to take a keek at that footage.' He hauled himself out of the chair. 'Come on, let's go to the control room.'

As they strolled round to the front of the Manor, it occurred to Marek that he'd have to keep his expression blank when Piero's image appeared on the screen, and act as though it was of no interest. The thought crossed his mind that he could ask Hayley to make him a copy of everything she had, and then look at it in his own good time, but he suspected that she'd bring up Data Protection. In fact, he was lucky he was getting to see anything at all.

They passed the man directing visitors, and took the path to the control room. Arron pressed the buttons on the keypad, and opened the door.

Hayley was standing just inside, fiddling with the controls on the wall. She turned quickly as the men entered. 'Hi Marek,' she said, with a warm smile.

'Good to see you, Hayley.'

'What are you doing, lovely lass?' Arron said.

'I'm adjusting the air con.' She stroked her small baby bump. 'Junior tells me it's too hot in here.'

'Let me do it. You take a seat.'

'I haven't seen you for ages,' she said to Marek. 'We need to get Glenna to hold another of her parties.'

'Ah, yes.' He raised an eyebrow. 'The last time I attended one of those, I had to be carried home.'

To his delight, he'd discovered that Glenna kept a selection of vodkas in her drinks locker. When he'd quizzed her, she'd confessed that it was Clare Conlee who'd suggested Glenna buy in a few, knowing that vodka was Marek's drink of choice. Yes, he'd definitely landed on his feet with Clare as a boss.

'Okay, that's the temperature turned down,' Arron said. His gaze lingered on his wife's face. There was such a look of tenderness in his eyes that Marek nearly turned away. He'd never met a couple who, after years of marriage, were still so hopelessly in love.

Arron seemed to remember himself then. 'Marek is looking for someone who came to the Maze last month. It's a drugs guy, and he's trying to hunt him down.'

'Good heavens,' Hayley exclaimed, her eyes widening. 'You're sure he came *here*?' she said to Marek.

'My source is convinced. I want to know who he met.'

'Is there an easy way of checking the camera footage?' Arron said. 'Have you done it before?'

'Only when the system was installed. The techie guy went through it all with me. It seemed straightforward at the time.'

'You've not deleted anything, then?'

'No, but if the drive starts to get full, I'll have to think about it.' She frowned at Marek. 'So, can we narrow it down? Do you have a rough idea as to when he was here?'

'We're in luck with that. It was June the seventh.'

'In the afternoon,' Arron added.

'Right,' she said, 'let's make ourselves comfortable.'

She sat down, and the men took chairs on either side. Marek

watched, his curiosity rising, as Hayley tapped at the screen, dismissing the images, and playing with the controls until she'd found what she was looking for. The date and time appeared in the top right-hand corner.

'June the seventh,' she said.

The screen filled with images of people in different areas of the Maze.

'Shall I start at midday?' she said, looking quizzically at Marek.

'A little later. How about two o'clock?'

'Righto. Two o'clock it is.'

She moved a slider at the bottom of the screen. 'See your guy anywhere, Marek? I can fast-forward.'

'That might be helpful.'

Hayley moved the slider and the people onscreen started to walk around more quickly, like something out of an old film. Then Marek saw him. 'Stop!' he called.

Piero was standing in front of a statue of Bonnie Prince Charlie. At least, that's who Marek assumed it was from the white wig, tartan outfit and blue sash. Piero by contrast was wearing jeans and a shirt in a milky-green colour. He was speaking angrily, and gesticulating to someone out of reach of the camera. The time on the screen was 14:56.

'Can we get the sound?' Marek said.

'We should be able to, I think, if I press this button here.'

But although Hayley tried everything, no sound was forthcoming. 'Sorry,' she said, in a small voice. 'It should have been recorded along with the images. I don't know what's gone wrong. I can certainly hear the sound when it's live.' She smiled thinly. 'I'll have to get the techie guy out again.'

'We've never needed to look at the recording,' Arron said.

Suddenly, he sat up straight. 'My God,' he added, in a hoarse whisper. He was staring at the screen.

'What is it?' Marek said.

He wiped his mouth with the back of his hand. 'Someone I used to know. I thought he'd left Dundee.'

Marek decided not to pursue it, as it was none of his business. But then Arron said, 'It was a writer I had a run-in with a while back. We were all set to sign the contract, and he pulled out without an explanation. Said he was moving to the US, where he'd get his book published. He never returned the advance, and we didn't think it was worth pursuing.' He was gabbling, as though he needed Marek to know the fine details.

'So, did you find your drugs man?' Hayley said to Marek.

'Yes, could you go back a bit, and then let it run at normal speed?'

'No problem.'

Marek watched in frustration as Piero walked around the Maze before stopping all of a sudden. To say he was stunned by what he was seeing was an understatement. He seemed to call to someone, then his look of amazement changed to one of anger. He mouthed off for several minutes, even raised a clenched fist. If Hayley and Arron had spotted this, they said nothing. Finally, Piero moved away out of reach of the camera, reappearing in several other areas, until he arrived at the entrance. Then he disappeared from view.

Marek continued to gaze at the screen, not wanting Hayley and Arron to suspect that it was Piero he'd been looking at. A minute or two later, he sat back with a sigh.

'I'm so sorry about the sound,' Hayley said.

He threw her a reassuring smile. 'Don't worry. I was able to get a good look at the person the drugs guy was meeting.'

'He didn't pass across any packets or anything, did he?' Arron said.

'Not that I could see. It was just a conversation.'

'We'll get the sound sorted, pal. If you hear that they're meeting in the Maze again, don't hesitate to get in touch.'

Marek ruffled his hair. 'Thanks for your time, anyway. I'll let myself out.'

As he was getting to his feet, his phone pinged. It was a message from Luca telling him that it would probably now be Wednesday before he came up to Dundee. Just as well, Marek thought glumly, since he'd learnt nothing new from the video.

At the door, he paused, wondering if he should ask for a copy of the footage. He glanced back.

Arron and Hayley were leaning forward, staring into the screen, whispering to one another.

CHAPTER 16

It was mid-afternoon on Wednesday before the pathology report landed in Dania's inbox. The only thing she learnt was that there had been no sign of sexual assault. Reports from Forensics were also in. There was no match for the victim's DNA in the database, nor for his teeth with dental records, which was a blow, as they'd thrown all the resources they could spare at that. The officer's comment that the teeth were in excellent condition, and so would have been checked regularly by a dentist, led to the suggestion that the man might have lived abroad. The toxicology report confirmed that no opiates were present in the bloodstream. To Dania's surprise, Jenn had left a message – much sooner than expected – to say that the results of the soil analysis had come through, and she'd been able to firm up slightly on the post-mortem interval. The man had died approximately six weeks earlier, with an error margin of about one week each way. That put the time of death at roughly the middle of June. Dania sent Jenn an encouraging message, thanking her.

Six weeks. Hayley had sacked two workers six weeks before, on 10 June. And one had dark hair and dark eyes. The men had changed address, but Honor had managed to track down where the fair-haired man – Martin Mason – was staying. There was no trace of the other.

Dania picked up her jacket, and was about to leave the incident room when her phone rang.

'Cosmo here, Inspector. I just wanted to say that I've finished the artist's impression of the shirt. I'll send it over now. And I managed to get the trousers in as well. They're an unusual shape. The two together might jog a few memories.'

'Brilliant, Cosmo. I owe you.'

'Is it too late to get it into the *Evening Telegraph*?'

'I don't think so. We'll put it out on the news as well.'

'Right, well, good luck.' He rang off.

Dania issued instructions to her team to get the image into the evening paper with a request to the public to come forward if they recognised the clothes. And to open a window, as the temperature in the incident room was becoming unbearable. Although she would never say it, it didn't help that the male officers seemed to feel the need to compete with each other for the most pungent aftershave. She left before anyone else collared her.

At three in the afternoon, the sun was cooking the ground, but mercifully it was a short walk to Constitution Street. Dania found the block of flats without difficulty. Several black bins stood on either side of the main entrance. She pressed the bell to Martin Mason's flat, and waited for a suspicious voice to ask who she was and what she wanted. To her surprise, she heard a man's voice say, 'Well, hello there, you're early. But that's okay. Come on in. I'm on the left, at the end of the corridor.'

Before she could reply, there was a buzz and the door opened. It had been surprisingly easy but, then, the man had been expecting someone.

The corridor was dim and smelt of antiseptic. She found the

apartment, and was lifting her hand to knock when the door opened suddenly.

A tall, slim-built man who looked in his late twenties was standing smiling. With his fair hair and magnetic blue eyes, he reminded her so much of Marek that she found herself staring. Hayley's photo didn't do him justice. In fact, had it not been for the large mole on his cheek, Dania would have said that this was not the man she was looking for. He was wearing a pale-green dressing gown in what could have been silk, and a pair of dark-blue slider sandals. Slowly, he removed the cigarette holder from between his lips, and gave a slight bow. 'Please, come in,' he said, stepping back.

Dania found herself in a sparsely decorated room. The furniture was old IKEA, and the pictures on the beige-coloured walls were cheap prints. A brown carpet worn to the weave, and in some places worn away completely, covered most of the floor, and she had to take care not to trip over it. The strong, floral scent she traced to the vase of white lilies on the sideboard. Two champagne flutes and an ice bucket containing a bottle of Prosecco stood on a glass coffee table. She became suddenly aware of the music playing in the background. A husky female voice that sounded like Marlene Dietrich was singing the 1920s song, 'Just a Gigolo'.

'Let me offer you a glass of fizz,' the man said. He had a quiet, silky voice, which she suspected was faked.

'I'm on duty, Mr Mason. You *are* Martin Mason, am I right?'

He drew his brows together, and his expression changed. 'So, you're not . . .'

'No, I'm not. I'm DI Dania Gorska.' She held up her warrant. 'I'd like a few words.' She glanced at his attire. 'If you're not too busy.'

'What's this about?' His voice was no longer silky, but thin and reedy.

'Would you mind switching off the music? It's a bit distracting.'

He fiddled with the CD player on the sideboard. Then he turned and glared suspiciously at her. 'I've done nothing wrong,' he said.

'I'm sure you haven't.'

He seemed to feel the need to explain. 'I entertain ladies, that's all. Some are lonely, and they just want a chat. With others, I provide them with a boyfriend experience.'

'And that is?'

'I take them places. Drinking, dancing, that sort of thing.' He glanced sideways. Through the open door, she glimpsed the double bed.

'Mr Mason, I'd like to talk to you about Alderwood Manor. You left your job there on June the tenth. Can you tell me why?'

He seemed taken aback by the question. 'I was given my marching orders,' he said, after a pause.

'What was your job there?'

He slumped on to the sofa. Dania took the seat next to him, as there was nowhere else to sit. He ran a hand through his perfectly groomed hair. 'I managed the zipwire. By that, I mean I made sure the mechanism was safe, and that the customers were securely strapped into the harness. That sort of thing. And if anyone got stuck, I had to get up there and help them. It came with a lot of responsibility. I went on a training course. I can show you the certificate,' he added, with a note of defiance.

She opened her notebook. 'Why did you get the sack? Was there an accident?'

'There almost was,' he said sourly. 'On my days off, someone else took over. His name was Jan Białek.' Martin's gaze wandered over her face. 'He had an accent like yours. Anyway, when I came

105

in one day after he'd been on the job, I discovered that the mechanism wasn't as it should be. A zipwire isn't as simple as it looks. There are all sorts of things that have to be tested. I won't bore you with the details, but each time I came in to work, I had to arrive an hour earlier to double-check that everything was in order.'

'Did you raise this with Jan Białek?'

'Yeah, and more than once. He just sneered that I didn't know what I was talking about.'

'Did he also go on a training course?'

'Not that I know of. Look, I've got nothing to hide,' Martin blurted, watching her write. 'If you're here to check my credentials, I can show you my certificate.'

Dania glanced up. 'I'm sure you did everything properly, Mr Mason.'

'Then why are you here? What do you want from me?'

'Tell me about Jan Białek. What was he like? Apart from not being a good zipwire operator.'

Martin lay back, and spread his arms over the edge of the sofa. The action caused his dressing gown to open, revealing his smooth white chest. 'What can I tell you? He seemed popular with the other workers.'

'And you weren't?'

'I'd say I was just as popular. We all got along.'

'Until this business with the zipwire mechanism.'

'We began to argue about it, I won't lie to you.' He sighed. 'In the end, we both got the sack.'

Dania looked up from her writing. He seemed agitated, but no more than most people who were questioned by the police, and weren't sure why. 'Why didn't you tell Hayley McGarry what was going on?' she said. 'After all, if Jan Białek was putting lives at risk, she ought to have been notified.'

'I suppose I should have gone to her. But I thought I could solve the problem myself without having to inform on him.' He leant forward, and rubbed his face. 'The others would have found out if I'd shopped him.'

'What sort of clothes did Jan wear?'

Martin looked at her as though she'd lost her marbles. 'He wore what we all wore. Jeans, sweatshirts. Why do you ask?'

'Nothing more stylish?' she suggested, thinking of the long shirt. 'Unusual colours?'

His blank look gave her the answer. 'Do you still keep up with the workers?' she said.

'We've been meeting for the odd drink.'

'And does Jan come along, too?'

'I never saw him outside work. He went back to Poland, according to one of the guys. Left pretty quickly after he was sacked. That's what they reckoned, anyway.'

Which told Dania – provided this intel was accurate – that the body they'd found in the woodland wasn't his.

'Well, I think I've kept you long enough, Mr Mason.'

'Was that all you wanted to talk about?'

'I'm trying to find the whereabouts of Jan Białek.'

'Why? Has he done something?'

'I can't discuss that, I'm afraid.'

'So, I'm off the hook?'

'You were never on it.' Curiosity got the better of her. 'What made you go into this line of work?' she said, resting her gaze on his clothes. Or lack of them.

'It's just something to keep me going until I decide what to do. I might go back home to Sussex, and try my luck there.' A smile touched his lips. 'Are you sure I can't offer you a glass of Prosecco? I can put the music back on. We could have a dance. And it's on the house,' he added, his smile widening.

'It's very tempting,' she said, hauling herself to her feet. 'But I need to get back to work.' There was a sudden, loud ring from the corridor. 'And I think you need to get back to yours.'

Dania wandered down the Marketgait towards West Bell Street. The afternoon was creeping to its end, and she hadn't yet had lunch. Her choice was either the work canteen or she could find somewhere in town. It didn't take her long to decide.

Minutes later, she was in the Overgate Shopping Centre, tucking into a Frankie & Benny's Classic Cheese burger, only realising how hungry she was when she gobbled her food so quickly that melted cheese dropped on to her plate. It didn't help that the place smelt of fried chicken. As she sipped her coffee, she thought through her meeting with Martin Mason. His explanation seemed plausible enough and, if Jan Białek had indeed returned to Poland, that was something they could check. But suppose he hadn't. Could Martin have shot him in retaliation for losing his job as a result of their bickering? And with a Beretta? It was an unconvincing hypothesis. And yet stranger things had happened. Her case files were full of them.

Dania finished her lunch, and was making her way past the shops towards the exit when she noticed that the lid of the baby grand was open. And no one was sitting playing. She couldn't pass up what she viewed as a rank invitation. She pulled out the seat, wondering what she should play. It was usually Chopin, which always drew the crowds, but today she fancied a change. It would be Schubert's 'Ständchen', the fourth song in his *Schwanengesang* collection. She began the piano solo version, and had reached the bar where the singer joins in when to her astonishment – and delight – she heard the rich tenor voice. She immediately switched to the accompaniment, slowing down slightly to accommodate the singer. He was standing somewhere behind her, but she didn't dare turn round in case she screwed up. The last time she'd played this piece was when she'd accompanied Marek, who also had a tenor voice, although nowhere near in the same league.

As she neared the end, she let the notes fade away dreamily. To applause and some whooping, she swivelled round to gaze at the singer. He was ignoring the crowd, and smiling at her, his arm outstretched.

Dania got to her feet and slipped her hand into his.

He shook it firmly. 'Thank you for accompanying me,' he said. He was tall, with broad shoulders and striking looks. His off-white linen suit and burgundy shirt looked newly pressed. Dania could see him playing any of the Wagner *Helden*, except that his voice was more suited to romantic tenor roles. Verdi or Puccini, then.

'I'm guessing you sing professionally,' she said.

'I don't, as a matter of fact. However, *I'm* guessing that you *play* professionally.'

Dania shook her head. 'But I always take the opportunity when I'm in the Overgate.'

'Then I'll have to come here more often.' There was warmth in his brown eyes. He must have noticed that he was still holding her hand because he released her suddenly. He glanced around. 'I think they're about to close up. May I take you somewhere for a drink?'

She was sorely tempted, but her shift wasn't over. 'I'm afraid I have to get back to work.'

'That's a pity. Perhaps, if our paths cross here again, we could tackle some more Schubert *lieder*.'

'I'll look forward to it. My name's Dania, by the way.'

He gave a slight laugh, as if he'd realised only then that they hadn't introduced themselves. 'Mine is Luca.'

And with a respectful nod, he left, striding towards the exit.

CHAPTER 17

'And that's what I learnt from Martin Mason,' Dania finished. 'We know the date he and Jan Białek were sacked, so we can check if Białek left the country. And didn't return. We may need to contact the Polish police.'

For a moment, no one spoke. Then Hamish Downie, who had recently been promoted to sergeant, said, 'I can do that, ma'am.'

'And what about the image from Cosmo? The clothes?' Dania said, looking round the group. 'Did anyone get it into the evening paper?'

'Aye, well, we were a wee bitty late,' someone at the back said. 'But it'll be in tomorrow's. And on tonight's news.'

'What happens if it turns out that this Białek isn't our babe in the woods?' Hamish asked. 'We've no other leads.'

'We might be able to do a facial reconstruction and get that out,' Dania said. 'But let's wait and see whether anyone recognises the victim's clothes.' She consulted her notes. 'Now we come to the background check on the McGarrys.' Seeing their looks, she suspected that had been a waste of time.

'Glenna McGarry was married,' a female officer said. When it came to checks, the woman had a track record of burrowing until she found what she was after. 'But Glenna ditched her husband after only a few years,' she went on. 'He was working his way through the family fortune.'

Dania tilted her head. 'His family fortune, or hers?'

'Hers. The estate was close to bankruptcy when they married. I've uploaded a photo of him if you're interested. He looks like a Hollywood film star, and no mistake.'

'What happened to him?' Honor said.

'He got a divorce settlement.'

'Don't tell me,' Honor said, lifting a hand. 'He worked his way through that as well.'

'Aye, he spent the money on fast cars and fast women. And then he disappeared.'

'And became a homeless vagrant?'

'He ran off with a girl half his age. Anyway, Glenna went into publishing. I think we all ken the rest of the history.'

'And what about Arron and Hayley McGarry?' Dania said. 'Anything there?'

'I checked out Arron,' someone chipped in. 'Nothing unusual. Went to Dundee High. Didn't really excel at anything, except playing in the Pipe Band.'

'What did he do when he left school?'

'He tried his hand at this and that, then joined Glenna in her business.'

'Is he a partner?'

'An employee,' the officer said meaningfully.

'And Hayley? She's the one I'm more interested in.'

'She's a Cambridge graduate. Engineering, apparently.'

'Cambridge?' Dania said, impressed. 'So, how did she and Arron meet?'

'She was the manager of the Maze renovation project. It took about two years. The McGarrys put her up in Alderwood Manor.

One thing led to another and . . .' The officer smirked. 'They were married even before the project came to an end.'

'What else do we know about her?' Dania said, trying to imagine the nervous Hayley presiding over such a large-scale undertaking. But maybe at the time she'd been a supremely confident young woman, and something had happened to change her.

'We didn't find anything of interest. She was schooled in England. Top in her class. Not really surprising she went to Cambridge.'

Yet there was something about her that didn't add up. Dania glanced at the clock. Half the team were nearing the end of their shift. 'Okay, that's it for now,' she said.

The officers leaving grabbed their jackets, while the others returned to gazing into their computers.

Dania found her thoughts drifting away from the McGarrys to Martin Mason. He'd lost his job as a zipwire operator and had taken up life as a gigolo. What would he be earning? Not as much, she guessed. But he didn't strike her as a murderer. Unfortunately, she was at that stage in the case where it had stalled, and they had little to go on. She twirled a lock of hair round her finger. Perhaps she should have accepted Martin's offer of a glass of fizz after all.

'Another one, Mr Terranova?' Marek said.

The men were sitting in the garden of a pub on the West Port, drinking beer and enjoying the relative cool of early evening. Clouds had started massing in the west, which accounted for the slight drop in temperature. The pub's owner, a balding Italian with a bull-like frame, had invested in cheap tables and chairs, an out-door pizza oven and a huge television screen. His gamble had paid off, as people flocked there after work, especially when there was a football match on. Tonight, however, they were to be disappointed. But it didn't stop them coming for the food, which was of high quality since the owner came from Naples. The smoky smell of cheese and pepperoni was what did it.

Luca got to his feet. 'It's my turn to get them in. And it's time you called me Luca,' he added, with a smile.

He disappeared into the pub, and returned a few minutes later with two pint glasses.

Marek had been surprised to receive Luca's phone call saying that he'd arrived in Dundee a day earlier than expected, and could they meet for a beer? Although Marek had hoped to attend a drinks party that Clare Conlee was holding at the East Dock Street premises, he suspected that Luca might have to leave the following day, and their time was limited. But the man had made small talk, quizzing Marek about Scotland, and Dundee in particular. He recognised this stalling behaviour: Luca was afraid that the investigator would be the bearer of bad news. Marek had learnt early on in his career that there were people who simply had to know the worst, however bad, and there were others who needed to psych themselves up before hearing the truth. Since he didn't know which category Luca fell into, he decided to wait until the man broached the subject himself.

'So, which part of Poland do you come from?' Luca said, wiping froth from his upper lip.

'Warsaw.'

'You know, my grandfather was living in Cassino when the war started. He was a young boy. But he never forgot the Polish soldiers. Have you visited the area?'

'I haven't, no.'

'Well worth a trip. Especially to the Polish cemetery on the side of the mountain.' He smiled. 'The locals know all about the Polish soldiers and what they accomplished. If you go anywhere in that region and tell them you're a Pole, you won't have to pay for a single drink in any of the bars.'

Marek laughed softly. 'That in itself is a reason for visiting.'

The pub owner had sauntered out, and was picking his way past the tables. Marek gulped his beer, watching as the man switched on the television and worked the controls. To his relief, he kept the volume low, and turned on the subtitles.

Luca was fidgeting with his shirt buttons. 'Is there anything further you've learnt about Piero?' he said finally.

'He visited the Maze at Alderwood Manor on June the seventh. Have you heard of this Maze? It's become something of an attraction because the hedges and statues can move.'

Luca paused in the act of bringing the glass to his lips. 'Isn't that dangerous?'

'It could be. But cameras have been installed. The person who operates the Maze can see everything that's going on. I say everything, but unfortunately there are some blind spots.'

'But we know that Piero was alive on June the seventh. How does this help us?'

'The camera caught him arguing with someone.'

'The operator saw this?' Luca said, lowering the glass.

'I saw it, too. I went to Alderwood Manor and asked if I could view the camera footage. It's stored on a hard drive. It's a pity there was a problem with the sound, or we would have heard what he was saying.'

'Did you see who he was talking to?' Luca frowned. 'You said he was arguing.'

'More like shouting. But it was at someone out of reach of the camera. I'm thinking that, if anything *has* happened to Piero, it might have had something to do with the episode in the Maze. If we could get the hard drive to a technical expert, they might be able to recover the sound.'

Luca was running a finger round the rim of the glass. 'And would the operators allow that?' he said slowly.

'They're friends of mine, a married couple. I know the family.' He tried to inject a note of urgency into his voice. 'Look, this is our best lead. Our *only* lead. If we could hear what Piero was saying, we might find out who he was yelling at. He could have used the person's name.'

Luca seemed lost in thought. While Marek waited for him to come to a decision, his gaze wandered to the TV screen behind Luca. On it was a drawing of a long, Elizabethan-style shirt in a honey-yellow colour. The sleeves were full, and gathered at the wrists. Next to it was a pair of pleated black trousers that tapered to the ankle. Marek couldn't hear what was being said, as a group of rowdy Dundonians had entered the garden. They passed in front of the screen, so he couldn't see the subtitles. By the time they'd taken their seats, the image had disappeared, and the newsreader was on to the next item: a fire that had been deliberately started in an empty building.

Luca was playing with his shirt buttons again. 'Well, if it's our only lead . . .' He glanced up. 'I could come with you in case they need to be persuaded to give up the hard drive.'

'That won't be necessary. As I said, they're friends.'

'But I'd like to.'

Marek smiled. 'All right. How about tomorrow morning? I could pick you up after breakfast.'

'Sounds perfect.'

But as they finished their beers, Marek had the impression that Luca was less than enthusiastic. Given that the man had engaged him to find his brother, and had even come up to Dundee, Marek couldn't help wondering why he wasn't urging him to finish his drink so they could go to Alderwood Manor straight away.

CHAPTER 18

Marek sauntered into the Hampton, scanning the crowded foyer. He caught the receptionist's eye. The man nodded towards the armchairs. Marek followed the direction of his gaze, seeing Luca, dressed casually in jeans and a navy T-shirt, sitting playing with his phone.

He got to his feet as Marek approached. 'Hi, Marek. I'm ready to go,' he said, without preamble.

'Great. I've just checked the website and the Maze is up and running today. So, there'll be someone there.'

Marek had decided against informing the McGarrys in advance, in case they put him off. But arriving with Luca might just persuade them to hand over the drive. After all, they could still operate the Maze, they just wouldn't be able to record anything. What had given him a sleepless night was that he'd have to come clean and explain that it was Piero he'd been looking to find on the footage, and not a drug dealer.

'I hope there'll be no problem,' Luca said. 'They might be wanting to use—' He stopped, staring at something behind Marek.

Marek wheeled round to see what had caused him to break off in mid-sentence.

On the large wall monitor, the ten o'clock news had just started, and the newsreader was asking if anyone could identify the clothes he was about to put up on the screen. Marek recognised the shirt and trousers as the ones on the pub's television the evening before. The reader stated that they were an artist's impression of the clothes worn by an unidentified man, whose body had recently been discovered in woodland outside Dundee. The police were looking for any information the public could give them.

The colour had gone from Luca's face. And in that instant, Marek understood.

'Are those Piero's clothes?' he said, gripping Luca's arm.

Luca seemed incapable of speech. He turned and gazed at him, his eyes brimming with tears. Marek felt a heartbreaking rush of pity for the man.

'They've found him,' Luca said, in a voice full of restrained emotion.

'I'm so sorry, Luca.'

He sank on to the nearest sofa and covered his face with his hands, weeping uncontrollably. 'Piero,' he wailed through his fingers. One by one, the guests grew silent, until the only sound in the room was the sobbing of a man who had just learnt that his brother was no longer alive.

The receptionist hurried over with a glass of water. Marek took it from his hands, and murmured his thanks.

'Shall I call someone?' the man whispered.

'It's okay, I'll deal with this. He's had some bad news.'

'Aye, he must have. He's greetin' like a bairn.' He nodded, and hurried away.

Marek took a seat next to Luca. 'Drink this,' he said softly.

Luca drew out a handkerchief and wiped his face. He took the glass with a trembling hand and drank down the water, gulping loudly. 'I'm sorry about that,' he said, setting the empty glass on the table. He tried a smile. 'A moment of weakness.'

'There's no reason to apologise. Anyone would have done the same.' Marek laid a gentle hand on his arm. 'Are you sure those are Piero's clothes?'

Luca took a deep breath. 'Absolutely.'

'Then there's only one thing we can do now. We need to go to the police. And we need to tell them everything.'

The man looked at his hands, then at Marek. 'Of course,' he said.

Marek pulled out his phone. He tried Danka's number but there was no reply. He got through to West Bell Street's reception, and explained the situation. He was told to come straight to the station. If Inspector Gorska wasn't available, someone else would be on hand.

'Come on, Luca,' Marek said gently. 'Let's go. It's not far.'

Dania was leaving her weekly meeting with DCI Jackie Ireland when a uniform caught her in the corridor.

'You're wanted at reception, ma'am,' the woman said. 'I'm told it's important. I was going to get you out of your meeting.'

'Something *that* important?' Dania said. 'What is it?'

She lifted her hands. 'I've no idea.'

'Okay, thanks.'

As Dania approached reception, she caught sight of Marek standing with a man whose back was turned.

'Ah, Danka, you're here,' Marek said breathlessly.

The man looked round then, and she recognised the tenor who'd sung Schubert the day before.

'Danka, this is Luca Terranova. Luca, my sister, Danka.' Marek paused. 'Inspector Gorska, I should say.'

'This is a surprise,' Dania said, smiling. Seeing Marek's blank expression, she added, 'We ran into each other at the Overgate yesterday. So, how can I help you?'

'Luca saw those clothes on the news this morning,' Marek said. He glanced at Luca, who was staring at the floor.

Dania lifted a hand. A corridor wasn't the place for a discussion. 'Let's go somewhere more private.'

She led the way to the nearest interview room. The scent of lavender polish suggested that it had been cleaned recently.

'Please do sit down,' she said, indicating the chairs. On the table were several pens and a pile of paper. Impromptu meetings were often held here, and someone had come up with the idea of supplying writing materials.

'You recognised the clothes, Mr Terranova?' Dania asked.

He had the look of a man reaching the end of his tether. He took out a handkerchief and dabbed at his eyes, then looked directly at her as though wanting her to think that he was in complete control of himself. 'They belong to my brother, Piero,' he said.

'Are you sure they're his?'

'There's no doubt. The trousers are Oscar de la Renta, if you want to check the label. Which I'm sure you already have.' He clasped his hands together. 'Inspector, I understand that a body has been found. Piero and I are identical twins. I can identify him.'

Dania thought of the face with the marbled skin and eyes pecked out. 'There's a better way. We can take a sample of your DNA.'

'Can't I at least see my brother?' Luca said pleadingly.

'It's not a good idea, Mr Terranova,' she said gently. 'He's been buried in woodland for several weeks. He's not in any condition to be viewed.' When Luca said nothing, she added, 'Is this why you're in Dundee? To visit Piero?'

He glanced at Marek. 'I engaged your brother to find him.'

The statement didn't surprise her. It wasn't the first time that her case had crossed with Marek's.

'Oh? When was this?' she said, directing the question at Luca.

'A week ago. Tuesday.'

Dania let her gaze rest on Marek. 'What can you tell me?' she said, pulling a sheet of paper towards her.

He fished in his jacket pocket, and removed the small book he used for note-taking. 'Piero was staying at the Hampton when his exhibition started at the V&A.'

'And that was?'

'June the fourth. He checked out of the hotel on June the ninth.'

'And the last time I was in touch with him was June the eleventh,' Luca said. 'I texted him and he messaged me back.'

'And nothing after that?' Dania asked, writing.

'My phone calls all went to voicemail.'

'And do either of you know where he went after he left the Hampton?'

'I had his address and phone number from someone at the V&A,' Marek said. He handed Dania the notebook.

'I'm assuming you went out there, Marek,' she said, copying the details.

When he didn't reply, she glanced up. He was fidgeting, and looking everywhere but at her.

'How did you get inside?' she said tonelessly.

'The back door was unlocked. I was careful to use gloves, and I didn't disturb anything. From the sell-by dates on the items in the fridge, no one had been in the cottage for some time. I was sure it was the right address because I sent photos of the clothes in the wardrobe to Luca, who confirmed they were Piero's.'

'I see.' She continued to write. 'I assume he had a car. Was it outside the cottage?'

'It was. A rented Mercedes. The sticker of the car-hire company is in the window.'

'Was the car locked?'

'Unfortunately, yes. There was a jacket on the passenger seat. I couldn't find the car keys anywhere in the house.'

'When did you go out there?'

'Last Wednesday.'

Dania sat back. 'What is it you're not telling me, Marek?' she said, after a pause.

He took a deep breath. 'I found a pistol and a packet of cartridges on the kitchen table.'

She gazed at the ceiling, then lowered her head. 'And you're telling me this only now?' she said angrily.

'Please don't be hard on him,' Luca blurted. 'I told him to keep it to himself until we decided on the best way forward.'

'The best way forward, Mr Terranova, would have been to inform the police.'

Marek ran a hand over his face, saying nothing.

'Tell me about Piero's fashion business,' Dania said. 'Was he successful?'

'He was just starting to make a name for himself in the US, where he lives now.' Luca smoothed back his hair. 'But there's so much competition. He'd brought his latest collection to the UK to see if he could make more of a splash here.'

'Do you know what he was worth?'

'I'll be honest with you, Inspector. Not much. There's always a cash-flow problem at the start of a new season. The clothes have to be made, then there are the transport costs to the fashion-show site, the venue hire and storage costs. On top of that, there's the insurance. It's only at the end that you know whether there'll be a demand, and you start to make sales. Or not. Piero always had to arrange a bank loan.'

'Were you involved in your brother's venture?'

'Me? Good heavens, no. I'm a voice coach. I'm currently working at Covent Garden.' The look in his eyes told Dania he had the same love for music that she had.

She recalled their encounter in the Overgate. He must have been thinking the same, because his expression softened.

'Was my brother murdered, Inspector?' he asked suddenly.

'We believe so.' She watched the emotions come and go on his face. 'Mr Terranova, do you know of anyone who might have had a grudge against Piero?'

For a second, a strange expression appeared in his eyes, and she thought he was going to give her a name. But he simply said, 'I don't. He was liked by everyone.'

'What about rival designers? Someone who might have wanted Piero to fail.'

'I really couldn't say. I'm sure he would have told me if there'd been any unpleasantness.'

Marek glanced at him, then said to Dania, 'There's something that might be relevant. One of the staff at the V&A told me there'd been an incident in Alderwood Manor Maze. It happened when Piero was there.'

'Go on,' she urged.

Marek consulted the notebook. 'It was on June the seventh. He started shouting at someone.'

'How do you know this?'

'The cameras in the Maze recorded it. I saw the video for myself.'

Dania leant forward. 'And what did he say? Did he call this person by their name?'

'That's the problem. For some reason, Hayley couldn't get the sound.' He looked intently into Dania's eyes. 'But I'm sure your technical department could recover it.'

'We were about to go and ask them if we could borrow their hard drive when I saw Piero's clothes on television,' Luca said. 'We came straight here.'

'Mr Terranova, I notice that you're right-handed. Is Piero also right-handed?'

'They're identical twins, Danka. Won't Piero be right-handed, too?'

'Not necessarily. When it comes to hand dominance, about twenty per cent of identical-twin pairs have one right-handed and one left-handed twin. Just one of those things detectives learn along the way.'

'My brother was left-handed, Inspector.'

She nodded slowly, appreciating the implication of his words. 'And how long are you planning on staying in Dundee?'

'As long as you need me to,' Luca said. 'I'll contact Covent Garden and explain the situation.'

'And where are you staying?'

'At the Hampton.'

'I'll need your mobile number.'

'Let me write it down,' he said, taking a sheet.

'And Piero lives in the US, you said?'

'New York.'

'Can you also write down his address there?'

A look of surprise crossed Luca's face, but he added it to the sheet.

Dania got to her feet. 'And now, I need to arrange for someone to take a cheek swab,' she said to Luca. 'Your DNA will confirm the identity of the man we found.'

Luca stood up.

'Can you stay behind, Marek? I'll just see to Mr Terranova.'

She saw her brother stiffen. He knew what was coming.

In the corridor, she turned to Luca. 'Would you like someone to come and stay with you? I can arrange for a family liaison officer.'

He smiled faintly. 'That's kind of you, Inspector, but it won't be necessary.'

'I will almost certainly have to speak with you again.' She handed him a card. 'Please don't hesitate to get in touch if you think of something that might help.'

'Thank you.' He pulled himself up. 'And when might you release my brother's body?'

'Not until the case is closed, I'm afraid.'

'I understand. But can you tell me how my brother died?'

She hesitated. 'I can't yet. I'm sorry.'

'Would it have been quick?'

'It would.'

He nodded slowly, but his expression suggested that he didn't believe her.

Dania escorted him to the reception desk, and explained to the duty sergeant what needed to be done. She waited with Luca until an officer arrived to take him to have his cheek swabbed. Before the men left, Dania shook hands with Luca, urging him to contact her if he needed anything. Then she hurried back to the interview room.

Marek was standing gazing at the ceiling, his hands in his pockets. He turned as she entered.

She leant against the wall, crossing her arms. 'So, you found a firearm and ammunition, and you didn't think to inform the police,' she shouted, in Polish.

'I know how it looks, Danka,' Marek said, making a calming motion with his hands. 'But I can explain.'

'What the hell were you thinking?'

'Luca asked me not to say anything for the time being.'

'You know the worst of it, Marek? You left that firearm in an unlocked building. I'm assuming you didn't lock up after yourself.'

'There was no key,' he said, looking at the floor.

'You're lucky I'm not charging you.'

His head shot up.

'But if you ever do this again, believe me, I will.' She paused to let him see that she meant it.

'Anything else, Danka?'

'Get out. Before I think of something.'

CHAPTER 19

Dania hurried into the incident room. 'Okay, everyone, gather round,' she said, holding up her arms to get their attention. She strode across to the incident board, and brought up the case details of the body in the woodland.

'We now have what I believe is a firm ID on the victim, subject to DNA analysis confirmation. Luca Terranova has identified these clothes as belonging to his brother, Piero.'

Someone whistled. 'Is that the guy whose dresses are on display at the V&A?'

'It is. I've just been speaking with Luca and Marek Gorski. Piero has been missing for some weeks, so Luca engaged Marek to find him. Here's what I have. Perhaps someone could add it to the board as I go through it.'

As quickly as she could, she told them what she'd learnt. 'Luca confirmed that Piero was left-handed,' she finished. 'So the fact that the Beretta was found in his *right* hand . . .'

'. . . nails the lid on the coffin of the suicide theory,' an officer known as Nessie said.

There were groans, and one or two muted guffaws. This officer, whose real name was Loch but everyone called Nessie, had a habit of coming up with morbid metaphors. He had large flabby cheeks, which shook when he laughed, which was often. But he knew Scots law better than anyone there, and Dania relied on him to keep her straight.

'If Piero lives in the US, it explains why we didn't find his dental records.' Dania glanced around. 'By the way, has anyone seen Hamish?'

'He's not on shift today,' Nessie said.

'When you see him, can you tell him to stop researching Jan Białek? He's not our babe in the woods,' she added, using the expression, which seemed to have stuck.

'And there was a firearm found in his rental?' someone asked.

'I intend to check that out. Right, we need to know everything about Piero Terranova.' Dania counted off on her fingers. 'Where he was born, what his life was like in the States, what he did before he became a fashion designer. And anything else you can think of. Oh, and talk to the staff at the V&A. I presume the exhibition is still on.'

'What about this Maze?' Nessie asked. 'The stooshie that was recorded? I reckon if Piero had been having an argie with his murderer, it might be our best lead, and no mistake.'

'We need to get absolute confirmation that it was his body in the woodland before we can lift the hard drive. That means waiting for the DNA results.'

Dania had been surprised to learn that, as part of a criminal investigation in Scotland, police have the common-law power to seize evidence without a warrant. That included articles like a recording device. Although Luca's confirmation based on the victim's clothes constituted reasonable belief, she wanted more than that, having been stung in a previous case, where a member of the public took legal action against her. The magistrate had ruled in her favour, but it had left her determined not to find herself in a similar situation again.

'Okay, everyone, you know what to do,' she said. 'I need to brief the DCI on these developments.'

They returned to their desks, all talking at once and deciding among themselves who would do what, a strategy Dania had tried early in her career and found that it worked brilliantly here, although less well at the Met. She hurried to the DCI's office only to find that the woman was in a meeting.

She ran into Honor on the way back. 'Grab your coat, Honor.'

The sergeant angled her head. 'We're going to the Maze, boss?'

'We're going for a drive.'

'Drumsturdy,' Honor said, as they turned off Kellas Road. 'Don't you just love these Scottish names.'

'At least I can pronounce this one.'

'I bet they're harder to say than Polish street names.'

'You think?' Dania then proceeded to come up with examples, having Honor repeat them until she gave up, dissolving into laughter.

They drove along the narrow road in silence. The landscape was typical of this part of Dundee: hedges and overhanging trees, and the odd cottage or homestead.

They hadn't gone far when Honor said, 'This must be it, boss. But I can't see anything.'

'Pull up anyway, and we'll have a walk around. It's not the first time the sat-nav has sent us to the wrong place.'

'Okey-dokey.'

'Hold on, I can see it now. Behind those trees.'

'You know, sometimes I wish crimes were committed only in

winter. There'd be no leaves to mask the view. It was all so much easier in London.'

The car bumped along the driveway. Beyond the curve was a white building.

Dania indicated with her chin. 'There's the Mercedes Marek mentioned.'

'How is your brother, these days?' Honor said, bringing the car to a halt.

'Not in my good books, I'm afraid. We had words. Or, rather, *I* had words.'

Honor said nothing. She switched off the engine.

Before they'd headed out of the city, Dania had visited the car rental company, and obtained a spare key for the Mercedes after explaining who she was, and why she wanted it. The manager had looked at her suspiciously, eventually handing over the keys, but not before he'd left the reception desk, probably to ring West Bell Street and check up on her. What she'd learnt on chatting to the secretary was that Piero had rented the car for two months from June the ninth, which Dania remembered was the date he'd checked out of the Hampton.

'So, which is it first, boss? The car, or the house?'

'The car.'

'You know what I don't get,' Honor said, as they approached the Mercedes. 'How come Marek couldn't find the car keys? They must be in the house somewhere.'

'He might not have looked carefully enough.' But the moment she said it, she knew it not to be true. When it came to searching, Marek was as good as any SOCO. SOCO had still to check out the place, but she doubted they'd find the car keys. Which begged the question: where were they?

They pulled on their gloves, and Dania pressed the key, hearing the clunk of the locks. She opened the passenger door. A linen jacket in a beige-grey colour lay on the seat. She checked the pockets. 'An Italian passport,' she said, holding it up. She opened it at the last page, seeing not one but two photos underneath the words REPUBBLICA ITALIANA.

'Is it Piero's?' Honor said, peering over her shoulder.

'It is. You can tell he and his brother are twins.'

'Cripes, he looks like a member of the Mafia.'

'Maybe he is.' Dania closed the passport. 'His brother speaks English without an accent. For that reason, I thought he was born here. According to this, Piero's an Italian national, so maybe Luca is, too.'

'We'll get it all from the background check.' Honor grinned. 'And I bet it's interesting. Born into a Sicilian Mafia family. Father killed. Luca and Piero smuggled as children out of Sicily, and brought up in a British convent school. Piero swears revenge on his father's killer, but the killer gets to him first.'

'You watch too much television, Honor.' Dania dropped the passport into an evidence bag. 'Piero's picture has been in the local papers with this fashion exhibition. If those damned birds hadn't pecked out his eyes, we might have had his identity sooner.'

'Glove compartment next, boss?'

But the only items inside were the manual for the Mercedes, and a foldable umbrella with the logo of the car-rental company. 'Let's try the boot,' Dania said.

Unsurprisingly, there was nothing there except a foot pump.

'Nice,' Honor said. 'I could do with one of those. So? The house?'

Despite having learnt from Marek that the back door was unlocked, Dania wanted to check the keys found in Piero's pocket. At the front, she inserted the Yale into the lock and pushed the door open with difficulty. 'Yes, I can see that anyone living here would prefer to come and go via the back,' she said, managing to pull the door shut.

They went round to the back.

'A glass panel, boss. Easy for a burglar.'

'It's too small. I suppose he could put his arm inside and reach for the key. Assuming it's in the lock.'

'Don't you think it's sad that, whenever we go somewhere, the first thing we think about is how a burglar would get in?'

'The downside – or the upside – of being a detective.' Dania tried the door, unsurprised to find it unlocked, then inserted the other key and turned it easily.

'Yep. It all fits. Are we going inside?' Honor added, peering through the window.

'We'll wait for SOCO. They won't be long.' She closed the door. 'What can you see?'

'It's the kind of kitchen I wish I had,' Honor said, with feeling.

'And the firearm?'

'On the table.'

Dania gazed through the window, trying not to touch the glass. She doubted Marek would have been as careful. He may have worn gloves, but he'd have left the imprint of his feet and who knows what else everywhere.

'Those flowers will be making the place stink, I bet,' Honor was saying.

'That looks like a milk jug. And if there's milk in it, it will add to the smell.'

'I see a pile of clothes in the washing machine. I can't tell if they're ready to wash, or ready to come out.' She stepped back. 'Why do you think Piero rented this place, boss?'

'Good question. He moved out of the Hampton. Okay, he

might have been short of money, but why move to somewhere so secluded? Why not find a cheap rental in the city centre? Near the V&A, perhaps. He wouldn't need a car. In fact, he didn't hire this one until he moved here.'

'You're thinking what I'm thinking, aren't you?' Honor said, after a pause.

'This would be a great place to shoot someone. Better than the Hampton, anyway.'

'Yep. And he could bury his victim in the woodland. There's plenty around here to choose from. Do you think, if that was his intention, that he botched it and his victim got to him first? Took him out into the woods and shot him there?'

'Maybe. But there's another possibility.' Dania gazed at her companion. 'Piero intended to kill someone else entirely.'

CHAPTER 20

Marek left West Bell Street feeling bruised. And yet what had he expected? He'd acted stupidly, and Danka had every right to reprimand him. At least she hadn't done it in front of Luca. She was too professional for that. But he wondered what he could do to get back into her good books because, if something was going to throw him off his stride, it was knowing that his sister was angry with him. If it was something trivial, it rarely lasted long. But this was different. He should have been firmer with Luca, and insisted on going to the police straight away. He was a complete imbecile, he thought miserably.

His phone pinged. Luca had sent a text message. He thanked Marek for his help and confirmed that he would be transferring the fee to his account. When Marek saw how much it was, he understood that the man had added a significant bonus. Yet he hardly deserved it. All he'd done was track down Piero's last-known address. Luca could have done that himself.

Marek was putting his phone away when it buzzed. It was Clare, asking if he could get himself to the office immediately, as they'd decided to move the meeting forward.

He straightened his tie, and hurried down the Marketgait.

* * *

The meeting was over, much to everyone's relief. Glenna had arrived unexpectedly, which had the unintended consequence of putting a damper on things due to the woman's forensic questioning. It also meant that the session had lasted longer than Clare had scheduled. It was now nearly 6 p.m.

Everyone was trooping out of the room when Clare said, 'Marek, can you stay behind a moment?'

He was gathering his papers together. 'Of course.'

'A drink? I definitely need one. Whether the sun's over the yardarm or not.'

He grinned. 'Sounds good.'

She opened the door to the cabinet, and removed a bottle of Glenfiddich and two tumblers. He watched her move with the assurance that comes with success. As usual, she was dressed in one of her tailored suits. Unlike Glenna, whose clothes were in what one of his colleagues had described as cartoon colours, Clare favoured neutral shades. Today, she was wearing a trouser suit in gun-grey. Her hair was loose, but tied back.

'Which investigations of your own are you working on at the moment?' she said, pouring. She handed him a tumbler.

Marek was surprised at the directness of the question. He was reluctant to share with Clare what he knew about Piero, as Luca had engaged him privately. And he had a gentleman's agreement with *Dundee Today* that only some of his cases would make it to the printing presses.

'I was asked to take on a missing person's case,' he said vaguely. He glanced at the wall monitor behind her. It was usually muted, with running text at the bottom. He was about to add that the person had been located when a photo of Piero flashed on to the screen.

Clare must have seen his fixed stare because she turned round.

A second later, she grabbed the remote and switched on the sound.

'. . . and his exhibition has been on display at Dundee's V&A for nearly two months. We have still to get a comment from the police, but Piero Terranova's brother, Luca, spoke to us today.'

Luca appeared, facing the reporter. 'That's right,' he was saying. 'As soon as I saw the clothes on the television, I recognised them as Piero's.'

'And have you reported this to the police?' the reporter said.

'I went there straight away.'

'Mr Terranova, have you any idea what might have happened to your brother?'

'None whatsoever. He was a lovely man. Everyone liked him.' Luca looked away briefly. 'All I know is that someone killed him and buried him out in the woods.'

'Can you think of anyone who might have done that?'

He shook his head, apparently too overcome with emotion to answer.

'And will you be returning to London now?' the reporter asked.

Luca looked up sharply, drawing his brows together as though disapproving of the question. He gazed directly into the camera. 'I'll be staying here for as long as it takes the police to find my brother's murderer. Then I'll take his body back to Tuscany to be buried in the family plot. One more thing,' he added, as the reporter made to speak. 'I would ask people listening to come forward if they have any idea as to what might have happened to Piero. Someone out there must know something. Even if it's just a suspicion. Go to the police. Or contact me personally, if you prefer. I'm staying at the Hampton by Hilton.'

'Thank you, Mr Terranova,' the reporter said respectfully. She turned to the camera and confirmed that she would be returning to this story as details unfolded, adding that Piero Terranova's exhibition was still on view at the V&A.

And no doubt the public would come flocking, Marek thought cynically. He took a gulp of whisky. Interesting that there was no mention of the firearm in the cottage. Or that Luca had engaged a private investigator to locate his brother. For that, Marek was grateful. He wondered if Clare had guessed that Piero was the person he'd been asked to find. Then again, he was often employed to track down missing people. But what had made Luca go directly to the press before West Bell Street had even issued a statement? Perhaps, like others in a similar situation, he thought the police would be hampered by regulations and forced to move at a snail's pace, whereas a direct appeal to people's consciences might deliver results. Marek could imagine Danka's annoyance: there would be a huge increase in nuisance calls, which would hinder progress.

The reporter was well into the next segment, an account of the increase in drug-related deaths. Clare was still standing motionless, facing the monitor.

'Clare?' Marek said, when the silence had gone on too long. 'What are you thinking? That we could run with this story?'

She turned slowly and gazed at him. She stood stiffly, like a statue, apparently deep in thought. Her expression was unreadable. He'd seen that look before – she was weighing up the time it would take to research this news item against the possible splash the resulting article would make. Perhaps she was waiting for him to offer his opinion. But before he could speak, she picked up her tumbler and downed the Scotch in one go. 'Might be sensible to leave off until the police have finished their investigation,' she said.

'We were stung once before when we leapt in too quickly, remember.'

'Okay, I can wait.'

Her smile had returned, which Marek put down to the restorative powers of whisky. Vodka would have done it faster, he thought, finishing his drink.

He nodded his thanks, picked up his folder and left the office.

As he was closing the door, he caught sight of Clare, her back to him again, flicking through the channels until she'd found the news. When Luca appeared, she paused the feed. Although Marek couldn't see her face, the way she stood rigidly told him that she had more than a passing interest in this story. Maybe it was the fact that Piero and Luca were twins. Those sorts of details always interested the public. Luca had mentioned taking his brother's body back to Tuscany. Perhaps there was a story there. Marek made a mental note to rummage around in the newspaper archives and see what he could dig up.

CHAPTER 21

Dania dropped her bag on to the desk. She didn't need to call her team together. As soon as she'd pushed through the door, the officers had sprung to their feet and made their way towards the incident board. Their faces suggested they'd had a productive time the previous day while she and Honor had been at the rented cottage. At the end of a long afternoon, Dania had travelled back with the SOCOs, leaving Honor to return to West Bell Street. She'd then spent the evening with Cosmo, discussing what they'd found.

'Who's going first?' she said, with a smile.

'DNA on Luca Terranova came in yesterday,' Nessie said. 'It's identical to that of the babe in the woods. There's no doubt now that he's Piero.'

'We can put that one to bed, then.'

'And we've been talking to the New York police. Piero rents an apartment in central Brooklyn. But they had nothing else to tell us. He's not on their radar.'

Dania nodded encouragingly. 'Okay, so SOCO found a couple of keys in one of Piero's jackets. There's a round fob engraved with the Statue of Liberty. We'll have to get Luca in and see if he recognises it, but my guess is that they're the keys to his flat in

Brooklyn. On the subject of keys, though, we couldn't find the ones to the Mercedes. And that's significant. The keys to the rental cottage were in the pocket of the trousers Piero was wearing when he was killed, but not the ones to the car.'

'What about the firearm in the kitchen, ma'am?' Hamish asked.

'It's another Beretta.'

'Like the one in Piero's hand?' Honor said.

'A different model. According to Cosmo, there are many types of Beretta pistols. And many people collecting them. The one in the rental is an M1923. It uses a nine-millimetre Glisenti, which is a different type of cartridge from that used in the Beretta Piero was holding.' Dania smiled. 'When it comes to Berettas, Cosmo is something of a connoisseur.'

'I always thought he was a gangster in disguise,' Honor said, grinning.

'The magazine takes seven cartridges. But the one in the kitchen was empty. Piero hadn't yet loaded it from his ammo box. And there's no firearm certificate for that Beretta either. Cosmo checked.'

They were looking at her expectantly.

'Right, so here's what I think happened. Piero is leaving the cottage, perhaps to go to the V&A, and has the house keys in his hand ready to lock up when he hears a vehicle pulling up at the front. The killer has arrived in his own car. Piero's left via the back, incidentally, as the front door sticks and is difficult to open. The killer gets out and pulls a Beretta, forces Piero into the Mercedes and tells him to drive. Piero slips the house keys into his pocket as he needs to have his hands on the wheel.'

'What about his jacket, boss?' Honor asked. 'The one we found in the Merc?'

'He throws it on to the passenger seat as per usual, which

suggests that the killer is sitting behind him with the gun thrust into the back of the driver's seat. That would attract less attention than sitting beside Piero and pointing the weapon at his head.'

'Okay,' Honor said, drawing out the word. 'And then he drives him straight to that car-parking area in the woodland.'

'And they take a walk through the trees. The killer shoots him, buries him, and then at the last minute decides to put the gun into his hand and make it look like suicide. But it's the wrong hand. He drives back to the cottage, locks the Mercedes, and leaves in his own car. But why he secures Piero's car and takes away the key is a mystery.'

'It could have been a reflex, right enough,' Hamish said. 'He's just killed someone, and isn't thinking straight.'

'But why go to all that trouble with driving out to the woods?' Nessie asked. 'Why not kill Piero at the cottage and be done with it?'

'Yes, I can't come up with a convincing explanation,' Dania said, 'unless he didn't want the body found quickly.'

Nessie stroked his chin. 'It's what some bad guys do when they kill. Unless they're wanting to leave a message, they bury the bodies of their victims somewhere remote.'

'We should check the farms and cottages near the rental. See if anyone saw anything unusual on or around June the eleventh.' But Dania doubted anything would come of this, given how secluded the place was.

'So, why didn't Piero have the *other* Beretta on him?' Hamish said, frowning. 'The one found in the kitchen? And why wasn't it loaded?'

'I can only think that he wasn't yet prepared to use it. He obviously knew enough about firearms to keep the magazine empty when not in use.'

140

Honor was gazing at the photo of Piero. 'He could have brought the Beretta with him from New York, boss.'

'Possibly. Certainly easier than trying to buy it here. By the way, do we know how long Piero lived in New York?'

'He moved there three years ago,' Hamish said. He consulted his notes. 'He made a big splash, and no mistake. His show was the talk of the town. Before that, he worked in a couple of London fashion houses, making clothes.' He looked up. 'Maybe that's where he got his inspiration, and decided to branch out on his own.'

'His passport shows him to be an Italian national. Do we know where he was born?'

'Aye, a place called Montepulciano, if I've pronounced that correctly.'

'His brother speaks perfect English without a trace of an accent,' Dania said half to herself.

'We saw that for ourselves, ma'am,' Hamish added. 'Luca was on television yesterday.'

'What? He was on *television*?'

'He was interviewed on the six o'clock. He's appealing for people to come forward. The switchboard has been taking the usual crank calls.'

After her long day with SOCO and Cosmo, Dania had gone straight to bed without catching up on the news. Perhaps it was just as well, as this would have given her a sleepless night. There was nothing that guaranteed putting the brakes on an investigation as much as members of the public taking matters into their own hands. She doubted Marek would have put Luca up to it. He was smarter than that. Mind you, he hadn't reported the firearm in the rental. She still hadn't made her peace with her brother and, if past experience was anything to go by, she was unlikely to any time soon. The muscles of her face tightened.

'It might not be such a bad thing, boss,' Honor said. She must have seen Dania's expression because she added quickly, 'It could give us a lead.'

Dania decided that it would be wise to put a lid on her anger. It wasn't the fault of her team that Luca had pipped them to the post with a public appeal. They'd been waiting for the DNA results before making an official statement. She rubbed her eyes. 'What about mobile-phone logs. According to Luca, Piero messaged him on June the eleventh. But there was no communication after that.'

'We've got records going back to June the first, which is when Piero arrived in Dundee,' a female officer called Orla said. She played with the controls, and the screen display changed to lines of data.

'Can you take us through it?' Dania said, hoping she would get a concise account. Where mobiles were concerned, Orla was the most technically experienced, but had an unfortunate tendency to stray off the subject. Enthusiastically.

'Aye. So, as you can see, Piero was one of those people who often switches off his phone when he isn't using it.'

There were groans from the room.

'These records show that during the first few days of June, he divided his time mainly between the Hampton by Hilton and the V&A. There are periods during the day where the phone is off, presumably because he doesn't want to be disturbed. Here we have him at the DCA in the evening.' She pointed to data that showed that Piero must have been in the vicinity of the Dundee Contemporary Arts centre.

'What about after he moves out of the Hampton?' Dania said.

'June the ninth.' Orla tapped the screen and brought up a map.

'Piero doesn't go directly to his cottage, but comes here first.' She traced the route with her finger. 'This is the car-hire place. Then he travels straight up north to his rental.'

'Ties in with what we know.'

'And the last time there was a signal was the morning of Saturday, June the eleventh.' She gazed at Dania. 'He was at the V&A. He messaged Luca, then switched off his phone at three minutes past ten.'

'I talked to the staff there,' Hamish said, 'but no one could remember the last time they'd seen him. He would just come and go. People like that tend to become invisible after a while.'

'SOCO didn't find his mobile anywhere,' Dania said. 'They searched the woodland around the cottage. I think they're still looking.'

'What about his bank account?' Honor asked. 'Did he have one in the UK?'

'He did,' Orla said. 'And he paid for everything using an app on his phone.'

'Which explains why we didn't find a wallet,' Dania said. 'Did you check his transactions? Anything unusual?'

'It all looked kosher. His biggest outlays were for his room at the Hampton, his car hire and rent for the cottage. But nothing after June the eleventh.'

'Right, tell us about June the seventh. According to the staff at the V&A, Piero went to Alderwood Manor Maze.'

'That's correct. And we're in luck. His phone was on that day. Here's the record. He leaves the V&A just before two o'clock, takes this route here, and arrives at Alderwood roughly half an hour later. Then shortly after three, he returns to the V&A.'

'So he stays, what, only half an hour?' Dania remembered her own trip to the Maze. She and Honor had spent much longer than that negotiating the paths and the moving hedges. But Marek had told her that Piero was shouting at someone. Could it have been so serious that he stalked out of there immediately? And the more she thought about it, the more she was convinced that this held the key to his murder. 'We need to lift that hard drive.' She picked up her jacket. 'I'll go now.'

'Haven't you got that review meeting, boss?'

Dania felt her shoulders slump. 'So I have.'

She was due to have a long session with Jackie Ireland to review the other cases she was working on. Which meant that she was unlikely to be out before the end of her shift. Before she left the room, she caught Honor's eye, the signal that the sergeant was to keep things moving in her absence.

CHAPTER 22

It was just before five when Dania left Jackie Ireland's office. The review meeting had been productive, and the DCI was more than satisfied with Dania's progress, urging her, however, to keep her more regularly informed, as the Polish detective had a tendency to wait until she had something substantial to report.

Dania left the building, and hurried to the Fiat, thinking only of reaching Alderwood Manor Maze before it closed for the day. There was more traffic than usual along the Strathmartine Road, and the large number of parked cars didn't help, with the result that she arrived at the estate later than she'd intended.

She drove through the ornamental gates, and passed the Lodge, noticing that, unlike the last time she'd taken this route, someone was at home, evidenced by the silver Hyundai parked in front of the building. A minute later, she pulled up in front of the Manor. This time, there was no man waving her down and instructing her to go to the car park, which made her suspect that the Maze had indeed closed. And that meant there would be no one in the control room. No matter. Someone in the Manor would take her there.

Dania rang the doorbell and waited, noticing that the flowers in the ornamental planters still hadn't been watered. After a minute, she pressed the bell again, with the same result. She was on the point of trying the control room anyway when she heard a car behind her. A Hyundai was cruising up the drive. It stopped beside the Fiat, and a blonde woman in a tailored light-grey suit climbed out. Even without the stilettos she would have been tall. Dania, who was tall herself and never wore high-heeled shoes as they were excruciatingly uncomfortable, wondered why the woman bothered. She would tower over most men. But then, perhaps that was the intention.

'Hello,' the woman said, coming towards her. She had a soft voice. 'May I help you?'

'I'm looking for Glenna McGarry. Or one of the other McGarrys.'

'I'm afraid they're all away today.' She glanced at the Fiat. 'I saw your car pass my window, and thought I'd better come over. I'm Clare Conlee. I live at the Lodge.'

'DI Dania Gorska,' she said, shaking the woman's hand. 'I believe my brother works for you.'

Clare's open expression changed. Dania was conscious that she might have been too abrupt. She was still feeling out of sorts over Marek's behaviour, and it seemed to manifest itself whenever she thought about him. 'There might be something you can assist me with,' she added, with a quick smile, remembering Glenna's comment that Clare sometimes operated the Maze. 'I'm here to collect the hard drive. The one that's in the Maze's control room.'

Clare looked surprised. 'May I ask why?'

'It's about the body found on the Alderwood estate. We believe that the man may have visited the Maze.'

'And do you have a warrant?'

'I have the power to seize evidence without a warrant if it's part of a criminal investigation. Which this is.'

'I understand,' Clare said slowly. 'In that case, we'd better go and fetch it.' After a long look at Dania, she led the way past the conservatory towards the Maze, then turned right and followed the path to the control room.

'That's strange,' she said, stopping abruptly. 'The door's been left open.'

'Does that happen often?'

'I've never seen it before. It's possible it's an oversight.'

'Was the Maze in operation today?'

'It wasn't. It certainly was yesterday.'

Dania recalled the equipment inside: the laptop and keyboard. And the ultra-large screen. Could there have been a break-in?

Clare must have had the same thought because she pushed the door wide, and flicked a switch, flooding the room with brightness. With a whoosh, the air conditioning fired up. The same faint smell of floral air freshener lingered in the air.

She hurried to the table. 'Everything seems to be here,' she said half to herself. 'Except the hard drive.' She lifted a pile of papers, then searched behind the screen. 'It's gone,' she said, turning to Dania.

'Are you sure?'

'Please see for yourself.'

Dania didn't need to be asked twice. She looked over, under and behind everything thoroughly. 'Do you know if the drive is taken to the house after the Maze is shut down for the day?'

Clare looked blank. 'Why would it be?'

'Maybe to back it up?'

'We don't bother doing that. At least, I don't think so. Although I could be wrong.'

'Who knows the key code to the door?'

'Just myself, Arron and Hayley. And Glenna, of course.'

'What about the engineer who set it up?'

Clare drew her brows together. 'He told us how to change the code. We did that after he'd left.'

'Is it written down anywhere?' Dania said, wondering if a cleaner might have come across it.

'Not as far as I know.' Her expression cleared. 'It's easy to remember, not because of the numbers we chose, but because of the pattern the fingers make when you enter them.'

'I see.'

'You're thinking that someone has broken in, aren't you? But there may be a simpler explanation.'

'Such as?'

'The drive could have stopped working. Electronics don't last for ever, do they?'

She had a point. 'And where do you take your electronic devices to be repaired?'

Clare's look told her what she'd feared: like most people, they simply threw a defective device away, and bought a newer model.

'Do you know where I can find the McGarrys?' Dania said.

'Arron and Hayley are at Ninewells. Hayley's having a scan. As for Glenna, I couldn't say. But I don't think they'll be long. You're welcome to stay and wait.' She smiled. 'I can offer you coffee in the Lodge.'

'That's kind of you, but I'm afraid I have to be getting back.'

'I'm sorry I wasn't able to help. I'll let the others know you were here.'

'Thank you.'

Inside the Fiat, Dania started the engine, and turned the car round. She drove away, gripping the wheel in frustration. She'd had cases like this before – one step forward, and two steps back.

But as she reached Emmock Road, the question at the forefront of her mind was: why was the drive missing?

Dania was approaching the Polish deli on Hilltown. The traffic was light, and the street was almost empty. The shop was due to shut shortly but, if she hurried, she might just make it. Her cupboard was bare, and she needed to get some food in. Pity it was all double yellow lines in that area.

She slowed to a crawl, and was thinking she might turn into Kinghorne Road and try to find parking there when she spotted a figure on the pavement opposite. He was strolling towards the city centre. Although he had his back to her, the gait and the light-coloured linen suit were unmistakable. His head was down, which meant that he was deep in thought.

As Dania was wondering whether she should stop and offer Marek a lift, a blue car came roaring along the street towards him. She watched in horror as it mounted the pavement. Marek must have heard the sound because his head jerked up. He immediately leapt to the side. The car narrowly missed him, then careered back on to the road and sped away.

Dania pulled up. Without bothering to switch off the engine, she jumped out of the Fiat and ran across the road. Marek was leaning against the wall, breathing heavily. His face was ashen.

She gripped his arm. 'Are you all right?' she gasped, in Polish.

For a second, she thought he didn't recognise her. But then his expression cleared. 'Yes, Danka. I'm okay.'

She glanced along the street. 'Do you know who it was?'

'All I saw was someone with a mobile pressed to his ear.'

'The passenger?'

'The driver. There was no one else in the car.'

149

'Don't worry. We'll find him on the cameras.'

Marek's colour was returning. He straightened, gazing at her. He looked as though he was about to say something, but seemed to think better of it.

'Let's go,' she said. 'I'm taking you home.'

She led him across the road, and bundled him into the passenger seat.

They drove in silence.

'I thought you were going to take me to my place?' Marek said, as Dania pulled up outside her flat.

'I think you need some TLC.' She studied him. 'I'll phone for a takeaway.'

She expected him to object, as takeaways weren't his thing, but he nodded in apparent resignation.

'So, are we good, Marek?' she said, searching his face.

'How do you mean?'

'You're no longer angry with me?'

He laughed softly. 'I thought it was *you* who was angry with *me*.'

'That never lasts long.' She squeezed his arm. 'Come on.'

Inside the flat, Dania phoned a Polish restaurant, which special-ised in nineteenth-century cuisine, and ordered two portions of ox tongue with horseradish. She'd eaten there once before, and was delighted to find that you could order by phone and they delivered to the door.

Marek had collapsed on to the sofa, and lay back, his eyes closed. 'Play something, Danka.' Suddenly, his eyes flew open, and he sat up. 'And I don't mean like "The Teddy Bears' Picnic". That was an affront to Chopin.'

'Okay,' she said placatingly. 'I'll play one of his nocturnes.'

Chopin had written twenty-one nocturnes, so there were plenty to choose from, but in the end she settled for Opus 55,

Number 2 in E-flat major. She played this with the emphasis on the right hand, keeping the left much softer, and more of an accompaniment. It wasn't how Rubinstein played it, with both hands given equal weight, but it was her piano teacher, Jakub Frydman, who'd encouraged her to try different techniques, and make the music her own. It had taken her some years before she'd felt confident enough to do this.

The piece was only six minutes long, and she was tempted to play it once more as tiredness had caused her to make the odd mistake, but a movement behind her made her turn. Marek was sitting up, smiling faintly.

'That was beautiful, Danka.'

'You didn't notice the slip-ups, then.'

'I'm sure even Rubinstein made them.'

'Shall I get us a drink?' she said, before he asked her to play something else. 'I'm all out of Żubrówka, I'm afraid.'

He looked scandalised, which she took to be a good sign. 'What else have you got?' he said.

'Whisky?'

'Okay. I'll have mine neat.'

At the sideboard, she poured two shots.

'What kind is it?' he asked, as she handed him a glass.

'Lagavulin.' She took a seat next to him. 'It was Hamish Downie who introduced me to the joys of malt whisky. He's a member of a tasting society. I went along as a guest, and really liked this one.'

Dania sipped the Lagavulin, savouring the intense, smoky flavour. She was about to ask Marek his opinion when the doorbell rang. 'That's our dinner,' she said, springing to her feet. 'Can you get the plates out?'

He smiled, his spirits evidently on the up at the thought of the rich Polish food.

But as they sat down to eat, it crossed Dania's mind that her brother might be in danger. His face was well known around the city, and more so since he'd started working for *Dundee Today*. There was always a small photo of him next to the titles of his articles. If one of the people he'd exposed had hired a hitman, he could find Marek easily. And maybe try to run him down.

'Marek,' Dania said, lowering her fork. 'Can you take some time off work? Perhaps leave Dundee for a while?'

He looked up in surprise. 'Why would I do that?'

'Whoever tried to run you over might try it again.'

'It was an accident, Danka. Pure and simple. Some idiot was using his phone while driving. It must happen all the time.'

She hesitated.

'Are you thinking it's someone I've outed in an article?'

'You've made more enemies in this city than I have.'

He reached across, and laid his hand on hers. 'It's all right. Don't worry about me,' he said.

'Just be careful.'

'I'm always careful.' He grinned. 'Now, is there any dessert?'

CHAPTER 23

'And you found this in a skip?' Chloe said, staring at the hard drive in her sister's hands.

'That's right,' Ailsa replied. 'It's in the field next to the Maze. Belongs to that grumpy farmer. You know, the one with the baldy heid and missing teeth.'

'And this was when I was at the dentist's?'

'Aye. I was hoping to check out that shed at the side of the Maze.'

They were seated in a coffee shop in the area of Perth Road frequented by students. As it was summer, the few students working at the tables were postgraduates. The walls were covered with graffiti, which Ailsa remembered had been sprayed on by the first customers who'd arrived when the café had opened. All the proprietor had to do was supply the aerosols. Ailsa had been one of the 'decorators', and remembered the fun she'd had doing what she would never dream of doing on the streets. The reliable Wi-Fi was the reason the place was crowded during term time, and made up for the lack of quality of the coffee. It hardly mattered to Ailsa and her sister, as they had ordered two glasses of 'Scotland's other national drink', i.e. Irn-Bru.

'I reckoned there must be something inside the shed that could tell us how to win this Maze competition,' Ailsa was saying.

'But it's always kept locked.'

'I ken that, but I'd come up with a plan. I got the idea from an American TV series, where a prisoner blew some powder on to a keypad, and then saw where it had stuck, and it told him that those keys had to be pressed to open the door. All he had to do was try every combination.' She threw Chloe a smug smile. 'So, I thought I'd do the same with the keypad on the shed.'

Chloe blinked rapidly in what Ailsa took to be admiration. Or maybe it was astonishment.

'The Maze was closed yesterday,' she went on, 'so I took Ma's face powder and sneaked in from the woods, the ones behind the rise. I was creeping up to the back of the shed when I saw someone running out.' She nodded at the hard drive. 'He was carrying that.'

Ailsa paused, remembering. The sudden appearance of the man had stopped her in her tracks. Seeing him had given her an enormous fright, but she wasn't going to admit that.

'Who was it?' Chloe urged.

'The guy who lives in the Manor.'

'Arron McGarry?'

'That's him. He was running as though the de'il was on his tail. I thought he was going to go into the house, but he made a left and went into the next field. There's a break in the fence.'

'Aye, I mind where you mean. That entire fence needs to be replaced. So, what happened then?'

'A few seconds later, he came out again.' She paused for effect. 'Minus the drive.'

Chloe sipped her Irn-Bru, gazing at Ailsa.

'I waited until after he'd disappeared into the Manor before sneaking into the field. The skip is right at the side. If he'd ditched the drive, it could only have been in there, right enough. It's one of those high skips, and I reckoned he'd simply thrown it up and over, then scarpered. I managed to get a keek inside. It was half full of branches and stuff. And the drive was lying on the top.'

'Did you climb in?'

'Ach, I had to. There was no other way. It was climbing out that was the problem. But here's the interesting thing. As I left the field, I saw that the door to the shed was open.'

'The guy must have been in a hurry if he forgot to pull it shut.' Chloe's eyes widened. 'And did you go in?'

'I just put my head round the door. I mean, he might have come back.'

'What did you see?'

'A table at the far end with stuff on it. Papers and that. And a huge screen.' Ailsa held up the drive. 'Anyway, I reckon what's on this might help us win the competition.' The date had been set for Saturday 27 August, which was in four weeks' time. She reached under the table for the rucksack, and pulled out her laptop. 'I'll just fire this up.'

A few moments later, the machine came to life.

'Right. Now, let's see what we've got.' Using a cable, Ailsa connected the hard drive to the laptop. 'Okay, here's the icon.'

'Then it's not damaged?' Chloe said, leaning over. 'Why did this Arron guy throw it away, then?'

Ailsa looked hard at her. 'That's a great question.'

'Could the disk be full?'

'It's not, according to this. And anyway, he could always delete files to free up space. Aye, so why would he throw it away?' she muttered to herself. She moved the cursor on to the icon, and double-clicked. 'Lots of video files, with dates. Let's take a keek.' She chose one at random.

The screen filled with squares. They were full of visitors walking around.

'Ailsa, they know our every move, and no mistake,' Chloe said, with a gasp.

'Ach, that's how they're able to position the hedges. Otherwise it would be too dangerous. They wouldn't want one of those crashing into people, ken.'

She tried another file, with the same result. They followed the visitors, some of whom were taking selfies next to the statues. The most popular seemed to be the Selkie, probably because she had huge breasts and was naked from the waist up.

'Try July the fifteenth,' Chloe said excitedly. 'We were there then. What time would it have been?'

'I reckon just after two.'

Ailsa found the file, and moved the bar until she reached 2 p.m. She let the recording run. 'There!' she said, loudly enough that a few heads turned. 'That's me, and there's you, Chloe.'

'Pity there's no sound.' They watched for a while, then Chloe said impatiently, 'What else is on the drive?'

'A couple of folders. This one says "ORIGINAL MAZE".' She double-clicked. 'Wow, there are loads of JPEGs.'

'Well, open them up.'

Ailsa ran through the first few. They were images of dark tunnels with walls lined in red brick.

'Stop!' Chloe said, making her sister jump. 'Look, there,' she added, more quietly. 'That's the Minotaur. It's different, though,' she added slowly. 'This one has only one axe. The one in the Maze is holding two.'

'Aye, you could be right. You know what I think this is? It's the original statue. The one the Victorians built, ken. The clue is in the folder's name: ORIGINAL MAZE. And look at the condition it's in. Most of the paint's peeled off, and bits of him are crumbling away.' She flicked through the photos, coming across more of the old statues. 'Is that William Wallace?' she said, glancing at Chloe.

'Aye, I think so. His sword is the same height as he is. And he's holding a shield. You can just make out the saltire.'

'These are the tunnels under the Maze. They must have stored the old statues down there.'

'Do you think there's a map of the Maze on this drive?' Chloe said softly.

Ailsa returned to the list of files. She scanned them quickly. Then she doubled-clicked, and a diagram filled the screen.

They stared at it for a long moment.

'Oh, Ailsa,' Chloe breathed.

CHAPTER 24

Marek woke early. He opened his eyes, resting his gaze on an unfamiliar scene. There was no ceiling rose in his bedroom, and that dusty white lampshade certainly wasn't something he possessed. Then he remembered that he was in Danka's spare room. They'd talked well into the night, and she'd suggested he stay over. He'd been too drained by the events of the day to walk home, and had promptly accepted her offer of a bed.

He hurried to the bathroom and showered quickly. The least he could do was to make Danka one of his special breakfasts. But when he reached the kitchen, not only did he find the remains of her breakfast – burnt toast – lying on the table, but she herself was gone. She must be on an early shift.

Marek set about making coffee, suddenly finding himself no longer hungry. He picked out one of the half-brown bananas from the fruit bowl. On peeling it, he was dismayed to discover that it was also half brown on the inside. Still, he preferred overripe bananas to the green varieties he found in supermarkets.

As he sipped the coffee, his mind harked back to Luca's comment about taking his brother's body back to Tuscany. Perhaps the man would be amenable to an interview about their lives there. An article about the brothers would keep their names alive, and might even lead to information that would help the police find Piero's killer. Luca could only say no. Marek sent him a text, then headed to the sitting room and switched on the TV. There was nothing further about Piero on the Scotland news channel. Marek wasn't due in at work till the afternoon. He might as well return to his apartment and finish off a report that had been languishing on his desktop.

He left Danka's flat, and was strolling down Meadowside when his phone rang.

'Marek Gorski,' he said.

'Marek? It's Luca. I got your message. I'm more than happy to get together for a chat. Are you free for a coffee in, say, half an hour?'

'Absolutely. Where would you like to meet?'

'I'm in your hands.'

'Are you at the Hampton? What about the DCA? It's not too far to walk.'

'Fine. I'll see you there.' He disconnected.

Marek put the phone away. That was a stroke of luck. Now all he had to do was think up some suitable questions. For an investigative journalist, that was child's play.

Luca got to his feet as Marek entered. He was wearing jeans and a black sweatshirt, which judging by the cut could have been designer. Unusually for him, his hair was tousled, with several strands falling over his forehead. It somehow made him look even more like an Italian gangster.

'Good to see you, Marek,' he said, extending a hand.

Marek smiled. 'Shall we sit outside? The weather's beautiful.'

'And it's been like this since I arrived in Dundee. I thought Scotland had nothing but rain.'

'I have to admit that this weather's unusual. So, what can I get you?'

'A large coffee will be fine. Thank you.'

Marek caught the eye of the Pole serving behind the bar, and mouthed their order. The men knew each other well, as the DCA was a favourite place for Marek to conduct his interviews. He led the way to the Jute Café Bar, grabbing the last free table. They settled themselves in the chairs, and made small talk until the coffees arrived.

'I saw your appeal on television,' Marek said. 'I'm wondering if anything has come of that.'

'I'm sure the police would have told me if it had. They called me in yesterday afternoon to identify keys found in one of Piero's jackets. They were to his New York apartment.' Luca took a sip of coffee. 'But it's early days. I've no idea how long the police take to solve murder cases, but we're talking a week or two, aren't we?'

Marek paused in the act of bringing the mug to his lips. He had a fair idea of how many unsolved murders West Bell Street had on their books. But he didn't want to discourage Luca so early on in the investigation. He nodded, smiling reassuringly.

'You suggested an interview, Marek. What would you like to talk about?'

'There's been quite a bit in the media about Piero and his exhibition, and his work as a fashion designer, but people will soon forget that when other stories start to take centre stage.' He leant forward. 'I'd like to keep Piero in the public eye, if you get my drift.'

'I'd welcome that,' Luca said eagerly.

'Tell me about your life in Italy,' Marek said, taking out his notebook. 'You're from Tuscany, I understand.'

A guarded expression crossed Luca's face, which surprised Marek.

'Yes, we're from the Siena area,' he said finally.

'Where exactly?'

'Montepulciano.' He waved a dismissive hand. 'But I don't think people will be interested in Piero's early life.'

'On the contrary, they'll be very interested. And in yours, too.'

He seemed mystified. 'Well, if you think so . . .'

'Your English accent suggests that you were educated in the UK.'

'That's correct.' Luca paused. 'Piero and I were sent to a boarding school in Kent. Our summers were spent back in Tuscany.'

'I take it this was a secondary school?'

'It did take in secondary-school pupils, but it also took in a small number of primary-school children. Piero and I were six when we enrolled. I'm guessing from your level of fluency in English that you had a similar childhood.'

'Not quite. We came over to Scotland when I was fourteen. I think, had it been earlier, I'd have lost my Polish accent.' Marek took a mouthful of coffee. 'What were your summers like in Montepulciano?'

'Our mother died when I was very young, so we were more or less left to ourselves. Have you been to Italy, Marek?'

'I covered the Venice Biennale for the *Courier* a few years ago.'

'Really?' Luca said, his eyes wide.

'One of the perks of the job.'

'Have you also reported on the Venice Film Festival?'

'I'm afraid not.'

'That really is a marvellous event. You'll have to find a way to visit Venice when it's on.'

As Luca began an account of his attendance at the festival, it came to Marek that the man was trying to move the topic away from his and Piero's early life in Tuscany. Marek would have to tread carefully if he wanted to tease that apart.

'The only film festival I'll be covering,' he said, as Luca came to the end of his narrative, 'is the Discovery Film Festival, which will be held here at the DCA. The films are intended for young audiences.' Before Luca could respond, he added, 'Tell me a little about your career. You said you're a voice coach at Covent Garden.'

'I should clarify that it's not a permanent position. I'm not on a salary, but paid hourly.'

'So, there are times when you have no work?'

'That's right. I'm hoping to get a salaried position either at the opera house or elsewhere, but I've had no luck so far.'

Marek looked at him with interest. 'How did you become a voice coach?'

'Well, we Italians have a great operatic tradition,' Luca said self-deprecatingly. 'I had wanted to become a singer, but had to eventually resign myself to the fact that my voice simply wasn't up to scratch.'

'Did you take singing lessons in Montepulciano?'

'Good heavens, no. There's nothing like that there.'

'What sort of a place is it?'

Luca turned the mug in his hands. 'It's a typically beautiful Tuscan town. It sits on a hill.'

'That must make driving interesting.'

'Most of the streets have been pedestrianised, so it's great for tourists.'

'And you lived where, exactly?'

'We had a villa outside the town,' he said, shifting in his seat. He glanced at his watch. 'I'm sorry, Marek, but I'm going to have to leave. I've only just remembered that I have a video call with Covent Garden. I need to get back to the Hampton.'

Marek got to his feet. 'Of course.'

'I suspect you have further questions, in which case do please email them, and I'll get back to you.'

They shook hands, and Luca left hurriedly.

Marek waited until he knew that the Italian would have reached the top of the stairs, and then followed him, seeing him leave by the front door. But as he watched Luca saunter down the Nethergate – no longer hurrying – he was forced to the conclusion that the man had something to hide. And he had a feeling in his waters that, whatever it was, it had a bearing on why his brother Piero had been murdered.

163

CHAPTER 25

It was midday, and Dania was cruising past Alderwood Manor Lodge and the pyramidal hedges. The lawns with their marble statues were being trimmed, and through the half-open window she could hear the sound of a petrol-operated machine. She wound the window right down, breathing in the sweet scent of new-mown grass.

The first thing she'd done on arriving at West Bell Street was to check the CCTV feeds for the previous day. Although she'd found the blue car that had nearly run Marek down, there was so much mud on the number plates that it was impossible to read the registration. She'd wondered if obscuring the plates had been deliberate . . .

Before she'd left the station, she'd rung Marek, as she was anxious to establish that he was safe. He'd been quick to reassure her that all was well, and he was about to go in to work. This wasn't the first time she'd had to check on her brother. He had a tendency to put himself in danger, and be blissfully unaware of it. As a police officer, she, too, frequently found herself in the same situation. The difference was, as Honor had once scathingly pointed out, that unlike Marek, Dania appreciated the predicament she was in and took steps to deal with it.

164

She pulled up in front of the Manor, glad that she'd rung ahead. The housekeeper had answered and confirmed that, aye, Mr Arron McGarry was at home, and could be found in the Maze. No, the Maze wasn't open today, but Mr McGarry often took advantage of that to do some general maintenance in and around the hedging. As the woman had started to ask why the polis wished to speak to him, Dania had disconnected.

She left the car. Inky clouds were beginning to gather, although so far the rain was holding off. But if the clouds emptied their load, that would be the myth of St Swithin's Day exploded.

To the left of the Maze's entrance, a giant aluminium stepladder was propped up against the hedge, suggesting that Arron had finished whatever he'd been doing in there. Dania made her way towards the control room, and knocked on the door. After several seconds, she tried again.

'Mr McGarry, are you there?'

No reply. He must still be in the Maze. With luck, she wouldn't have to go too far in. She returned to the entrance and tried to remember the route she and Honor had taken – when was it? – a fortnight ago. Not that it was likely to help her as, although the Maze should be back to the 'base state', some of the hedges had moved around during their visit.

Dania turned left, soon meeting the Minotaur on its plinth. As she approached, she caught the sharp smell of wet paint. So, Arron was doing a bit of touching up. She continued through the Maze, coming across statues she'd not seen before. One that would probably give her sleepless nights was a velociraptor, its head angled towards her, its open mouth showing a red tongue and more teeth than a creature ought decently to have. A huge horse's head, which she guessed was a kelpie, was round the next corner, and tall enough for the sun to burnish the stippled silver paint.

She pushed further into the Maze, and was beginning to ask herself whether this had been such a good idea when, to her great relief, she found the gap that took her out. Ahead was the field, with woodland beyond the rise.

Dania followed the path at the side of the hedging, wondering where Arron could have got to. She was on the point of ringing the Manor when she saw him strolling towards the control room. His head was down, and he seemed deep in thought.

'Mr McGarry?' she said.

He stopped short. 'Aye, I'm Arron McGarry.' An expression of surprise appeared on his face. He was a tall man with a nest of fair hair, and was wearing a Dundee United sweatshirt identical to one that Marek owned. The sleeves were rolled up, exposing his suntanned arms.

Dania held up her warrant. 'DI Dania Gorska. Could I have a word?'

The surprise turned immediately to suspicion. It was a reaction Dania had seen many times from the guilty and the innocent alike, and thought nothing of it. 'I'd like to talk to you about your hard drive. The one you use with your Maze system.'

He hesitated, and for an instant Dania thought he was going to refuse, but then he said, 'In that case, you'd better come in.' He paused at the control-room door, and punched in the code. 'I hope you haven't been waiting long, Inspector. I've just grabbed a quick lunch. I've still got a few things to do here.'

'I'll try not to keep you too long.'

'Ach, it's okay. There's plenty of time before tomorrow.'

He switched on the light, stepping back to let her enter.

'Now, what do you wish to ask me, Inspector?' he said, moving towards the table. 'Do you want to look at the drive, eh? In that case, let me power up the laptop.'

So, the drive was back in action? This was better than she'd expected. 'Actually, I'm here to take the drive away. I want our Tech department to look at it.'

Arron's head shot up so rapidly that she heard the bones in the neck crack. 'Take it away?' he said. 'But why?'

'To see if Tech can restore the sound.'

'Aye, but there's nothing wrong with the sound. Wait, hold on. You're talking about the *old* drive.' He glanced at the device on the table. 'This is a new one, which I put in yesterday evening. The sound's fine on this.'

'And where's your old drive?'

'As you said, it wasn't recording the sound, so I took it to one of my mates. He does repairs.' Arron paused for so long that Dania suspected he was thinking up a narrative. But maybe she was being too cynical. 'He couldn't get the sound back,' Arron continued. 'He tried everything. And while he was fiddling, something went badly wrong.'

'How do you mean?'

'When we tested the drive, not only did it fail to record the sound, it didn't even record video. I thought the disk might be full, but we checked and it wasn't. We need to record what's going on in the Maze for health and safety reasons, in case there's an accident and we're asked to produce the footage. That's happened before. A lady fainted once. Nothing to do with us, of course, but we needed to be able to demonstrate that she hadn't been hit by a hedge or – God forbid – a statue.' He was gabbling now, which convinced Dania that he was lying, or at best massaging the truth.

'And then what?' she said.

'Aye, well, the guy took it apart, and did something to the magnetic disks. He ended up wiping them completely, saying something about a factory reset. I didn't understand all the techie stuff, but he seemed to think it was the disks that were causing the fault rather than the software.' Arron ran a hand over his brow. 'But then he couldn't get anything to work. He concluded that the disks were corrupted. Personally, I think he was careless and it was something he did. Aye, and he seemed to think so too because he gave me this new drive for free. It works fine, by the way,' he added.

'Did you by any chance back up the old drive?'

'We didn't, no.' He straightened. 'But we'll be backing up this one at the end of each day, and no mistake.'

'What about the laptop?' Dania said, glancing at it. 'Does the recording go on to that first, and then to the drive?'

'It doesn't. There's not enough space. We have other things on the laptop, like the layout for the Maze. There's also a copy of that on the hard drive, actually. But the live footage from the Maze cameras goes directly to the hard drive. It has a huge amount of storage.'

'And where is the old drive now?' she said, thinking that, if she had the magnetic disks, Tech at West Bell Street might be able to salvage the data.

'My mate said he'd recycle what he could, but the magnetic media was trash. He fed it into his industrial-strength crusher.' Arron grinned. 'I once saw him crush a skateboard in that thing.'

Dania felt her heart sink. This wasn't what she'd hoped to hear.

'What was it you wanted to look at, anyway?' he said, his hands in his pockets.

'It doesn't matter now.' She tried to keep the disappointment out of her voice. 'I need to go, Mr McGarry. Thank you for your time.'

He smiled. 'Goodbye, Inspector. Sorry I wasn't able to help.'

But as Dania sat in the car, thinking through the conversation with Arron, the realisation that she'd failed to get what she'd come for suddenly overwhelmed her. She slammed her hands hard on the wheel, and let out a yell of frustration.

CHAPTER 26

Marek sat back, loosening his tie. He'd spent the last hour quarrying the internet for every Terranova who had – now, or in the past – a connection to Tuscany. His first attempt involved checking Italy's *Pagine Bianche* or White Pages – the residential phone directory. Several names had come up, but his phone calls quickly made it clear that these Terranovas had no links to Piero and Luca. Of course, since the brothers had been schooled from an early age in the UK, and had then made their lives outside Italy, he was unlikely to find phone numbers, or even residents of Tuscany who had known them. He widened the search, coming across more Terranovas than he could reasonably deal with. Time for a new approach.

He grabbed himself a coffee from the machine in the corridor, and settled down to think laterally. So, what else had Luca told him?

We're from the Siena area. Montepulciano.

Montepulciano.

Back to the internet. What Marek learnt was that the mediaeval town of Montepulciano sat on a high ridge, south-east of Siena, and tourists were encouraged to visit the ancient churches and elegant palaces, relax in the squares, bathing in sunshine and drinking cappuccino before wandering to the outskirts of the town to take in the stunning views of the Val d'Orcia and the Val di Chiana. Montepulciano even boasted underground passageways, something Marek had heard was not unusual in Tuscany.

He flicked through the many images, wondering what Piero and Luca's father had done for a living that enabled him to send his two sons to an English boarding school. Luca had been remarkably unforthcoming about their lives in Italy. Maybe his father had been a Mafia boss.

We had a villa outside the town.

Exactly where a Mafia boss would reside. Marek pictured the building, surrounded by a high stone wall, with the odd mafioso lolling against it, a cigarillo in one hand and a machine gun in the other. Then again, maybe not. Perhaps the father had taken up an honest profession.

Marek was flicking through the images looking for inspiration when he came across a photo of a group of men rolling wine barrels up a street. It transpired that this was the famous *Bravìo delle Botti* – a barrel race through the city – that takes place in Montepulciano every August. What made it challenging was that the barrels were rolled uphill. The winning district would receive a painted cloth bearing the image of the patron saint of Montepulciano. As with other such historical competitions in Italy, there were accompanying events such as processions, dressing up in mediaeval costumes and flag waving.

But it was the image of the huge wine barrels that held Marek's attention. A little more sleuthing told him that Montepulciano is a wine-producing region famous for, among others, the red wine known as *Vino Nobile di Montepulciano*. The grapes are grown in the vineyards that surround the town.

Marek sipped his coffee. Perhaps he should check Italy's business directory, the *Pagine Gialle*, or Yellow Pages. He entered the phrase 'wine production in Montepulciano', and trolled through the returns, finding only one entry with the name Terranova in the title. It was possible to send an online message direct to the business, but he decided to phone. In his halting Italian, he was able to determine that the company had been owned by a Riccardo Terranova, who had sold up some years before on the condition that the business kept his name. The new owner wasn't able to tell Marek much more, except that Riccardo had been fabulously wealthy, and had also owned vineyards in Sicily. As for family, he could tell Marek nothing.

Marek got himself another coffee. He wondered if he should go down the obvious route of applying for vital records at the registry office at Montepulciano. But when it came to records, he'd come up against Italian bureaucracy before. He could contact Luca, and ask him if the Riccardo Terranova who owned these vineyards was indeed his father. But something held him back. It was the niggling feeling growing inside him that Luca might put obstacles in his way, or try to steer him down another path. No, he was better off leaving the Italian out of it.

He gazed at the screen, pondering his best line of attack. It would have to be newspaper archives. Searching was something he excelled at. It was that combination of patience and quick skimming that always paid off. And he suspected that, if Riccardo Terranova had been a successful wine producer, he would have made it into the local newspapers.

By the end of the afternoon, Marek had found what he'd been looking for: an article featuring wine merchant Riccardo

Terranova. Using Google Translate, he learnt that Riccardo was expanding his business to Sicily, and had just taken possession of land to the west of Palermo, where he intended to grow the grapes needed to make red wine. He would have to divide his time between Montepulciano and Sicily. The article was dated 1999. The accompanying photograph showed Riccardo with two young boys. Although the image was grainy, there was no doubt that these were twins. The caption read: Riccardo with his sons, Piero and Luca. Result!

Marek glanced at his watch. He had no plans for the evening. He could continue his search, but he wanted to tell his sister about his find. He powered down the laptop, and left the building.

'Danka!'

Dania paused in the act of opening the car door.

'I'm glad I caught you,' Marek said. 'I've got some information that I think would interest you. It's about the Terranovas.' He glanced around. A number of officers were leaving the building in a group, presumably because their shifts had ended.

'Perhaps this isn't the best place,' Dania said. 'Why don't you come to mine?'

'Are you going to phone for another takeaway?'

She laughed. 'How well you know me.'

'That last one was excellent. Can we have the same again? The ox tongue with horseradish?'

'I'll phone them now. It should arrive shortly after we do.'

Because of the delays caused by the early-evening traffic, they reached Dania's flat at the same time as the delivery. She thanked the Pole, who chatted briefly, then left with a tip from Marek and a huge grin.

Inside, she picked up the note that her Polish neighbour Arkadiusz had slipped under the door. She'd discovered that they shared a wall: her piano was on one side, and the sofa in his living room on the other. Which meant that – provided he didn't have his television on – he could hear her practising. After a while, he'd apparently summoned up the nerve to suggest pieces she could play, doing this by leaving notes. She did her best to accommodate his wishes, although she couldn't always find the sheet music and was reduced to listening to the piece online and then trying to play it from memory. Today's suggestion was 'Flight of the Bumblebee' by Rimsky-Korsakov, arranged for the piano by Rachmaninov. She'd have to wait until Marek had left, as this type of music wasn't to his taste.

'Now, what is it you wanted to tell me?' Dania said, when they were in the kitchen.

'I've tracked down the name of the Terranova father. It's Riccardo.'

'Wouldn't Luca have told you that?'

'Actually, Luca's being evasive.'

She paused in the act of taking a bottle of wine from the cupboard, and gazed at Marek.

'I think he's hiding something, Danka.'

She thought back to her meeting with him and Marek. He'd been more than helpful, but then, he'd just seen his brother's clothes on television.

Marek took the bottle from her hands, and pulled the cork. 'I met with him to see if I could get information for an article about him and Piero. When I tried to probe his background, he kept moving the conversation on to something else. Then he left all of a sudden on some pretext.'

Dania unwrapped the food. Marek was as good at spotting

evasive behaviour as any police officer. 'What did you uncover about this Riccardo?' she said.

'He was a wine-grower.'

'*Was?*'

'Was. Is. He may still be alive. I didn't get that far. He had vineyards around Montepulciano, and also in Sicily. Filthy rich, according to the man I spoke to. He sold up a few years ago.'

'I wonder if he's still living. Because if he isn't, what's happened to his money?' She brought plates to the table. 'Anything about a wife?'

'Their mother died when the boys were very young. I think the vital records are the place to go.'

Dania could tell from the way he said it that for an investigative journalist it would be something of a chore. The police, on the other hand, might be better placed to lift those stones and look under them, although having encountered Italian bureaucracy in the past, she wasn't hopeful of a rapid return. 'Send me what you have, Marek.'

'And how are you getting on with the investigation into Piero?' he said, picking up his fork. 'Did you manage to get that hard drive? Ah, I see from your face. So, what happened?'

He listened without interrupting as she went through the events of the previous day.

'Unbelievably bad luck,' he murmured.

'Where Piero's murder is concerned, it was our only lead. Unless anything comes out of Montepulciano.'

'There is one thing you could try.'

'Go on.'

'It was June the seventh, right? In the afternoon?' He set down the fork. 'Loads of people must have taken selfies when Piero was in the Maze, and made video recordings, and so on. You know what people are like these days. And they'll probably still have them on their phones. Why not run an appeal, and ask the public to come forward with anything they have? You could show them a photo of Piero, although after Luca's TV appearance, I suspect Dundee will have Googled him by now.'

Dania stared at Marek. 'You know, that's not a bad idea. The sound quality on mobiles gets better with every new model. We might just strike gold there.'

And the more she thought about it, the more she realised that this could get them back on track. She'd speak to the DCI and see if the woman was prepared to offer a reward for information that would lead the police to Piero's killer. It had worked in the past. Her spirits rose.

'Now, before you ask,' she said, as they finished the ox tongue, 'I ordered dessert.'

Marek raised an eyebrow. 'What is it?'

'*Chrust.*'

He looked at her in amazement. 'You've found someone who knows how to make it?'

'This restaurant is something else. We'll have to go there one evening.'

Dania carried the empty plates to the sink, and returned with a cardboard box tied with a thin red ribbon.

Marek closed his eyes. 'Ah, I can smell the vanilla icing sugar.'

She laid a hand on his. 'Just one thing.'

His eyes flew open. 'There's a condition?'

'I need you to keep burrowing in the archives. Time allowing, of course.' She untied the ribbon, and pushed back the leaves of the box.

He stared at the pile of *chrust*. 'Of course,' he said, his voice drifting.

CHAPTER 27

Dania was finishing her appeal, which would go out that evening on *STV News at Six* as well as in all the city's newspapers. Honor had been quick to set it up as soon as she'd heard the idea. They'd been able to source some high-resolution images of Piero and, thanks to Honor's media contacts, had got it under way quickly. Dania had been cagey about what might have happened in the Maze, saying only that they were trying to track down Piero's associates and they thought that one or more might have been with him in the Maze that day.

'So, to be absolutely clear,' she finished, 'we're looking for images, and particularly video footage taken by anyone who was in Alderwood Manor Maze at any time on June the seventh. Whatever you can give us will be gratefully received, and may eventually lead us to Piero Terranova's killer.'

Dania had discussed with Jackie Ireland the advisability of limiting the time to the afternoon, but the DCI had pointed out that whoever Piero was shouting at might have arrived well before and, if he wasn't seen clearly when Piero was losing it, there might be other better images of him taken earlier. They'd also discussed the possibility of obtaining the visitors' names. Tickets had to be bought online, so there would be a record of transactions, and the police could contact the visitors if no one came forward. Dania had decided to wait and see what came of the appeal, as it was a less intrusive way of getting the intel. They could always fall back on the transactions. But try as she might, she was unable to persuade the DCI to let her offer a reward.

The cameraman indicated with a raised hand that he'd stopped filming. His female assistant came over and removed the microphone from Dania's jacket.

'I hope that gets you what you need, Inspector,' she said, smiling. With her skinny jeans and spiky hair, she reminded Dania of Honor.

Dania thanked everyone, then hurried back to West Bell Street. She phoned Marek.

'Anything to report, Danka?'

'I'm just checking up on you, that's all.'

'Nothing's going to happen to me,' he said, before she could continue. 'If it were, it would have happened by now.'

She had to admit that he had a point. 'All right, Marek, I won't keep you any longer. But if you see anything that makes you suspicious, don't hesitate to call me.'

'Okay.'

'By the way, my appeal will go out on tonight's *STV News at Six*.'

'Let's hope it gets you somewhere.'

She ended the call. The video recordings made by the public simply had to lead them to Piero's killer because – as she'd told the DCI – she was completely out of ideas.

Hayley was perched on the edge of the sofa, rocking slightly as she watched the news. She recognised the Polish detective who had come poking around asking questions. And here she was again, making an appeal for people to come forward. Her final words – *whatever you can give us will be gratefully received, and may eventually lead us to Piero Terranova's killer* – told Hayley that they now had the victim's identity. The news anchor finished by providing a contact number for the police.

Hayley sat back, unplaiting and replaiting her hair. Arron had told her of the inspector's visit and the woman's request to take the old hard drive away. These events must be related. They *must* be. In other words, the inspector knew that there was something on the drive important enough that she'd made this television appeal. Yet how did she know? Hayley got to her feet and hurried into the study. The laptop they used at the Manor was open on the desk. She went through the transactions for June the seventh, finding a group booking for staff at the V&A. The names were all there, including Piero's. That must be it. The inspector had learnt from someone at the museum that Piero had visited the Maze. And she was now following it up, trying to find his killer. It was what detectives did, if the TV crime series were anything to go by. They left no stone unturned even if all that was underneath was sand.

Hayley returned to the living room, deep in thought. She lay back on the sofa, her eyes closed, trying to make sense of it all.

A noise dragged her out of her reverie. The front door had opened, followed by footsteps in the hall. A second later, Arron sauntered in. 'There you are, lovely lass,' he said, leaning over the sofa to kiss her. 'How did it go with the Maze today?'

She sat up. 'It went fine. But Arron, something's happened. Did you see the *News at Six* on STV?'

'I didn't.' He frowned. 'What's the matter, eh? You're looking a wee bit peely-wally.'

She struggled to her feet, her gaze sweeping his face. 'We need to find it on the catchup player.' She was conscious that she was trembling.

He took her in his arms. 'Hey, whatever it is, it's all right,' he said soothingly.

She pushed him away. 'Oh, Arron,' she wailed, 'we're in so much trouble.'

'No, we're not.' He paused. 'Okay, let's go and look at the news,' he said, taking her hand.

In the study, he fiddled with the laptop. It seemed to take him ages to find the right segment. Hayley watched his expression change as he listened to the Polish detective making her appeal. She herself tried not to listen, because she was starting to feel unwell.

The segment came to an end. Arron switched off the player. He stared through the window, saying nothing.

'Well, what do you think?' she said, when she could bear the silence no longer. 'We have to tell them everything.'

He turned and gazed at her. 'No, lovely lass,' he said gently, stroking her hair. 'We don't.'

It was Wednesday before the first photos and videoclips started to trickle in. Dania was finishing a meeting with her team. At West Bell Street's request, the New York police had been to Piero Terranova's flat and itemised what they'd found, which, apart from a number of stylish clothes in the wardrobe and a few books in Italian – *and, yeah ma'am, no sweat, we checked through them in case there were any loose papers inside* – there was nothing that would move the case forward. The only other item of news was that a check made on Piero's bank transactions going back several weeks before his arrival in Dundee showed no large cash withdrawals. There followed a lively debate as to how he'd found the money to pay for the Beretta, because one thing illegal gun dealers never did was accept credit cards.

It was as they were discussing this that the alert arrived on Dania's laptop.

'Okay, everyone. This is from Tech.'

Dania had arranged for the photos and videos to go directly to Tech with the proviso that they copied them back to her. Tech were then to try and piece together Piero's journey through the Maze. The timestamps on the media should help. Her questions were: was there anyone tailing him? Or anyone behaving in a strange manner, whether Piero was in the frame or not? The Tech guys had exchanged looks, which told Dania that this would not be an easy assignment. But she already knew that. And she also knew that they would give it more than 100 per cent. Like all techies, they relished a challenge. And to give them a head start, she'd rung Arron, although it was Hayley who'd answered, and requested a copy of the 'base state' plan of the Maze. After a brief discussion as to why the police wanted this, and Dania having to explain that, yes, she knew it would have been different when visitors were there on account of hedging and statues moving, but it was the best they could come up with, Hayley had relented and sent the plan. It was now up on the incident board, with the positions of the statues clearly marked. Dania had suggested to her team that time allowing they, too, should try to piece together Piero's movements, perhaps even beating Tech to the finishing line. She could tell from their faces that the officers were itching to roll up their mental sleeves.

'Right,' she said, 'the first photo is in.' She tapped the board, and the image appeared at the side. 'This shows Piero arriving at just after two p.m. Note what he's wearing. That green shirt is distinctive, and should help us track him.' She swiped the image across to the Maze entrance, and added the timestamp. 'Right, over to you. And don't try to do it on your own. It's better as a group, so talk to each other.'

Dania returned to her desk, listening to the chatter as the team set to work. Although there were things she needed to write up, she found herself watching over the top of her screen as the officers moved images about and added notes. In a short time, she'd given up all pretence that she was dealing with her reports, and left the desk to join the others.

CHAPTER 28

By Friday, the photos and video footage from Tech had dwindled to one or two submissions. The incident board showed – as far as was possible – the route Piero had taken through the Maze. Many of the stills were selfies that had accidentally captured people behind the photo taker, and they happened to include Piero. In a few photos, he was facing away from the camera, and it was by his clothes that they recognised him. There were invariably statues in these selfies which, given that they didn't move a great distance from their base positions, allowed the team to outline Piero's route reasonably accurately. The timestamps added hugely to their confidence in knowing broadly where he was at any time. As for someone tailing him, that was proving to be problematic. Various people popped up again from time to time, but none was constantly in Piero's vicinity.

Interestingly, Dania recognised some of her Polish friends. And DCI Jackie Ireland had visited the Maze, although she was there only in the morning. But the two girls, Ailsa and Chloe, were absent, which was not surprising as June the seventh was a Tuesday, and the Dundee schools hadn't yet finished for the summer.

'Boss, have you see this?' Honor jumped to her feet and hurried to the incident board. She pulled up a photo. 'This is Luca Terranova, isn't it?'

Dania stared at the image. The dark hair brushed back over the head was instantly recognisable. And he was in a tailored linen suit, not the jeans and green shirt that Piero was wearing. He was standing near the velociraptor. A couple were taking a selfie, their teeth bared in solidarity. Whoever was holding the phone had caught Luca turning his head.

'Someone sent it in,' Honor went on. 'I reckon they thought he was Piero.'

Dania cast her mind back to the meeting with Marek, when she'd learnt about Piero shouting at someone in the Maze. Luca had been present. And yet he'd said nothing about being there himself. So, why had he kept quiet? And why hadn't he chummed up with Piero? It could, of course, have been a coincidence, the two of them in the Maze at the same time. But it didn't explain why Luca had kept his visit a secret.

'Put it on the map, Honor. And what's the timestamp?'

'Fourteen thirty-two.'

The door opened then, and a uniform popped his head round. 'Inspector,' he called. 'There's someone here who wants to speak to you personally. He said he's got a video that you need to see. It's from the Maze.'

'Send him in, please.'

The uniform ushered in a man in black jeans and a red sweatshirt. He had thick brown hair and a delicate, serious face. He glanced around, his gaze falling on Dania. He must have recognised her from the television appeal, because his expression softened. He smiled. 'Inspector Gorska?'

'That's right,' she said, returning the smile. 'What have you got for us?'

He pulled out his mobile. 'As soon as I remembered where I'd seen that man on your telly appearance, I came straight over. I was in the Maze that day. This guy was mouthing off. I mind he was using threatening language, and no mistake.' He tapped the phone and a still image of Piero appeared.

'Can you remember what he said?'

'It was something like he now had all the evidence to put the other person behind bars for a very long time. I took this quick photo. I dinna ken why. And then something made me turn on the recorder. Here, let me find the clip.' The man played with the phone, and the video started.

But Piero had switched to Italian. He continued to mouth off, even raising a fist. Finally, he stood and stared, then he turned away. The recording came to an end.

'Isn't that Bonnie Prince Charlie behind him?' Honor said.

The statue was of a young Scotsman in a white wig, tartan outfit and blue sash.

'Looks like it,' Dania said. 'At least we know where he was when this happened, and at what time. Did you see who he was yelling at?' she said to the man.

'By the time I turned to look, whoever it was must have vanished. A few people had gathered to listen, mind. They always do when there's a stooshie.'

'We might be able to find who else was in the vicinity, boss.'

'Could we take a copy of this?' Dania asked, turning to the man.

'Of course. There are several other photos there that might help. Make copies of them all, if you like.'

'Here, I'll do it.' Honor took the phone from his outstretched hand.

The man was beaming at Dania. 'I've heard you play at the Overgate, Inspector.'

'Oh?'

'I own the mobile coffee van not far from the piano. All the shop workers round there look forward to your performances.'

'That's kind of you to say.'

'Next time you're passing through, stop by and have a coffee. It'll be on the house,' he added shyly.

'Thank you, Mr . . . ?'

'Just call me Mick.'

'Thank you, Mick.'

'The last time I heard you was when you played for that Italian tenor. He's this Piero's brother, isn't he? He was also on the telly.' He watched Honor transferring the images. 'I've caught him in one or two selfies.'

Honor returned the phone. 'Here we go.'

'Thanks, Mick,' Dania said, holding out her hand to shake his.

To her surprise, he lifted it to his lips. 'That's how they do it in Poland, I believe,' he said, with a cheerful grin. 'If that's all, Inspector, I'd better be on my way.'

'We're grateful to you.' She nodded to the uniform at the door.

'And don't forget my invitation to coffee,' Mick said, over his shoulder.

As the door closed behind him, the whistles and chortling started up.

'Looks as if you've got a fan, boss,' Honor said, smirking.

'Never mind that. Does anyone here speak Italian?'

'I have a smattering of Dundonian,' someone said. 'Will that do?'

'What about Luca?' Honor said. 'We could ask him for a translation.'

But Dania's instincts were telling her otherwise. 'No, not Luca. In fact, once you've adjusted Piero's route using these new images, I want you to go back to the beginning and map out his brother's.'

'But why?'

'Two reasons: when Marek told me about Piero being in the Maze on June the seventh, Luca was present. And yet he said nothing about being there himself. I find that strange.'

'And the other reason?'

'Marek tried to quiz him about his background, particularly his life in Italy, but he kept changing the subject. And I've just thought of a third reason.'

They looked at her expectantly.

'Piero switches to Italian,' she said. 'Now, who else do we know who speaks the language?' When they said nothing, she added, 'I think it could be Luca he's shouting at.'

By late afternoon, there was a red line – albeit with several gaps – showing Piero's passage through the Maze. In some places, he appeared to be standing where a hedge should be, but Dania put that down to the fact that the hedging would have been moving. This was the 'base state', she reminded everyone. Luca's route was much more patchy, and it was impossible to tell if he'd been anywhere near Piero when the man had been shouting. But what they could establish of Luca's movements didn't rule him out, either.

One of the officers had contacted an academic who taught Italian at the University of Dundee. When he read out the translation, it silenced the room:

Don't walk away from me. You won't escape the consequences of your actions. Do you hear me? You won't get away with this.

It was Honor who finally spoke. 'Given that Mick said Piero

claimed to have all the evidence to put the other person behind bars for a very long time . . .'

'. . . a threat like that might have made this person want to dispatch Piero at the earliest opportunity,' Dania said slowly.

'You really think it's Luca, boss?'

'It might be. Then again, it could have been another visitor.' She chewed her thumb. 'There's only one thing to do. We need a list of names of everyone who came that day.'

'Tech have uploaded the names and addresses of the people who sent in the photos and videoclips,' someone said. 'And they're all Dundonians.'

'There may have been people who either didn't record anything, or did, but decided not to submit it. Something makes me suspect that the person Piero was shouting at was one of them. But everyone in that Maze bought a ticket online. Alderwood Manor will have the names.' She glanced at her watch. 'There should be someone at home.'

'Are you going to phone ahead?' Honor said.

'I think it would be better to arrive unannounced. But there's something I need you to do. Can you meet with Marek and get whatever he's been able to dig up on Riccardo Terranova?' Seeing the woman's look of puzzlement, she added, 'He's been doing some research for an article he wants to write about Piero and Luca. Riccardo is their father. Given Luca's reluctance to talk about the past, I'm wondering if the key to all this lies there. Marek was going to send me his findings, but it must have slipped his mind. And, with everything that's going on here, it slipped mine, too.'

'On it, boss.'

As Dania left the building, she reminded herself how lucky she'd been with her team. Honor had had a recent, brief spell with the Drugs Squad, something which Dania had observed with growing anxiety in case the woman asked to be transferred permanently. But to everyone's relief, she'd returned to the Murder Squad when her stint had come to an end. Having Honor on this case made Dania appreciate that the Drugs Squad's loss was her gain.

Dania had made good time despite it being rush hour. As it was well after five, the Maze would be closed, which meant she wouldn't have to confront the man near the entrance. Part of her was disappointed. It wasn't the first time she'd been challenged simply because she was 'polis', and she doubted it would be the last. But she always gave as good as she got.

She turned off Emmock Road into the estate grounds, noting as she passed the Lodge that the silver Hyundai was absent. This suggested that Clare Conlee was still at work at the East Dock Street building. Would Marek be there? And more to the point, would he have time to meet with Honor? The two of them were old buddies, and had worked together before. Dania had wondered whether they'd start up a relationship but, so far, they hadn't. She wasn't sure how to feel about that, but maybe it was for the best.

She pulled up in front of the Manor. A light-blue BMW was parked nearby. Was this a visitor, or did the car belong to one of the McGarrys?

Dania pressed the doorbell. She waited, hearing the sound reverberate through the building. There was no response. Given the size of the house, anyone in might have a trek to the front door, so she rang again. Unfortunately, patience had never been one of her virtues. After reaching the conclusion that there was no one at home, she considered her two options: she could call one or all of the numbers she had for the McGarrys, or she could go hunting.

Instead of taking a left towards the conservatory, Dania turned right and followed the building round to the back. She stumbled immediately on to a patio paved in red-and-brown herringbone. The stylish outdoor furniture consisted of a huge yellow parasol and a table and chairs in a quiet grey. Stone steps led to an empty car park.

She stood uncertain as to whether to continue. But she might as well carry on, as there was another wing to the huge building. If she found no one around, she'd resort to phoning.

She was reaching the far end of the wing, which would curve round to the conservatory, when she spotted a wooden door. Unlike the other doors, which were solid and stained the same rose-brown as the windows, the wood was unvarnished and splintering at the bottom. The rusting hinges indicated that it opened outwards. There was a large black handle, but no keyhole. Which could only mean that the door couldn't be locked, unless there was a bolt on the inside.

After a furtive glance around, Dania gripped the handle and pulled. The door opened with a creak. She'd expected a scullery or a passageway into the house, but what she saw was a red-brick wall a few metres away, and a flight of stone steps leading down into darkness. Another time and place, she would have used the torch on her phone and gone exploring. But the BMW at the front entrance suggested that there was someone in the vicinity, and she daren't risk being caught snooping. She shut the door firmly and turned to gaze out over the landscape, wondering if the McGarrys were out for a stroll.

Beyond the wilted fields was a line of trees, their branches entangled. As Dania peered into the distance, she became aware of a white figure leaving the woodland and walking in her direction. Whoever it was wore a wide-brimmed hat and veil, and long gloves, and was carrying a plastic bucket. The gait suggested a woman, and the fact that she was tall made Dania suspect it was Glenna McGarry.

As the woman drew closer, she raised an arm and called, 'Inspector.'

Dania recognised the voice. 'Mrs McGarry, I hope I'm not disturbing you.'

'I'm just finishing up. You've come at a good time.'

She lifted off her hat and veil, letting them drop against her back. Despite the fact that she'd worn something on her head, there wasn't a hair out of place. Glenna McGarry looked as elegant as always. And her make-up was perfect.

'I had no idea you kept bees,' Dania said.

'We have several hives just in front of those trees. There's always something that needs attention.' She lifted the bucket so that Dania could see the contents. 'Today, I've been harvesting the honey.'

'How much do you take?'

'Only an amount that would be considered an excess for the bees. You need to leave them enough to get through the winter.' She smiled. 'So, what can I help you with, Inspector?'

'It's to do with the visitors to the Maze. I'm after the names of those that were here on June the seventh.'

Glenna set down the bucket. 'I take it this is in connection with your television appeal.'

'It is.'

'Arron told me about the hard drive failing. A pity. You would have seen everyone who came and went.'

'But you keep a record of who bought tickets, I understand.'

'I'm not sure there's a list *per se*. But the names on the credit-card transactions should be on the laptop.'

She hesitated, and for a second Dania thought she was going to ask to see a warrant, and Dania would have to refer to the common-law power to seize evidence without one. But Glenna picked up the bucket, and said, 'Let's go round to the front.'

Something made Dania say, 'Wouldn't it be quicker this way?' She indicated the wooden door with the rusting hinges.

'Oh, that doesn't take you into the house. Here, let me show you.' She gripped the handle, and pulled. 'Those steps lead down to a network of tunnels. They go right under the Maze. In fact, it's how the original Maze was operated. Some poor sod had to wander around moving the statues and hedging. When we upgraded to the new Maze, we took down the old statues and stored them there.'

'Why don't you have the tunnels filled in?'

Glenna pushed the door shut. 'We thought about it, but the engineers told us that if anything ever went wrong with the tram lines, it would be easier to fix them from underneath. So we left the tunnels. And it would have cost us a fortune to have them blocked up.'

They made their way round to the front. Inside, Glenna ushered Dania into an old-fashioned study. The only items on the desk's leather surface were a laptop, mouse and printer.

'Take a seat, Inspector. I'll just find where we keep the record of the transactions. June the seventh, was it?' She played around with the mouse, then said, 'Ah, here we are. Shall I print them off for you?'

'Actually, would you mind downloading everything on to this USB?'

'No problem.'

Dania watched the drag and drop.

'I do hope this helps you,' Glenna said, handing back the stick. 'Knowing we might have had a killer in the Maze is rather disconcerting.'

'I hope it hasn't resulted in a fall in visitor numbers.'

'On the contrary. We've had record sales. The Maze was teeming today.' She rolled her eyes. 'People are such ghouls.'

'Well, thank you for this. I won't keep you any longer.'

In the corridor, they ran into Hayley. 'Inspector,' she said, her voice tailing away. Dania could almost hear her add, *What on earth are you doing here?*

Dania nodded respectfully. 'Mrs McGarry.' She turned to Glenna. 'Thank you again for your help. I'll see myself out.'

She left quickly, but not before she'd heard Hayley say to Glenna, 'That Polish detective. What did she want?'

It was a pity that Dania had to close the door before she could hear Glenna's reply. More to the point, why had Hayley not opened the door to her? Had she spied her from an upper window and decided to stay in her room, hoping the detective would give up and leave? But why?

CHAPTER 29

'Thanks for making time to see me, Marek,' Honor said.

'It's my pleasure. And I needed a break.'

They were sitting at a table outside the Bank Bar on Union Street. Honor had hoped to meet at the V&A but it closed at five, which was a bit of a bummer as she hadn't seen Piero Terranova's exhibition, and now really wanted to. For some reason, it was still on, although it was supposed to have wrapped up at the end of July. Perhaps Luca had arranged with the museum to keep it going for a while longer. Honor would have bet good money that even more people would be coming to view it. By now, the whole of Dundee knew that Piero's was the body found in the woods.

She sipped her cappuccino. 'The reason I wanted to meet up with you,' she said, getting straight to the point, 'was that the boss thought you might have some more intel on this Riccardo Terranova.'

'I have, as a matter of fact. I found a newspaper article saying he'd died a few years ago.'

'Do you know *how* he died?'

'It didn't go into detail. It was from the local paper. I've got it here.' He opened his folder and handed her a sheet. 'The translation's underneath.'

'Crikey, he looks just like his sons.' Honor read the text quickly. 'Says he was born in 1964, and died in Montepulciano at the age of fifty-two. Which means he passed away in 2016, if my arithmetic is correct.' She glanced up. 'Relatively young, I'd say.'

'I understand that Italian death certificates don't list the cause of death, although there have been exceptions.' Marek ran his spoon over the cappuccino froth. 'I have a contact – Bruno – in Italy, who owes me a few favours.' He raised an eyebrow. 'I decided to call them in. This contact travelled to Montepulciano and asked around. He sounded as though he'd spoken to almost everyone,' he added, with a smile. 'What he learnt was that after Riccardo sold up, he became unbelievably wealthy.'

'How wealthy?' Honor said.

'I don't have the exact sum, but vineyards and wine businesses together can sell in Italy for tens or hundreds of millions. Some of the well-known names have been valued in the billions. But here's the thing: no one knows what happened to the money on Riccardo's death.'

'But *would* they know? Aren't wills usually kept secret?'

'Indeed they are. Italian Succession Law is firm on how they're written and signed, and so on, but witnesses don't always keep their mouths zipped. What Bruno told me is that there was something suspicious about the whole thing. Yes, Riccardo left a fortune on his death, enough to keep his heirs in the lap of luxury for the rest of their lives without having to work. The witnesses blabbed that it was to be divided equally between his children. And yet it never was. They didn't receive a penny, apparently, or only what they got from the sale of Riccardo's retirement flat.'

'That would explain why Luca and Piero had to find employment.' Honor crossed her arms. 'So, what happened to the fortune?'

Marek shrugged. 'I've no idea.'

'There must be bank records.'

'That's what I said to Bruno. His reply was along the lines of: good luck with that. The process of following money in Italy is unbelievably turgid, and can take months, sometimes years. But there may be other ways of finding out.' He smiled. 'Bruno's remarkably resourceful.'

'And will he keep looking?'

'Oh, yes. He sees a story of his own. He, too, is an investigative journalist. And, anyway, he says he's loving it in Montepulciano.'

Honor closed her notebook. 'Will you update us the instant his intel comes in?'

'Of course.' Marek pushed the folder across. 'Everything I've learnt is in this. You're welcome to keep it. I have my own copy.'

'Thanks. I'd better go. The boss will be back soon.'

'You're still on shift?'

'Can't you tell?' She lifted her coffee mug. 'I'd have ordered a cocktail otherwise.'

Dania hurried into the incident room. She held up the USB. 'Okay, everyone, on this stick are the names of the people who purchased tickets for the Maze for June the seventh. Now, some will have ordered more than one ticket if they were coming with others, but you'll be able to tell from the cost on the credit-card transaction how many they bought. We can then ask them to supply the names of the others in their group.'

'And then check if any of them are Italian. Or can speak the language,' Honor said, taking the USB. 'By the way, I'm not long back from my meeting with Marek. He's got a contact digging around in Montepulciano.'

Dania pulled off her jacket. 'Tell us what you learnt.'

They listened as Honor went through the main points. 'This Bruno may be our best bet if it takes weeks or months to get vital records,' she finished.

Dania knew how well connected Marek was. If Bruno was as good an investigative journalist as her brother, he might stumble upon the truth faster than they would themselves. Vital and bank records could be requested later.

'What are you thinking, boss?'

'A fortune that was to be divided equally between Piero and Luca has gone missing. And now Piero is dead.'

'Do you think he stole the money?' someone asked. 'And Luca found out and killed him?'

'Maybe. But there's another possibility.' Dania turned to the incident board. What Piero had been shouting in the Maze was up on the board in English:

Don't walk away from me. You won't escape the consequences of your actions. Do you hear me? You won't get away with this.

'Could it have been *Luca* who managed to steal the money,' she said, 'and Piero found out? And decided to kill *him*?'

'It would explain why there was a Beretta in Piero's rented cottage,' Honor said. 'But it went pear-shaped. Piero stumbled upon Luca in the Maze, lost it and threatened him. Big mistake. Luca felt he had no choice but to finish off his brother. And all this stuff about trying to find Piero's killer is intended to throw us off the scent. Remember how he kept quiet about being at the Maze on June the seventh. I wonder why?' Honor added, with a sneer.

'A question I intend to ask him,' Dania said. She glanced at her watch. 'Now's as good a time as any. Bring him in, Honor.'

'What about checking these names on the credit-card transactions?' someone said.

'Carry on with that. And as quickly as possible. After all, Luca may not be our perp.' And as she said it, she remembered that the brothers had exchanged text messages in recent weeks. Would they have been so chummy if Luca had defrauded Piero? There was only one way to find out.

Half an hour later, Dania and Honor were sitting in the main interview room, facing an anxious-looking Luca Terranova. With his fearful expression, and the way he kept running his tongue over his lips, he couldn't have looked less like a gangster.

'Thank you for coming in, Mr Terranova,' Dania said.

'Am I under arrest?'

'Not at all. We just want to ask you a few questions.'

He ran a slightly shaking hand over his hair, smoothing it back.

While Honor had gone to the Hampton to fetch Luca, Dania had taken the opportunity to study the contents of Marek's folder. She was therefore well prepared.

'I'll come straight to the point, Mr Terranova. Your father died a few years ago, I believe. Is that correct?'

Diving straight in was a technique she'd used before, and it always paid dividends. The expression on Luca's face changed from one of extreme anxiety to one of growing perplexity.

He stared at his hands before speaking. 'You must surely know that, or you wouldn't have asked the question.'

'Can you tell me what the cause of death was?'

He took a deep breath, and looked directly at her. 'His heart stopped.'

'Mr Terranova, everyone knows that the heart stops on death, but what I want to know is what *caused* the heart to stop?'

'I really have no idea. I was on the other side of the world when he passed. It happened suddenly.'

Dania leant forward. 'Are you saying that you didn't make enquiries as to why he'd died?'

A look that could only be described as cunning crossed Luca's face. 'I didn't, Inspector. It was Piero who dealt with all that. My father was ailing. We didn't expect him to live long.'

'And that was because . . . ?'

'He had a congenital heart condition. It was why he sold the estate. He could no longer run it.'

'Why didn't you and Piero keep the estate going?'

'Neither of us had any aptitude for wine production. Or business in general,' he added dismissively. 'We were more interested in the creative industries. Our father knew that, which is why he disposed of everything.'

'What happened to the proceeds?' Honor said.

Luca directed his gaze at her. 'I really have no idea.'

'Seriously?' she said, injecting a note of amazement into her voice. 'You surely must have expected to inherit.'

He said nothing. The expression on his face suggested that he was struggling to come up with a suitable explanation. There was now no doubt in Dania's mind: he was lying or, at best, concealing the truth.

'Did you see the will, Mr Terranova?' she asked.

'I didn't.'

'And you didn't ask to see it?'

'As I said, Piero dealt with all that.'

'I understand you received a relatively small inheritance.' Dania opened the folder. 'From the sale of your father's retirement apartment in Montepulciano.'

'You've been meddling in my affairs,' he said, through gritted teeth. 'You had no right.' Now, with his eyes blazing and his fists clenched, he looked exactly like a gangster.

'We have every right,' she said. 'We're investigating your brother's murder.'

'And how is knowing where my father lived in his last years going to help with that?'

'It's not where he lived that is important. You see, I'm trying to understand what happened to his assets. His retirement flat was only one small part. The rest was the proceeds of the sale of his vineyards and wine-production business. How much did it come to, Mr Terranova? Tens of millions? Hundreds? That money seems to have vanished without trace.'

For an instant, she saw something pass across his face, a look of panic that made her realise she was close to getting her answers. But then it was as if a mask had come down. His face became expressionless. He sat motionless, like a statue. It was time to try another tack.

'Mr Terranova, when you and I met with Marek on the Wednesday before last, he told me he'd learnt from one of the staff at the V&A that Piero had been in the Alderwood Manor Maze on June the seventh. And that he'd been shouting at someone. You were in the Maze that same afternoon.'

'Was I?' he said, before she could continue. 'I can't remember. But I don't think so.'

Which was the answer she'd expected.

'There's something I'd like you to see. It's a video recording.'

Honor played with the controls on the laptop.

'Please look at this clip,' Dania said. 'It was taken on June the seventh. Do you deny that this is you?'

There was no getting away from it. The clothes he'd been wearing in the Maze were the ones he was wearing now. 'Yes, that's me,' he said quietly.

'Now, the next clip was recorded a little later.'

Honor moved the mouse and, after a moment, Piero appeared in front of the statue of Bonnie Prince Charlie. He was shouting in English, then switched to Italian. As Dania had watched this clip several times, she took the opportunity to watch Luca instead. It must have taken a monumental effort, but he managed not to show any emotion.

'We have, of course, obtained a translation,' she said, after the clip had come to an end. 'What I want to know is this: is it you that Piero is shouting at?' When Luca said nothing, she added, 'We know from the timestamps that you were in the vicinity.'

For one fleeting moment, she thought she saw a look of resignation in his eyes. He seemed undecided.

'I want the truth, Mr Terranova. The unvarnished version.'

'It wasn't me,' he said, rubbing his face. 'Yes, I was there. But I didn't run into Piero. He's not shouting at me. I swear on my life.'

'In that case, can you think who it might be?' Dania said.

His reply came quickly. Too quickly. 'Absolutely not,' he said firmly.

And now she knew that he was both lying *and* concealing something.

They gazed at one another. She took a sheet from the folder and laid it in front of him. It was an article that Marek had found in an Italian newspaper.

'Your father, it seems, was a collector of Berettas,' she said. She turned the sheet round so that Luca could read the text. 'This item is about his bidding for a Beretta M1915 in an auction in Siena. Successfully, it appears.'

Luca scanned the article. 'It's no secret. My father had a large collection.'

'What happened to it?'

He lifted his hands. 'I really don't know.'

'Did he sell it along with the estate? Or keep it when he retired?'

'As far as I remember, he kept it. Why are you asking me these questions?'

'You once asked me how your brother had died. I can tell you now. He was shot with a Beretta M1934.'

Luca frowned. Why didn't he look surprised? Dania thought.

'Was there a Beretta M1934 in your father's collection, Mr Terranova? Or an M1923, perhaps?' she added, thinking of the model found in Piero's rental.

'I've no idea. He owned several. He was always going to auctions.'

'Do you own a Beretta yourself?'

'Of course not,' he said, in distaste. 'I've never owned a firearm. I haven't even fired one.'

She closed the folder. 'We may need to speak to you again. I take it you have no immediate plans to leave Dundee.' She paused for effect. 'Or the UK.'

'Is that a question,' he said quietly, 'or a statement?'

'A question.'

'I intend to stay in Dundee until you find Piero's killer, Inspector.' He hesitated. 'I do understand why you've asked me these questions. But I loved my brother. I didn't kill him.'

Dania kept her gaze steady. 'I didn't say you had.'

'So, may I go?'

'DS Randall will take you to the main entrance. Thank you for your time.'

Honor stood up, and left with Luca.

She returned a couple of minutes later. 'What do you reckon, boss? Guilty?'

'Guilty of something, definitely. The problem is, what?'

202

'Do you think it might be worth trying to follow the money? Start with the bank in Italy?'

'Have you any idea how long that would take? And it's probably been laundered so many times that it's whiter than white.'

'It's a pity that guy Mick didn't record who Piero was shouting at. He might have caught Luca.'

Dania ran her hands through her hair. 'Without hard evidence, we can't detain him. And I'm beginning to think he might not be the perp.'

Honor must have heard the dejection in her voice because she said, 'We've still those transactions to check, boss. You never know, we might find some Italian speakers. But why do you think it isn't Luca?'

'Okay, the pieces fit in that being cheated out of one's inheritance – a huge inheritance – is certainly a motive for murder. And Luca is definitely hiding something. No, it's only a feeling, but I'm convinced there's something else going on. Something we're missing. It's as though we're taking wrong turnings all the time.'

'Like in a maze?'

'Exactly.'

It was now down to Marek and Bruno, she realised then. Two professional investigators working together might succeed where the police were singularly failing. Yes, with a bit of luck thrown in, the men might find the key to this puzzle, and help her find the way out of her own maze.

CHAPTER 30

Hayley was walking around the living room in a state of great agitation. She knew that, for the sake of her sanity, she had to unburden herself, so she'd come to a decision. And there was only one person she could talk to. She'd phoned her close friend, Clare, who at this time on a Sunday evening would be in the Lodge, and invited her over for a drink. Arron was closing up the Maze, and would be here shortly. What Hayley was fretting over was not the confession she was about to make, but how Arron would react when he'd learnt what she'd done. She'd therefore decided to wait until he arrived, then come straight out with it before he could stop her.

The sound of his voice in the corridor, followed by Clare's, told Hayley that they were both here. It was time to pull herself together. She badly wanted a drink, but couldn't, since she was pregnant. She took several deep breaths, steadying herself.

'Hi there, lovely lass,' Arron said, breezing through the door. He took her in his arms. 'What's the matter? You're shaking,' he said, as she pulled away.

'Where's Clare?' she blurted.

'In the study, leaving a report for Glenna for when she returns next week.' He gazed at her, frowning. 'She said you'd invited her over.'

Hayley forced a smile. 'I think the time has come, Arron.'

'What do you mean?' he said slowly.

Clare appeared in the doorway. 'Hello, Hayley,' she said brightly. She was dressed casually in tight-fitting jeans and an oversized cream top. 'How are you?'

'I'm fine,' Hayley said, avoiding Arron's gaze. 'Can I fix you a gin cocktail?'

Clare laughed softly. 'Need you ask?'

Hayley hurried to the sideboard, and busied herself with the alcohol and mixers. She knew the kind of cocktail Clare liked. For Arron, she made a whisky and ginger wine. After adding ice to the drinks, she carried them to the right-angled sofa where the two had settled themselves.

'What are you having, Hayley?' Clare said.

'There's some non-alcoholic wine.' She didn't think she could manage the cork. 'Could you open it, Arron?'

'Of course,' he murmured.

She took advantage of the fact that his back was turned to say, 'Clare, there's something we need to tell you.'

Arron wheeled round. 'Hayley! No!'

She sank into the armchair. 'Arron, we *have* to tell her. *You* have to tell her. This is making me ill.' She started to sob.

He rushed back, and dropped to his knees beside her. 'Oh, Hayley, it's all right, darling, it's all right. Please stop crying. I'll tell her, if that's what you want.'

'Tell me what?' Clare said.

'We know who killed Piero Terranova,' Hayley wailed.

Clare set the gin down on the table, spilling it on the glass. 'My God,' she whispered. 'But *how* do you know? Did you see it happen? Who was it?'

'Tell it from the beginning, Arron,' Hayley said, wiping her face with her fingers. When Arron looked uncertain, she shouted, 'Please!'

'All right, all right.' He slumped on to the sofa. After a pause, he began to speak. 'It started in June. June the eleventh to be precise. I'd just closed the Maze. Everyone had gone, and I was locking up the control room when I felt something hard pressed into my back. Then I heard a voice.' He ran a trembling hand over his eyes.

'What kind of voice?' Clare urged.

'A man's. It was deep, and he spoke in short sentences, as though he didn't want me to identify it. He said he had Hayley.'

Clare turned to her. 'This man kidnapped you?' she gasped.

'That's right. It was in the morning. I'd gone for a walk on the estate grounds, like I try to do every day, you know, in the woodland. Anyway, the same thing happened, something was pushed into my back. The man told me it was a gun, and I had to do everything he said, or he'd kill me.'

Clare was staring at her, an expression of horror on her face. It somehow gave Hayley the strength to carry on. 'He pulled something over my head, then grabbed my wrists and tied them behind my back. He ordered me to walk. Of course, I couldn't see anything, so he gripped my arm and guided me. We didn't go far, then I heard a car door open. I was bundled inside and made to lie on the back seat. I heard the engine start, and we drove away.'

'Wait, wait,' Clare said. 'Didn't you manage to shake the thing off your head?'

'He'd tied it. I could hardly breathe.'

'Oh, Hayley,' Clare said, closing her eyes briefly.

'After a while, we stopped. He dragged me out of the car. I could hear birds and things. I guessed we were still in woodland.

Then he took me into a shed. That was when he pulled off my hood.'

'Did you see his face?' Clare said eagerly, leaning forward.

She shook her head. 'It was dark, and he was wearing what looked like a balaclava. And he was tall. I suppose most men are. He tied a rag round my mouth and put the hood back on, but he didn't fasten it this time.' She glanced at Arron. He was sitting staring at the carpet. She remembered his reaction when she'd told him all this before. Poor love. He'd been in a state of shock.

'There was an old mattress on the floor,' Hayley went on. 'He helped me lie down, and then he tied my ankles and put something round my waist. It was a rope. He attached it to the wall, I discovered later. He told me he'd be returning with something to eat, and that I'd be free the following day.' She closed her eyes, remembering that heady mix of relief and terror. She opened them to see Clare with her hands over her face. The woman let them drop slowly, and gazed at her.

'He did return later. I saw then that he was wearing blue workmen's overalls. He had a thermos with soup. And some bread. And a bottle of water. He didn't untie my hands. He fed me as though I was a child.'

'Ach, the bastard,' Arron said, through clenched teeth.

'When I'd finished, he put the gag and hood back on, and told me to try and get some sleep. He assured me again that I'd be free the next day.' She took a huge breath. 'I couldn't sleep at all. I might have dozed for a bit. I could tell through the cloth when the sun had come up.' Her gaze slid away. 'I'd soiled myself in the night.'

'And the man came back for you?' Clare said.

'It was Arron who came.'

'Arron?' she said, glancing at him.

'I need to tell you my side of it,' he said. A vein was pulsing in his temple. 'After he told me he'd taken Hayley, and I'd have to follow his instructions to get her back, he pulled out his phone and showed me the photo. She was lying trussed up like a chicken. Although she had a hood over her head, I recognised the dress she was wearing, ken.' He gazed at the floor. 'He told me that if I contacted the polis, he'd kill her.'

Hayley was watching Clare, trying to gauge from her expression how she would deal with this. Because what they needed was for her to take the reins and guide them through what they had to do. Neither she nor Arron had the capability to think straight in this matter. Strangely, though, just unburdening herself had left Hayley feeling stronger.

'Carry on, Arron,' Clare said softly.

'He told me I'd have to kill someone if I ever wanted to see Hayley alive again. I couldn't believe what I was hearing. Then he ordered me round the back of the Maze and up into the woodland. He gave me a pistol, and showed me how to use it.'

'A pistol? You didn't actually fire it, did you?'

'No, no. He told me how to rotate the safety catch, and that I was to keep it on until I was ready.'

'And he had this balaclava on?'

'All the time.' Arron played with his fingers. 'He told me the mark was Piero Terranova, and then he gave me instructions on how to get to his place. He had a photo of what it looked like.' Arron closed his eyes briefly. Hayley reached across and squeezed his hand.

'I was instructed to force him to drive us out to the Dundee countryside, and find a suitable place to do it. Then I was to return in his car, and leave it where I'd found it. Aye, and the man gave me an unregistered phone saying I had to take a photo of the body to prove I'd killed him.'

'Did he tell you where to send the photo?' Clare asked.

'I was to leave the phone in the field next to the Maze. There's that old potting shed in the corner. I had to put it inside the big plant pot, the man said. And then I was to return to the Manor, and wait by the landline for further instructions.'

'Looks as if he thought of everything.'

'And he knew something about forensics, right enough. Ach, that's not difficult these days with all the CSI stuff on telly. He said that, after I'd done it, I was to burn all the clothes I was wearing and also my beanie hat and gloves – he was very insistent I wear those. I was to do it somewhere way out in the boonies, and make sure that there was no trace of the clothes left.

'The following morning, I drove over to Piero's first thing.' Arron rubbed his eyes. 'He was just leaving the cottage. A few minutes later, and I'd have missed him, and no mistake. I levelled the gun at him, and told him to get into the car and drive. He was holding his jacket. He reached inside to get the car keys, and asked me what this was all about, and did I know who he was, and he could give me money if that's what I was after. I couldn't bear all that blethering, so I told him to shut it. I sat behind him, and told him the gun was pressed against his car seat, so there was to be no funny business. Then I gave him instructions as to where to go.' Arron glanced at Hayley. 'It was a place we sometimes go walking. Pretty secluded, so I reckoned it would be safe to do it there, eh. And at that time of morning, there'd be no one around. And there's a car-parking area, which is convenient.

'I told him to pull up, and we went for a wee walk. When we'd gone far enough, I ordered him to stop.' Arron paused. 'Christ, I need that whisky.' He grabbed the drink and downed it in one, spilling some on his shirt. 'He began to greet like a bairn, begging me not to kill him. You know, for a second, I considered throwing the gun into the bushes and legging it out of there. But then I thought of Hayley, and our unborn wain. I'd do anything for her. Even kill a stranger.

'I pushed back the safety catch, and placed the gun against the back of his head. He must have felt the muzzle, because he swung right round just as I pulled the trigger. The bullet went in here,' Arron added, tapping his forehead. 'The noise was unbelievable. All the birds charged out of the trees. Once I'd steadied myself, I looked down and saw him in a heap on the ground. Something changed in me then, right enough. I couldn't leave him like that, I had to bury him. But I didn't have a spade. I found a piece of branch that was splintered at one end, and I started to dig out the soil. It took me ages. I put him in the ground and covered him with earth and leaves.'

Hayley was gazing at Clare, who was sitting with her head in her hands. She'd be imagining how it would all feel. Hayley herself had done that when Arron had described what had happened.

'I was leaving the area when I remembered that I was supposed to take a photo,' Arron went on. 'I had to scrape the soil away from his face. He was staring at me with those dead eyes. I pulled out the burner phone and took a couple of photos. Then I covered him again. That was when I remembered something else. I was supposed to make it look like suicide. I'd got that wrong by aiming for the back of the head. And burying him. But it was too late. And I needed to get away from there because I was losing it. I scrabbled around and found his arm. I pulled it out of the soil and placed the pistol in his hand. In some strange way, that was the worst of it, having to curl his fingers round the grip. And then I ran to the car park. I drove like a maniac to the cottage. I locked the car – I don't know why – then I got into mine and hightailed it out of there. It was only when I'd reached the Manor that I realised I still had his car keys.'

'What did you do with them?' Clare said quietly.

'A few days later, I drove out to the Tay Bridge, and halfway across I opened the window and tossed them out.'

'Tell her the rest, Arron,' Hayley said, squeezing his hand again.

'I took the burner phone to that potting shed and left it there. Then I went home.'

'Why didn't you hide somewhere and see who came to the shed?' Clare asked.

'Because I was afraid to. I reckoned that, if he phoned here and no one answered, he'd suspect that I'd either gone to the polis or, as you say, was waiting to catch him in the act. And he'd kill Hayley. I couldn't take the risk. I just sat by that landline. And then, what seemed like a million years later, he rang and told me that Hayley was safe and well in the bothy on the estate.'

'So, she was on the *estate*?' Clare said, her eyes wide.

Arron smiled faintly. 'All that time, she'd been only a few hundred metres away. I ran there like a maniac. I think I was in more of a state than she was.'

'He took me home, and put me in the bath,' Hayley said, smiling bravely at him. 'And then life sort of went on.'

Clare was silent for so long that Hayley said, 'What are you thinking, Clare?'

She frowned. 'This was carefully planned. Whoever kidnapped you knew everything they needed to. About the two of you, about where Piero lived, about all your movements. And about the estate.'

'He must have been watching us for ages before making his move.'

'That's why they call this a "tiger kidnapping".'

'Tiger kidnapping? I've not heard that expression.'

'Imagine a tiger stalking his prey before pouncing. He strikes only when he has all the information he needs. In our human world, kidnapping and blackmailing are part of the piece.' She gazed at Arron. 'You must have been living in limbo all this time.'

'We had a bit of a wobble when Marek came asking to see old footage from the Maze.'

'Marek?'

'Aye, he'd had a tip-off that there was a drug dealer coming, something like that. Anyway, it was while we were running the recording – minus the sound due to a technical fault – that I saw him. Piero. He was shouting at someone. I thought I was going to faint.'

'Did Marek notice him?'

'I don't think so. He was looking only for this drugs guy.' Arron chewed his lip nervously. 'But he must have seen my reaction.'

'We were able to make up a story,' Hayley said quickly, 'so he was none the wiser.'

Arron nodded. 'Aye, well, we decided it would be wise to get rid of the footage, so I threw the hard drive away and bought a new one.'

'Seems a bit drastic. What else was on the drive?'

'Just things backed up from the laptop. You know, the plan for the competition, the base state, that sort of stuff.'

'And another thing. That Polish detective has been round wanting information,' Hayley said, stabbing a finger at Arron. 'She came looking for the hard drive.'

'I know, I know.' He sighed heavily, then gazed at Clare. 'After Piero's body was found, things began to move quickly. There was the interview with the brother, Luca. But what really shook us was the detective's television appeal. She was asking for photos and videoclips from anyone who'd been in the Maze the day Piero was there.'

'We can't go on like this, Clare,' Hayley said. She could hear the anguish in her own voice. 'Tell us what we should do. Because we don't know.'

Clare got to her feet, and paced the room. She stopped and stared at Hayley, then at Arron. 'There's only one thing you *can* do,' she said promptly. 'You need to go to the police. Tell them exactly what you've told me.' She sat down and leant forward, taking Hayley's hand. 'As you say, the police have started a wide-ranging investigation. They may soon come and interview you. Better to confess before that happens. It will work in your favour.' She paused. 'If you like, I'll come with you.'

Relief flooded through Hayley. She closed her eyes, feeling the tears welling. She'd always known that Clare would come up with the solution. And Arron would be excused in view of the kidnap, and they could get their lives back.

'Hold on a wee minute,' Arron said. 'I'd be confessing to murder, wouldn't I?'

'It wasn't murder,' Hayley said. 'You were forced into it. It's the kidnapper who's the murderer, not you.'

Clare lifted a hand in the manner of someone trying to prevent an argument. A shadow crossed her face. 'Actually, Arron has a point. I must admit that I'm not an expert in criminal law, but now that I think about it, if he confesses, he'll be the one charged with murder, not the kidnapper.'

'But kidnapping is a crime,' Hayley wailed.

'And that will be taken into account. But I believe that Arron would still receive a custodial sentence.'

The relief that Hayley had felt earlier evaporated. She started to sob uncontrollably.

'Look, let's not do anything rash,' Clare said. 'We won't go to the police just yet. We'll think this through. Every problem has a solution.'

Hayley wiped her eyes, and glanced at Arron. He was growing

increasingly agitated. Clare must have noticed because she said gently, 'You did what many others would have done to save a loved one, Arron. It wasn't your fault. You do know that, don't you?'

He nodded, playing with his fingers and tearing at the cuticles, which Hayley knew he only did when his nerves got the better of him. 'Aye, I think Clare's right,' he said. 'We keep shtum. Only . . .'

'Only what?' Hayley said.

'I listened to Luca Terranova's interview. He seems like a decent man. I'd like to be able to tell him what happened.'

'Oh, but why?'

'To put his mind at rest. I'm sure he'd understand about the kidnapping. I'll tell him about our baby. He'll realise that I'm not the real murderer.'

'Don't you think he'll go to the police?' Clare said warily.

'I'll try and persuade him not to.'

'But surely he'll want to find this kidnapper,' Hayley said. 'He *will* go to the police. He'll think they'll be able to question you, and get some sort of lead.'

'Hayley's right,' Clare said. 'Personally, I wouldn't do it, but it's your call. If you do decide to confess to Luca, and the police arrest you, you could tell them you're willing to put yourself at their disposal to find this man. The more help you give the police, the better it will play in court. I think a jury would be highly sympathetic, and your sentence would be reduced.'

Hayley stared at Arron. He seemed to be taking this on board. But if he went to either the police or Luca, then if Clare was right he'd end up in prison and not be there when their baby was born. This wasn't the way she'd wanted the conversation to go. Everything was spinning out of control.

Clare got to her feet. 'Look, you two need to have a good talk about this. I'll leave you to it. I do of course hold anything you've told me in the strictest confidence. You have my word on that. Once you've made a decision, let me know, and I'll give you whatever support I can.'

'I'm sorry we've burdened you with this,' Arron said, standing up.

'You haven't.' She laid a hand on his arm. 'I'll let myself out.'

Hayley now realised that this had been a huge blunder on her part. Panic threatened to overwhelm her. She didn't even wait for Clare to reach the door before blurting, 'Arron, you *can't* talk to Luca. You simply *can't*.'

'But I have to, lovely lass. The Maze is closed tomorrow, and I need to do some repairs in the morning. One of the birds is coming loose. I'll ring Luca first thing and ask him over in the afternoon. He's staying at the Hampton, according to his telly appeal.'

'No, Arron, no,' Hayley murmured.

'It might be best for you not to be here. Look, why not take yourself over to Edinburgh? You said you wanted to look at baby clothes and stuff. You could meet up with your friends, have lunch, make a girly day of it.'

She nodded, unable to think of a suitable reply. Or indeed any reply. His mind was made up. She stared through a blur of tears, hearing Clare closing the door behind her.

Clare let herself into the Lodge. Her mind was in turmoil. This was the last thing she'd expected to hear when she'd accepted Hayley's invitation. The couple had come to her for advice before, but it had been to do with the financial side of running the activities at the Alderwood estate. Hayley and Arron's confession was something she'd never have anticipated. But now that they'd told her everything, she would have to decide what to do. Had a loved one of hers been kidnapped, and she'd been forced to commit a crime, she'd have kept quiet. Assuming, of course, that she didn't go to pieces. Arron seemed to have been able to cope, which was remarkable given how long he'd had to keep this terrible secret. But Hayley was in another place altogether.

Clare busied herself preparing a light supper. It would be seafood salad, and a couple of cannoli, which she'd bought in Edinburgh. As she moved around the kitchen, she wondered what the McGarrys' decision would be. By the end of the conversation, Hayley had been firmly of the opinion that going to the police was the wrong thing to do, whereas Arron was determined to call Luca, thereby risking the police finding out. Clare took a bottle of Donnafugata from the fridge, and poured a small glass of the white wine. She'd left it to the two of them to think about the best course of action. But if Arron confessed to Luca, then it would be out of their hands. Events would take their course, and it was clear exactly what that course would be.

Clare drank down the wine, then poured another. She picked out a prawn from the salad bowl, examined it, and popped it into her mouth. She had meetings the following day, otherwise she could have talked to Arron on his own, since Hayley would be away. But perhaps that might make the situation worse. She sipped the wine, unable to see a way forward. Dear God, what a mess they were all in.

CHAPTER 31

Dania woke panting, and in a sweat of fear. She'd dreamt that she'd been running through the Maze, not knowing which route to take, and being pursued by someone with a Beretta. Whenever she paused to get her breath or decide which way to go, another shot rang out. Finally, she'd made it to the end, only to find all exits blocked. She'd turned to face her attacker. But before she could see his face, she woke up.

She staggered out of bed, tripping over her shoes. The alarm clock chose that moment to sound off, shredding her nerves further. She felt a chill pass through her. Time for a shower.

But as she stood under the hot jet, working shampoo into her hair, she wondered what had brought on such a God-awful dream. Sometimes, it was eating too much the night before, yet she'd had only a light salad and half a chicken breast. Not that she was in the habit of making such a small supper, but she had nothing else in the fridge.

Another possibility was her earlier worry about Marek, but he seemed not to be in danger, and was responding promptly to her phone messages. Her anxiety had subsided when she'd concluded that whoever had nearly run him over seemed not to be interested in trying again. Marek must have been right, and it was just a mistake on the part of an idiot driver. Her problem was that she was always in a state of high alert when it came to her brother because he never looked out for himself. But her bad dream could also be the result of stressing about her piano playing. A request had come in from the Polish consul general. Could she give a concert in Edinburgh in a few weeks' time? He would, of course, leave the choice of music to her, but it was understood without his having to say it that at least one of Chopin's compositions would be on the programme. Dania had chosen the Polonaise Opus 26, Number 1 in C-sharp minor. It started with a few fierce chords, then grew more gentle. However, it was the section with the arpeggios that had tested her. She was clearly out of practice. Yet she would persevere and play this at the concert because, of all the polonaises, this seemed to her to be the most 'Chopin'. Her neighbour Arkadiusz's latest suggestion – a piece by Paganini – would have to wait.

The only other explanation for her nightmare was that her cases weren't moving forward as quickly as she'd have liked, something that always gnawed away at her. Fortunately, the DCI wasn't breathing down her neck, but if Dania didn't deliver results, the woman soon would. Perhaps, given that this was the start of a new week, there might be something positive on her desk to cheer her up.

After wolfing a banana and gulping an instant coffee, Dania left the flat and made the short journey to West Bell Street.

She signed in and headed for the incident room. At her desk, she draped her jacket over the chair, and sat down to read the latest reports. Minutes later, she pushed them away. It hadn't taken long for the team to track down everyone who'd bought tickets for the Maze for June the seventh. The result of their investigations was that the only Italian visitors to the Maze that day were Piero and Luca Terranova. All the others were Dundonians. Some confessed to a few words of Italian, but they were the ones a typical British tourist would use. This suggested that Luca was the target of Piero's rant. The words were still up on the incident board:

Don't walk away from me. You won't escape the consequences of your actions. Do you hear me? You won't get away with this.

They'd discussed this ad infinitum. Mick had heard Piero say he had evidence that would put the other person behind bars for a very long time. If this was Luca he was shouting at, then the most likely 'actions' were that Luca had stolen Riccardo's money and laundered it. And yet the police had no proof of this, and that meant they couldn't arrest him. Dania wondered idly what Luca would have done to hide the money. Probably squirrelled it away in an offshore account. No, if they were to indict him, they'd need something solid. It was now down to Marek and Bruno. Failing that, she'd have to start the torturous process of requesting Riccardo's bank records, and then following the money.

'I can't believe we found the base-state plan *and* the plan for the competition on that drive,' Ailsa said.

The girls were sitting on the rise of the hill, gazing down at the Maze. It was just after two, and thin shards of sunlight were filtering through the branches. The heat was such that the air was full of tiny flies, which had somehow managed to get under their clothes.

'The best part is that they're not too different,' Chloe replied. 'It's just the final leg, where one of the hedges has been moved. I've memorised it now, but I need to keep checking it out in case I forget.'

Ailsa picked up a twig and ran it over the ground. 'What now? We go through the Maze again?'

'But starting at the main entrance. I'll lead, and today we're going to time ourselves. Remember that we need to get through in the fastest time if we're to win.'

Ailsa sighed. 'Let's get it over with, then.'

They slid down the rise and crept round to the front of the Maze.

'Right,' Chloe said, pulling out her mobile. She felt a tingle of excitement. 'I'll set the stopwatch. Are you ready?'

'I suppose so,' Ailsa said, sounding bored.

Chloe played with the phone, then barrelled through the gap in the hedge. She turned left, hearing Ailsa running to keep up. But then she stopped so suddenly that Ailsa piled into her.

The body of a man lay on the ground, his legs slightly apart. From where they were standing, Chloe couldn't see his face because someone was bending over him. It was when he straightened, giving them a better view, that Ailsa let out a small scream.

The man spun round. Chloe realised with a prickle of fear that he was holding an axe. He dropped it, and ran towards them. For an instant, she thought he was going to attack, but he pushed past them and rushed out of the Maze.

She raced after him, taking photos as he ran to the car parked in the driveway. Admittedly, it was his back view that she'd captured, but he might be recognisable from his light-coloured suit. She took a few more snaps as the vehicle backed away, turned and disappeared down the drive. With luck, the polis would be able to trace the registration.

She ran back to Ailsa. The girl was leaning against the hedge, shaking uncontrollably. Now that they had an uninterrupted view of the figure on the ground, Chloe recognised the owner of the Alderwood estate, Arron McGarry. Behind him was the statue of the Minotaur. Her gaze travelled upwards, and she realised that the creature was missing an axe. She stared again at Arron's body, his shirt a mass of red, the ground underneath soaked with blood. It had even reached the edge of the Minotaur's plinth.

She suddenly became conscious of Ailsa's whimpering. The urgency of dealing with her sister's needs caused her own fear to evaporate. 'Come on, Ailsa,' she said gently, putting an arm round her shoulders. 'Let's go, eh.'

It was Honor who took the call. 'Boss,' she said, 'there's been a 999 call from Alderwood Manor. A girl has rung in saying that Arron McGarry has been found murdered. He's lying in the Maze. An ambulance is on its way, just in case.'

Dania jumped to her feet, her heart pounding.

Minutes later, they were heading north out of Dundee. The uniforms had had a head start. Dania called Milo, urging him to get an incident van out to Alderwood.

'Arron McGarry,' Honor said, shaking her head. 'What the hell's going on?'

'Did this girl give her name?'

'The sergeant who rang the station didn't say. She's waiting for us at the Maze entrance. She said she has something to show us.'

'And she used the word "murdered"?'

'Yep. I wonder if Arron was shot with a Beretta.'

'We'll find out soon enough. Okay, here's the turn-off.'

They headed up the drive, meeting the ambulance on its way back. The driver slowed and gave a thumbs down, the signal that it was now over to Milo and his team. As they approached, she spotted a group of uniforms standing beside a police car. The back door was open, giving Dania a view of a figure sitting sideways, her feet on the ground. A girl with curly hair was standing speaking to one of the uniforms. Dania recognised her as Chloe.

She and Honor left the vehicle. A glance into the police car revealed a sorry-looking Ailsa, her hands clasped round a bottle of water, her head bowed.

'Inspector,' a uniform said, approaching. 'This lassie has something you need to see.'

'It's Chloe, isn't it?' Dania said. 'I saw you in the Maze.'

A fleeting look of recognition crossed the girl's face. 'Aye, I'm Chloe.' She looked past Dania. 'That's my sister, Ailsa.'

'Was it you who called this in?'

She nodded, and held out her phone. 'I took these photos of the guy who did it.'

Dania swiped through them, seeing a man in a light-coloured suit running away from the camera, scrambling into a car, then turning it round and driving off.

'Did you get a look at his face, Chloe?'

'I did, and I ken who he is. He was on telly talking about his brother, the one who'd been found in the woods.'

Luca Terranova? Dania exchanged a glance with Honor. 'You're sure?' she said to Chloe.

'Aye, I'm sure. He was standing in front of the Minotaur. He was holding an axe and leaning over the guy. When he saw us, he dropped it and ran off. I chased after him.'

'That was brave of you,' Honor said.

'Ach, he'd ditched the axe by then.'

'Even so.'

'We've got the lassie's statement in full, ma'am,' the uniform said, lifting his notebook.

'Great. Let's have a look.' Honor pulled out her phone, and took snaps of the pages.

'Is there anyone in at the Manor?' Dania said to the uniform.

'We rang the bell, but there was no reply.'

She turned to check on Ailsa. A female officer was kneeling beside her, talking softly.

'Ailsa's had a wee bit of a shock,' Chloe was saying. 'She's sensitive, ken.'

Dania wondered whether Chloe, who seemed to be putting on a brave show, would go to pieces later. She'd need to see that the girls weren't left on their own.

'Chloe, I'm going to get someone to take you and Ailsa home. And we'll arrange for a family liaison officer to stay with you for as long as you need them. Are your parents at home?'

'They'll be out working.'

'One of these officers will call them.' Dania paused. 'What were you and Ailsa doing in the Maze?'

Chloe looked at the ground. Then she said, 'We were timing ourselves.'

'And why would that be?'

It was a moment before she spoke. When she did, there was a note of defiance in her voice. 'We were practising. We're going to enter the competition.'

'I see.' Dania held up the girl's phone. 'We'll need to hold on to this for a while longer, but I'll make sure it's returned to you as soon as we've finished with it.'

Chloe nodded reluctantly.

Dania called the female officer over and issued her instructions. The woman was someone Dania had worked with before, and knew that she was more than competent.

After they'd gone, she beckoned to one of the uniforms. 'I want you to go to the Hampton by Hilton, and arrest Luca Terranova on suspicion of murder.'

'Aye, ma'am.' He left, almost running.

Dania handed Honor a pair of gloves. 'We'll need overshoes. There are some in the car.'

When they were ready, they headed for the Maze.

'The Minotaur was the first statue we came across,' Honor said. 'We shouldn't have to go far.'

Dania indicated the bloody footprints. 'We'd better watch where we tread.'

The further into the Maze they ventured, the bloodier the prints became.

'There he is,' Dania said, as they rounded the corner.

'Christ,' Honor murmured.

Arron McGarry was lying on his back, gazing sightlessly into the sky. The Minotaur towered threateningly over him. Had it not been for Arron's hoodie and jeans, this could have been a scene straight out of a sword-and-sandals Hollywood blockbuster. Dania paused to take everything in, mentally reconstructing what had happened. Next to the sprawled body lay an axe, which was almost certainly the one that was missing from the Minotaur's left hand. She forced herself to look more closely at Arron. It was hard to be certain from this distance, but most of the damage seemed to be to his chest.

Honor made to move forward, but Dania put out her arm. 'This is as far as we go. We need to wait for Milo and Lisa.'

They returned to the entrance.

'Killed with an axe?' Honor said, shaking her head. 'Why did Luca do it?'

'I intend to find out,' Dania said grimly. She badly wanted Milo and the SOCOs here so she could get back to the station.

They watched the uniforms constructing a cordon. Dania wondered if they had enough police tape to encircle the Maze. And officers would have to be posted around the entire perimeter.

As soon as she returned to West Bell Street, she would arrange for notification that the Maze and all the other Alderwood activities were to be closed until further notice.

'Here he is,' Honor said.

The incident van rumbled towards them. It came to a stop, and Milo and the SOCOs emerged. They immediately started to pull on their over-suits.

'Ladies,' Milo said, approaching. He gazed at Dania. 'What am I to expect?'

'A man killed with an axe.'

He drew his heavy brows together. 'It's a long time since I've seen that.'

He glanced at the photographer. Dania knew what he'd be thinking. Although Lisa was made of stern stuff – she had to be – there were limits to what anyone could bear. And she had to get up close and personal to take the photos. Milo was protective of his staff, and Dania understood that he was wondering how well she would cope.

'I'll take you to the Maze's entrance, Milo, and then we'll be off.'

'So soon?'

'The perpetrator will have been arrested by now.'

'And you're keen to get his confession?'

'I'm keen to charge him. And if he confesses to this one, he may confess to Piero's murder, too.'

Milo nodded slowly. 'Take us in, then, Dania.'

'Actually, I don't need to.' She pointed to the bloody footprints. 'Follow these, and they'll lead you to the body.'

He smiled. 'And there was I thinking I'd have to lay down coloured beads to guide us in and out.' He peered at the footprints. 'But these are better.'

CHAPTER 32

When Dania and Honor arrived at the station, they were greeted by the officer who'd been sent to arrest Luca. Relief swept through Dania. She'd had a vision of the Italian escaping, even though she'd called West Bell Street en route and told them to put out an All-Ports Warning.

'Is he in the cells?' she said.

'No, ma'am. He wasn't at the Hampton. They said they hadn't seen him all day. But when I got here, I learnt that he'd handed himself in. He wants to speak to you.' The man grinned. 'Even better, eh? He'll confess for sure.'

Dania stared at him. This wasn't at all what she'd expected. But then, Luca must have known he'd been spotted, and his actions possibly even witnessed. Maybe he'd concluded that it would be almost impossible to do a runner.

'Okay, can you have him brought to the main interview room in half an hour?'

'Aye, ma'am.'

In the incident room, she and Honor went through Chloe's statement.

'He was definitely holding the axe,' Dania said. 'Let's look at those photos.' She swiped through them. 'No gloves, so we'll have his prints.'

'I'd say that's Luca, boss. No question.'

'I'm inclined to agree.' She enlarged one of the photos. 'And we have the registration number of the car.' She sat back, chewing her thumb. Then she pushed the chair back. 'Okay, time for a chat.'

When they entered the interview room, Luca was already sitting at the table, his head in his hands. He glanced up and, seeing the officers, made to get to his feet, but the uniform behind him laid a firm hand on his shoulder and pushed him down.

Dania and Honor took the seats opposite.

'You asked to speak to me, Mr Terranova,' Dania said.

He nodded. Perspiration had gathered on his upper lip.

'Before we go any further, you have the right to legal representation. We can arrange for the duty solicitor to attend. There'll be no charge.'

'I don't want a solicitor. I've done nothing wrong.' He ran a hand over his face. 'I know how it looks. But I didn't kill him.'

'Didn't kill whom?'

'Arron McGarry.'

'So what were you doing there?'

'McGarry rang the Hampton this morning, wanting to speak to me. The call was put through to my room. He asked me to come round after lunch. Said he had something he urgently needed to tell me. It concerned my brother, Piero.'

'If it was about a man who'd been murdered, why didn't you come straight to the police?'

Luca looked surprised. 'It didn't occur to me.' He spread his hands. 'You could have asked Arron the same question.'

'Go on.'

'I decided I couldn't wait until two, so I went immediately.

I arrived at the Manor, and rang the bell.' He took a deep breath. 'There was no reply. I walked round the building, looking into the windows. No one seemed to be in. I tried the bell again. After a while, I came to the conclusion that maybe Arron was out for the morning, and that was why he'd told me to come in the afternoon. I left, and returned just after two. Again, there was no one in the house. So I tried the Maze.'

'And you didn't have his mobile number?' Honor said.

'I didn't. I decided that, if he wasn't in the Maze, I'd get the contact number from the website.' He ran his hands over his hair. 'I went into the Maze, calling his name. It wasn't long before I stumbled across him.'

Dania leant forward. 'What did you see? Exactly.'

'A body lying on the ground. There was an axe partly covering his face. I couldn't see who it was, so I picked it up. I recognised Arron McGarry immediately.'

'Had you met him before?' Honor said.

Luca shook his head.

'Then how did you know it was him?'

'When I booked the Maze last month, his photo was on the website. His wife's too. There was a whole section on the history of the Maze and the McGarry family.'

'Could you tell that he was dead?' Dania asked.

'I guessed he was. That wound in his chest. And the blood.'

'Yet you still picked up the axe. And contaminated a crime scene.'

'Inspector,' he blurted, 'I wasn't thinking. I was in a state of shock.'

'Do you know what *I'm* thinking, Mr Terranova? You went to Alderwood Manor to kill Arron McGarry for reasons as yet unknown, found him in the Maze, grabbed one of the Minotaur's axes and put it through his chest.' It sounded far-fetched even as she said it, but her intention was to rattle him.

'Why would I kill him?' Luca exclaimed. 'Give me one good reason.'

Before Dania could reply, the door opened and an officer hurried in. He whispered something into her ear and handed her a note. It was from Milo, and marked as urgent. She read it quickly before passing it to Honor.

'It seems that Arron McGarry was *not* killed with an axe,' Dania said. 'He was shot.' She sat back, folding her arms. 'When we spoke before, you denied ever owning a firearm. Would you care to revise that statement?'

Luca's eyes glittered with anger. 'I would not,' he said nastily. 'I stand by that statement.'

'I put it to you, Mr Terranova, that you do indeed own a firearm. We've still to do the forensics, but my guess is that the bullet came from a Beretta, one of your father's Berettas now in your possession.' She paused. 'Where is it? I'm guessing not in your room at the Hampton. Did you stop somewhere on the way back from Alderwood and hide it in the woodland, intending to retrieve it later? It was such bad luck that those girls stumbled upon the scene, wasn't it?'

'And where does the axe come in, Inspector?'

'Did Arron grab it when he saw you pull out your gun? And it fell on to his face when he collapsed?'

'If I'd just shot him, why would I pick it up?' He was almost shouting.

Dania had no immediate answer. Milo's message confirmed that the bullet wound was the only injury they'd found so far. He would check once back at Ninewells, of course, but there was no evidence of tears or cuts in Arron's clothing to suggest an attack with an axe. Dania glanced at Luca's suit. It was the same one he was wearing in the girl's photos. They would check it for gunshot residue.

'I think that's all for now, Mr Terranova.'

'So, I'm free to leave?'

'I'm authorising you to be held in custody.'

She nodded to the uniform, who escorted a dazed-looking Luca out of the room.

'We need to move quickly, Honor. I want his prints, his hands and clothes swabbed for GSR and his room at the Hampton searched. Talk to the staff there about his movements. And check the phone records, because we need to know when – and if – Arron McGarry made that phone call. And where's Hayley? And Glenna?'

'On it, boss.'

Back in the incident room, Dania rang Milo. 'Are you still at Alderwood?' she said, without preamble.

'I'm at Ninewells,' came the deep voice.

'And the post-mortem? When will that be?'

'Rigor is coming on so we'll need to wait until it wears off. Give it forty-eight hours.'

'Rigor is coming on?' she said slowly. 'So, what about the time of death?'

'I'd say some time this morning. I can't be more specific.'

'Could it have been shortly before you arrived, early afternoon, say?' Which was when the girls had found Luca leaning over Arron's body.

'It was definitely earlier than that, Dania.'

'Is there anything else you can tell me?' she said, after a pause.

'When we removed the victim's clothes, we found a bullet

wound. But only one. The shot was fatal. Nothing to suggest an axe attack.'

'Are SOCO still out there?'

'Indeed they are. From what I overheard, they'd found the cartridge casing.'

'Thanks, Milo.'

'I'll be in touch.' He rang off.

Dania stared straight ahead. Something didn't add up. Chloe and Ailsa had seen Luca in the Maze around two o'clock. Yet Milo was convinced that Arron had been killed much earlier. Luca stated that he'd arrived in the morning, but couldn't find Arron. Could that be a lie, and he'd killed him then, and returned to the scene of the crime later? But if so, why?

Honor came in, and slumped at her desk.

'You look tired,' Dania said, dragging her gaze from the screen. She'd been writing reports, a necessary but thankless task.

'Just back from the Hampton, boss.'

'And?'

'They remember a call coming in for Luca after breakfast this morning. Then he left, and wasn't seen again all day.'

'Milo puts Arron's time of death in the morning. My guess is that Luca killed him then, and returned in the afternoon. I'm racking my brains as to why.'

'Maybe he dropped something? Or thought he had.'

'Maybe.' Dania paused. 'It's interesting he told us from the off that he went to Alderwood in the morning.'

'No point denying it. We can follow his movements from the phone masts.'

'Tech will confirm all that soon enough. They're checking his mobile. They've got Arron's phone as well. And what about the search of Luca's room?'

'Nothing. No Beretta. Not even a cartridge box.' Honor massaged her temples. 'Do you think he has more Berettas hidden somewhere? His father owned a collection, remember.'

'He may well have. We just don't know where they are.'

'I get that he put a pistol in Piero's hand in a clumsy attempt to make it look like suicide, but there was nothing like that with Arron.'

'I think Arron's murder was rushed,' Dania said. 'My guess is that he told Luca something about Piero that made him go crazy and shoot the man.'

'Luca did come into the station of his own accord, boss. Mind you, he'd been spotted. Maybe he even saw Chloe taking those photos. He'd have had nothing to lose.'

'What about his clothes?'

'We took all of them to be tested for GSR. As well as the ones he was wearing at the interview. It's now down to Forensics.'

Dania played with her pen. 'What about the McGarry women?'

'Turns out that Glenna is in China. We've left a message on her phone to get in touch.'

'And Hayley?'

'Voicemail only. We've left a message for her, too.'

Dania was aware of a growing sense of unease. Was she wrong about Luca, and someone else had targeted Arron? And was also targeting the two women? 'Do we know where Hayley is right now?' she said.

'I can talk to Tech.'

As Honor was reaching for the phone, the door opened and an officer appeared.

'Message from one of the uniforms at Alderwood Manor,

ma'am. Hayley McGarry has just arrived. The man is still on the line. He's wondering what's the best thing to do.'

SOCO would still be working in and around the Maze. Dania thought of the highly strung Hayley rattling around in that big house, having just had the news from the police that her husband had been murdered. 'Ask him to bring her here,' she said.

CHAPTER 33

Half an hour later, Hayley arrived at West Bell Street, carrying a number of shopping bags. Dania was waiting to greet her at reception, having arranged for coffee to be sent to one of the less intimidating interview rooms. She didn't relish the task ahead, but it wasn't the first time she'd had to deliver bad news. Honor had offered to be present in case an emergency arose. Although Dania would have preferred to have her sergeant brief the team on developments, she accepted gratefully.

Hayley looked around, an expression of bewilderment on her face. Seeing Dania, her eyes widened. 'What's happened, Inspector?' she said breathlessly.

'Let's go somewhere more comfortable, Mrs McGarry,' Dania said. She ushered Hayley into the nearby room. The smell of hot coffee greeted them as they entered.

Hayley sat down on the sofa, setting her bags on the floor. Honor took the seat next to her. Dania knew that she'd be ready in case Hayley broke down. In her time as a detective, Dania had seen every type of reaction, ranging from complete calm to manic rage, with despair somewhere in between. She guessed where on the spectrum Hayley would lie.

'Would you like some coffee, Mrs McGarry?'

Hayley shook her head vehemently. 'Why are those people at Alderwood? There were police, and vans and people in white suits.'

'There's no easy way to say this,' Dania said slowly.

'Then, for God's sake, just say it!'

'I'm afraid your husband's body was found earlier today.'

In the crushing silence, the only sound was from the large clock on the wall. Hayley gazed at her.

'I'm so sorry, Mrs McGarry.'

Hayley continued to look steadily at her, saying nothing. Dania couldn't decide if she'd understood what had just been said, or whether she was on the brink of collapse. But then she replied calmly, 'When was this?'

'In the early afternoon.'

She took a deep breath. 'Was it a heart attack?'

Dania glanced at Honor, the signal that she needed to ready herself.

'Your husband was murdered, Mrs McGarry.'

A strange expression crossed Hayley's face. Dania couldn't tell what she was thinking. Her breathing was becoming laboured but, other than that, she seemed in control of herself.

'Was this in the Maze?' she asked, almost in a whisper.

'It was. Why do you say that?'

'Arron told me he was going to make some repairs there. In the morning.'

'To the Minotaur?'

'No, to the birds on top of the hedge.' She focused her gaze on Dania. 'Why do you think it was the Minotaur? Is that where you found him?'

'That's right.'

'And was he shot? Like the man in the woods?'

'I can't tell you that,' Dania said gently. She was becoming concerned by Hayley's manner.

'I know who killed him, Inspector,' she blurted suddenly. 'It was Luca Terranova.'

'Luca?'

'It was because my husband killed his brother, Piero.'

For almost a minute, no one spoke. Then Dania said, 'How do you know this, Mrs McGarry?'

'I need to start at the beginning. Perhaps I'd better have that coffee after all.'

Honor reached over and poured a cup. Without being prompted, she added three teaspoons of sugar. Hayley drank it down greedily. Then she began to speak, slowly at first, as though unsure of the officers' reactions, then apparently gaining in confidence.

As Dania listened, her thoughts in turmoil, she looked not at Hayley, but at Honor. The stunned expression on the woman's face mirrored her own.

After Hayley had come to the end of her account, she said, 'It's my fault that my husband is dead, Inspector. I couldn't take it any longer. That's why he was going to tell you everything. But first, he decided to tell Luca.'

'Didn't either of you confide in Glenna?' Dania said.

'We talked about it, but decided against it. We didn't want to burden her with the knowledge that her son had murdered someone.' She picked up her shopping bags. 'And now, I need to go home and make a start on dinner.'

Honor caught Dania's eye, and gave her head a small shake.

'Mrs McGarry,' Dania said, 'we can't let you go back to the Manor. Our Forensics team will be working there for some time yet. We'll put you up in a comfortable hotel. And someone will stay with you in case there's anything you need.'

A look of surprise crossed Hayley's face. 'But Arron will expect dinner on the table.' She stood up, then her hand flew to her mouth as she realised what she'd just said. She started to tremble violently, and collapsed on to the sofa. Staring straight ahead with a wild expression, she rocked back and forth, keening softly.

The shopping bags had dropped from her hands, spilling their contents.

Dania felt her heart clench. The floor was littered with toys and baby clothes.

Dania and Honor were drinking coffee, having left the traumatised Hayley in the expert hands of a family liaison officer. Dania had given strict instructions that Hayley was to be guarded day and night until further notice. Arron's killer – and it might not be Luca – may have decided to do away with Arron *and* his wife, and it was simply luck that Hayley had been in Edinburgh the entire day. Dania urgently needed to speak with Glenna, but the woman was still in China and hadn't yet responded to their messages.

'That was the last thing I expected to hear, boss,' Honor said. 'A tiger kidnapping.'

'Poor Hayley. Living with that knowledge all this time. No wonder she was so nervous whenever we ran into each other.' Dania set down her cup. 'This changes everything. We're no longer searching for Piero's killer. We're searching for Arron's.'

'Hayley's account answers some of our questions, though. Why Piero was buried the way he was, with his arm above ground and the Beretta in his hand. The wrong hand, as it happens.'

'Arron wouldn't have known that.'

'Yep. And we now know that the keys to the Merc are at the bottom of the Tay.'

'Arron must have had a huge shock seeing Piero on the control room's recording.'

Honor smiled knowingly. 'No wonder he threw the hard drive away.'

'So, let's think about what might have happened today. Luca arrives in the morning and finds Arron – alive – in the Maze. And Arron tells him what Hayley told us just now. Including that he himself had shot Piero.'

Honor poured herself another coffee. 'One possible scenario is that Luca, on learning that Arron was Piero's murderer, killed him in a rage. But if that were the case, it couldn't have been Luca who kidnapped Hayley and had Arron kill his brother.'

'Alternatively, if Luca was the tiger kidnapper, he might well have decided to silence Arron when the man told him he intended to come clean to the police. The whole point of a tiger kidnapping is that the killer never confesses.'

'My money's on that one, boss. Hayley did say that the kidnapper had a deep voice. And so does Luca.'

'I wonder why he chose Arron to be the one to kill Piero.'

'My guess is that he saw Hayley. It's obvious she's pregnant. It would be reasonable to assume that her husband would agree to kill a stranger if he thought his wife and unborn child's lives were on the line. And doing all the kidnapping and stuff would be a damn sight easier on an estate as big as Alderwood than in the city centre. Luca could have prowled around the place, and had a good recce before he made a move. Just like a tiger.'

Dania glanced at her watch. Their shifts had finished an hour ago. 'We could interview Luca now, but I suggest we leave it until tomorrow. A night in the cells will soften him up. And Forensics may have something for us by then. In fact, if we have hard evidence to present to him, he might cave in.'

'You still think Riccardo's missing money is behind all this?'

'I can't think of a better motive.'

The following day, Dania arrived at the Forensic Science Laboratory just after noon. She'd rung ahead to let Cosmo Denison know that she was on her way, but had resisted the urge to ask what he'd uncovered. She'd also resisted the urge to get there first thing, as she needed to give him enough time to do his work in peace.

She'd spent the morning with Tech, going through phone records. Luca's account held up insofar as Arron's call to the Hampton early the previous day was logged in the phone-mast records. Although the hotel's receptionist remembered taking the call, the police would need the logs to present to court, if they ever got that far.

Arron's mobile placed him at Alderwood Manor shortly after he'd made the call. And Luca's put him at Alderwood roughly half an hour later. And again after two in the afternoon, just as he'd said. But if they were to charge him, they'd need something solid from Forensics.

A further check of Luca's mobile revealed the text messages between him and Piero: the usual stuff, wishing Piero the best with his exhibition, letting him know when he would be in Dundee etcetera. But nothing after June the eleventh.

As Dania pushed through the doors of Cosmo's lab, she saw him sitting at the far end, frowning into his screen.

He looked round as she approached, and rewarded her with his dreamy smile. 'DI Gorska.'

'Hi, Cosmo.'

His wiry hair seemed more dishevelled than usual, and the dark circles under his eyes had crept further down his face. But his expression suggested that he had something for her. He brought over a chair.

'Okay, look at this,' he said, indicating the screen.

'It's a cartridge casing.'

'But not just any old casing. This is from a nine-millimetre Glisenti.'

'Ah, like the cartridges we found in Piero's rental?'

'Precisely.'

'Tell me about the Glisenti, Cosmo.'

'The dimensions are the same as that of a Parabellum, but a Glisenti uses less powder.'

'Which presumably makes it less powerful?'

'That's right, Inspector. You need to get close to the mark with this one.' His lips curved into a smile. 'The cartridge was developed for the Glisenti Model 1910, which was in service in the Italian army during the two world wars. But there's a number of firearms that can use this. The Beretta M1915 version, for example. Also the M1923, which was the model you found in Piero's rental.'

'Great work, Cosmo,' she said warmly. 'And have you had time to look at anything else?' she added, guessing the answer.

'I hared on over to Ninewells this morning to get Arron McGarry's dabs.'

Dania hoped that her alarm didn't show. She'd been with Cosmo when he was behind the wheel, and knew how fast he went. If he himself had stated that he was 'haring', then he would have been driving at breakneck speed. She wondered if he'd ever been issued with a speeding ticket.

'We've examined the axe,' he went on. 'No blood on the blade, but there were fingerprints on the handle. We found Arron McGarry's and Luca Terranova's.'

'We have a witness who saw the axe in Luca's hands. My guess is that Arron grabbed it to defend himself, but was shot before he could use it. Were there any other prints?'

'Just a few old ones.' Cosmo was looking at her strangely. 'There's one thing I should tell you before we continue,' he said, in a way that suggested he was choosing his words. 'As soon as the call came in from DS Randall yesterday afternoon, we moved quickly to swab for gunshot residue. I don't need to tell you that it doesn't hang around on surfaces for very long. We're still working on the suit and other clothes, but what we've found so far might be significant.' He hesitated. 'There was no trace of GSR on Luca's hands.'

'None at all?'

Cosmo shook his head.

'Milo told me that Arron was shot in the Maze yesterday morning,' Dania said. 'Luca would have had plenty of time to wash his hands before turning himself in.'

'That's true, Inspector, but there's something else. I understand that he went out to the Maze in his hired car. When DS Randall told us that it's parked at West Bell Street, I sent my team out immediately. We've put all our efforts into that car.'

Dania pictured the scene at Alderwood: Luca shoots Arron in the Maze, then hurries to his car. As he isn't wearing gloves, any GSR from his hands is transferred to the steering wheel, and rubbed well in as he drives away.

Cosmo had guessed her thoughts. 'We found nothing on the steering wheel, Inspector. Not a single trace.'

Dania stared at him.

'We checked the driver's seat, and the floor in case some residue dropped off his clothes.' He glanced at the image of the cartridge casing on the screen. 'Old cartridges are liable to flake. As you can see, this doesn't look in pristine condition. I'd have expected to find tiny metal fragments.'

She said it for him. 'And you've found nothing.'

'But we're still checking the clothes.'

'When will you know?' Dania said, thinking that they had until five that day to charge Luca.

'Mid-afternoon. I'll phone you as soon as we have the results of the analysis.'

'If he'd worn gloves . . .'

'It might explain why there's no GSR on the steering wheel. But we'd still have expected to find traces from his clothes on the car's upholstery, and possibly even on the wheel. Oh, and there's no GSR on the axe he picked up, either.' Cosmo paused. He seemed to feel the need to cheer her up. 'SOCO are out in the Maze again today, Inspector. They're giving it a thorough going-over.'

Dania thanked him and left the building. SOCO might well turn up something. But she knew that, without firm forensic evidence, she would be powerless to charge Luca with anything, let alone murder. Her shoulders sagged as she realised that not only was time slipping out of her hands, but so was the case.

CHAPTER 34

Dania was coming to the end of her briefing when the call came in from Cosmo.

'Sorry to be the bearer of bad news, Inspector, but we found absolutely no trace of gunshot residue on any of Luca Terranova's clothes.'

'Okay, Cosmo,' she said, trying to keep the disappointment from her voice. 'Thanks for letting me know.' She ended the call.

The team were looking at her expectantly.

'That's it, then,' she said. 'No GSR.'

'If there's no GSR, then we're looking for another perp,' Nessie said.

'But if Luca killed Arron in the morning, he could have worn a hazmat suit,' Hamish suggested. 'And removed it before he got into his car. If he's our tiger, he'd know about GSR, right enough. Didn't Hayley say he'd told Arron to wear gloves, and burn his clothes after shooting Piero?'

'Good point,' Dania said encouragingly.

'If it were me, I'd have bundled everything into a huge plastic bag, weighted it down and thrown it into the river under cover of night.'

243

Dania had always admired Hamish's imagination. Sometimes, he went over the top, but she had to admit that what he'd just proposed was more than plausible.

'Is Luca likely to confess without the forensic evidence?' Orla asked.

'I doubt it,' Dania replied, remembering the man's intransigence when interviewed. 'But we should maybe consider that it might be someone else,' she added, choosing her words.

Hamish cracked his knuckles. 'And how do we find this person, ma'am?'

'We go back to the beginning,' she said, ignoring their groans. 'Go through everything again. But we've still to hear from SOCO, remember.'

'What about CCTV? I know there's none around the Alderwood estate, but maybe we could look at cars that were heading north on Strathmartine Road the morning Arron was killed.'

Dania knew that this would eat up a huge amount of time, and probably lead nowhere. But she didn't want to discourage them. 'We could certainly try that,' she said.

'Going back to Piero's murder,' Honor said, 'Hayley was kept on the estate. Could our tiger have been one of the estate workers? And then he killed Arron to silence him.' She didn't wait for a reply. 'Although I can't think why any of them would want to have Piero killed.'

'Neither can I.' Dania shook her head. 'I keep coming back to Riccardo's missing money. There's no other motive that's even remotely credible. It would rule out an estate worker. Unless any of you can think of a reason?'

She listened as they tossed ideas back and forth. She remained unconvinced and, judging by Honor's comments and suggestions, so was she. Time was moving on, and they would soon have to decide whether to charge or release Luca.

A uniform put his head round the door. 'Ma'am,' he said, addressing Dania. 'The DCI wants to see you.'

She left the team to it, and hurried to Jackie Ireland's office.

The woman was at her desk, writing. She looked up as Dania entered. 'Ah, good, you're here, Dania.'

Jackie Ireland was one of those no-nonsense types who came straight to the point. Some officers found that disconcerting, but Dania appreciated it, as she was inclined that way herself. The woman had recently had her blonde-grey hair dyed silver, which surprisingly made her look younger. Knowing her, Dania doubted that had been the intention.

The DCI indicated the chair opposite. 'Glenna McGarry called our main number a while ago, and it was put through to me. She's only just clocked your voicemail messages.' She set down her pen. 'I've explained the situation regarding Arron's murder.'

'How did she take it?'

'As well as can be expected. She's cutting short her trip and arranging to return on the first available flight.'

Dania was relieved that for once it wasn't she who'd had to break the bad news. It was difficult enough doing it in person, but on the phone was worse. There were no facial clues to help you decide the best way of responding. 'Did you tell her about the tiger kidnapping?'

'I didn't. That's for another time. The reason I've asked you here is to get an update on the forensics on the Arron McGarry case.'

'I heard a short time ago from Cosmo. They've finished the tests. There's no trace of GSR.'

'I'd agreed to extend Luca Terranova's custody to give the test results a chance to come through. That time's nearly up.'

She held Dania's gaze. 'Do you have anything you can charge him with?'

'I don't.'

'Then you know what to do.'

Dania nodded. She got to her feet and left the office.

Silence descended as she entered the incident room. From their faces, they'd guessed what was coming.

'What news on Luca, boss?' Honor said.

'Release him.'

Wednesday morning saw Dania at her desk earlier than usual. In fact, she wasn't even on shift, but she'd reached the stage in her investigations where she worked whether on shift or not. And she'd had another sleepless night, brought on by the fact that she was no further forward with any of her cases. And as someone had so eloquently pointed out, the bodies were starting to pile up.

Dania sipped her coffee as she ran through the reports. There was a message from Milo confirming that Arron's autopsy would take place in the afternoon. She replied to say that she would attend with the fiscal. The DCI had also left a message: Glenna would be arriving in Dundee the following day, and hoped to meet with Dania at the earliest opportunity. Which reminded her that she needed to check on Hayley. She contacted the liaison officer who was staying at the same hotel. The woman informed Dania that Hayley was as well as could be expected, but was prone to episodes where she broke down uncontrollably. That wasn't unusual in the circumstances, she added. Dania guessed that the first thing Glenna would want to do when she arrived the following day would be to take Hayley home. SOCO would have finished their sweep of the Maze by then, if they hadn't already.

There were a few old reports still on her desk. At the bottom of the pile was the folder that Marek had given Honor. Dania slid it out and leafed through it again. Maybe the key to Piero and Arron's murders lay somewhere in these papers. As she read through the Montepulciano newspaper articles, she was reminded again of how thorough her brother was in his research. He'd make a great addition to her team, she thought, until she remembered that he wouldn't be quite so keen to give up the freedom afforded to him as an investigative journalist. And, anyway, he helped her often enough when their cases crossed.

At the back of the folder were several articles that she'd only briefly scanned previously. They were from a paper called *Giornale di Sicilia*. In the first, there was a photo of Riccardo standing with a couple. The man beside him was stockily built and scowling into the camera. The woman, whose dark hair was tied up in a scarf, was smiling blissfully, as though determined to ignore what appeared to be her husband's bad temper. Behind them, rows of vines stretched to the horizon. Marek's translation informed Dania that the couple were Aldo and Anna Girifalco, and they and Riccardo Terranova had gone into the grape-growing business together, and set up their first vineyard in the Trapani region of Sicily. The Girifalco dynasty was already well established in the wine business, their main product being Marsala. In another photo, there was a display of bottles of their famous brand of the sweet wine. The labels showed a bird holding a branch. The date of the article was June 1999.

The remaining articles were about this joint wine venture, which expanded in the years following the merger. Riccardo was in all the photos, suggesting that he'd arranged for publicity whenever he was in Sicily, which seemed to be often. In one article from 2002, Anna was standing with a young girl, whose face and hair were hidden under a wide straw hat. A quick look back at the Montepulciano articles told Dania that, in Tuscany, Riccardo was sole owner of his vineyards. Given that he'd sold up eventually, perhaps his stake in the Sicilian enterprise had been bought up by the Girifalcos.

She closed the folder, wondering if any of this was relevant to her case.

Dania returned from the post-mortem having learnt nothing new. Apart from the entry and exit wounds in the chest and back, there were no other injuries of any kind on Arron McGarry's waxy-white body. The bullet had torn through the heart, resulting in almost instantaneous death. That was something she'd be able to tell Glenna. Nothing else in the autopsy raised a flag, Milo confirming that Arron had been fit and healthy prior to his death.

Dania showered, but turned down the offer to take coffee with the fiscal. She needed to get back to West Bell Street as she was waiting for the report from the SOCOs, and it might have arrived in her absence.

She was in luck. The folder was on her desk.

'That came in while you were at Ninewells, boss,' Honor said, looking up. She was the only other officer in the room. 'And Cosmo rang asking for you,' she added. 'He's away now, but he said he'd catch you soonest.'

'Did he say what he wanted to talk about?'

Honor grinned. 'You know Cosmo. He never talks to anyone but the boss lady.' Her grin widened. 'I once asked him why, and he said that if he talks to the hired help . . .' she pointed at herself, '. . . he always ends up having to repeat it all to you. He obviously doesn't trust anyone to pass on the intel accurately.'

'I think I know why that is. He once *did* tell the number two, but the man left out a significant piece of information when relaying it to his DI. It resulted in a huge delay in catching the killer, who went on to butcher two more women before he was caught.'

'Yikes. I didn't know.'

'So, I guess we need to respect Cosmo's decision.'

'Yep, I get that.' Honor nodded at the folder. 'Anything useful in there?'

Dania could see that the woman was itching to read it. She'd been with Dania in the Maze when the body had been found, after all. 'Bring over a chair, Honor,' she said, opening out the folder.

Honor leant over the sheets. 'Cripes, look, they've mapped out the Maze.'

'Useful. I wonder how long it took them?'

'I bet they used a drone.'

'Okay, they've marked this area here, for some reason. It's further inside the Maze, where those huge birds are, the ones on top of the hedge.'

There was a photograph attached. It showed an aluminium ladder lying on the ground next to an open toolbox, its contents scattered.

'Didn't Hayley say that one of the birds was coming loose, and Arron was going to fix it?' Dania said. 'If he had, then surely he wouldn't have left the ladder lying around.'

'Maybe his attacker found him there first, and he dropped the ladder and ran. Or could he have tried to defend himself with it, and accidentally kicked the toolbox over? What else has SOCO got?'

Dania removed the pages and spread them out. 'They found the bullet that killed him. It had gone right through the hedging by the Minotaur and out the other side of the Maze.'

'Crikey! Just as well there was no one on that path.'

'Ah, but look at this. They've found *another* cartridge casing. And a *second* bullet lodged in the wood of the hedging. But this bullet is near where the birds are.'

'So, he fired once when Arron was standing beside the ladder. And missed. And then again when he'd reached the Minotaur.'

'And here's a diagram showing the two trajectories, and where Luca would have been standing.'

'You still think it's Luca, boss?'

'I'm swithering. Considering the motive, there's no one better who fits the bill. The problem is that the lack of GSR excludes him. I mean, would he really have brought a hazmat suit with him?' Dania laid out the diagrams. 'I recognise Cosmo's hand in these. He's an ace when it comes to this kind of forensics.'

In the case of the first bullet, Cosmo had set out three possible scenarios for where Arron and Luca could have been standing, given the track of the projectile through the wood.

'It's clear from the height of the bullet track that Arron would have come down off the ladder before the shot was fired,' Dania said. 'Or hadn't yet gone up it.' She ran her hands through her hair. 'How would Luca have known where he was, though?'

'If it were me, I'd have hidden somewhere where I could keep a watch on the front door. Then I'd have seen him fetch the ladder from wherever, and tiptoed after him. Better to kill him in the depths of the Maze than risk doing it just outside the Manor. You never know who might be coming up the drive.'

Dania studied her. 'You know, Honor, with a mind like that, you'd make a great criminal.'

'You need to have a mind like a criminal to make a great detective.'

'True, true. So, what about the second shot?'

'Yep, okay, so Luca misses with the first. But before he can fire again, Arron rushes away. Luca barrels after him, following the sound of pounding feet. Arron sees the Minotaur, and decides to make a stand. He reaches for the axe, thinking he can surprise Luca, but by the time he's pulled it out, Luca has got there, and it's game over.'

'I agree that's the most likely scenario,' Dania said. 'Right, let's see what else SOCO have marked up.'

'They've indicated where objects have been found in the Maze. Here, by the Selkie, there's a coin. And an empty crisp packet by the Frog. And there are similar items elsewhere.'

'What about near the birds?'

'Aha!' Honor said. 'A crumpled white handkerchief. Here's the photo.'

'What do you think? A man's or a woman's?'

'Hard to tell.'

'Where was it, exactly?'

'According to the map, it was near the toolbox.' Honor glanced up. 'Could it be that Arron dropped it?'

'Or his killer did. Maybe there was a fight.'

'Did Milo find anything under Arron's fingernails?'

Dania shook her head.

'If I was fighting someone who was trying to kill me,' Honor said, 'I'd be grabbing at his arms, especially the one holding the gun. I wouldn't bother scratching his face.'

'There you go with that criminal mind again.'

'I've missed my calling,' Honor said, with a grin.

'What I still don't get, though – and I'm sorry to sound like a broken record – is that, if it *was* Luca, why did he return in the afternoon?'

'Maybe he's telling the truth, boss. Maybe the killer is someone else. When you were with the DCI, we discussed this ad infinitum.' Honor rubbed her cheek thoughtfully. 'It's not the absence of GSR on Luca, it's that he came back, as you've just said. Chloe saw him leaning over Arron's body. Why would he even do that? He'd have known Arron was dead when he killed him earlier. Forget the massive blood loss. Those staring eyes would have done it. And he picked up the axe. Why?'

Dania played with her fingers. She had to concede the point. She was slipping into that mindset that detectives try to avoid: being so fixated on one theory that she ignored everything else, especially the evidence.

'You're right, of course,' she said, with a sigh.

'And, going back to Piero, we're assuming that Luca is the tiger, but that might not be the case. Yes, he could have embezzled Riccardo's money and Piero found out, but the motive for Piero's murder could lie in the past. In Italy. And what we need now . . .'

'. . . is for Marek and Bruno to deliver the goods,' Dania said, finishing the sentence.

CHAPTER 35

Dania let herself into the flat, and dropped her bag on the hall chair. She was ravenous, having had only a light lunch, as eating was something she avoided before an autopsy. As she hung up her jacket, she wondered if Marek would like to join her. She could phone the Polish restaurant and order two portions of that ox tongue with horseradish he'd liked so much. Or they could try something else, the tenderloin in Madeira sauce, perhaps.

But before she ordered the food and rang Marek – the two would arrive at more or less the same time – she needed to make the place presentable. As she washed the dishes piled up in the sink, her mind slipped back to her conversation with Honor, and the woman's comment that the team were convinced Luca Terranova wasn't Arron's killer. Honor had been right about conducting a deeper check of Arron's background. Maybe there was more to the man than everyone had thought. Hayley was unlikely to be in a condition to help, assuming she knew anything, or was prepared to divulge it. But Glenna had struck Dania as sensible enough to reveal secrets about her son if she thought they'd lead the police to his killer. Dania was hoping to see her on Friday, which, as this was Wednesday, gave the team the following day to dig up anything relevant on Arron. The

253

background check they'd conducted a couple of weeks earlier might not have been as thorough as it should have been . . .

In the living room, Dania plumped up the cushions, and tidied away the old newspapers. As she carried them to the recycling bin, her gaze fell on a copy of *Dundee Today*. It might be bad karma to throw that into the bin, as it was the paper Marek worked for. She flicked through the pages, seeing Clare Conlee's name at the bottom of the editorial. She would read it some other time, she thought, stuffing it into one of the drawers. She mopped the kitchen floor, then ran the vacuum cleaner over the living-room carpet. It wasn't up to Marek's standards, but it would have to do.

Dania flopped on to the sofa and rang Marek. She was on the point of giving up when he answered.

'Danka! This is a surprise.'

'I was wondering if you'd like to come over for supper,' she said, before sneezing. The living room was obviously dustier than she'd thought.

'Well, that could be problematic,' he said slowly.

'Why? Have you had a better offer?'

He laughed. 'I wish. No, I'm in Montepulciano. It's glorious here, but unbelievably hot. I'm sitting in my shirt sleeves.'

She sat up. 'Montepulciano? What are you doing there?' Stupid question, she realised then.

'Actually, I'm on annual leave. I'm staying with Bruno.'

'That's nice,' she said sourly. 'Does your boss know you're there?'

'Clare? No. The research I'm doing here is freelance, and won't appear in *Dundee Today*.'

'So, have you got anything on Riccardo?'

'Give me a chance, Danka. I only arrived on Monday evening.'

'And it's Wednesday evening now. You're usually quicker off the mark.'

'Bruno's the one doing most of the work. What he's discovered from his various conversations is that the people here remember Riccardo with great fondness. They worked in his vineyards.'

'And Riccardo's money?'

'They all looked blank when he asked. But he's not finished yet. He's got a few contacts of his own.'

'How long do you expect to stay?'

'I'm not sure yet. I've not booked a flight back. It depends on what we dig up.' A pause. 'Any news from your end?'

'It's in the papers here, so I can tell you. Arron McGarry's been murdered.'

'*Arron?* My God. What happened?'

'He was shot. In the Maze. We don't know much more at this stage.'

After a silence, Marek said, 'Is this to do with Piero's murder?'

'I think it is. But we're still at the start.'

'I understand. Look, keep in touch, Danka, and I'll do the same. As soon as I have something, I'll let you know. I have to go. Bruno's just arrived.'

'Okay.' Dania ended the call. She lay back on the sofa, her eyes closed. So, Marek was in Montepulciano. Lucky Marek. Her last holiday had been in March, in Orkney, where the wind had blown under the sash windows of her Airbnb. She imagined her brother sitting in a pavement café, sipping wine and watching the Italians go by. But the news about Arron would have shaken him.

She hauled herself off the sofa and padded into the kitchen. Her piano practice could wait until after supper. The polonaise was proving more challenging than she'd thought, but she needed something to take her mind off work. In fact, it was often while deep in the music that the ideas for moving her cases forward presented themselves. But first she had to eat. Since Marek wasn't joining her, she wouldn't bother with a takeaway. She opened the fridge and looked inside.

There was half a pack of stale cheese, and a bottle of Wyborowa.

It was Friday before Dania finally saw Cosmo. After calling to check that he was free, she hurried to the Forensic Science Laboratory.

He looked up from his desk as she pushed through the lab doors. 'Inspector,' he said, with his enigmatic smile. 'Thanks for coming over.'

She took the seat next to his. 'I read your report, Cosmo. It was the usual thorough analysis, and extremely helpful.'

He acknowledged the compliment with a nod. 'A team effort.'

'Led by yourself.' She paused, surprised to see him looking uncomfortable at being praised. 'Honor said you rang asking to speak to me.'

'It's the handkerchief. I wanted you to see it,' he said, getting to his feet.

He returned with an evidence bag. A white handkerchief was spread out inside.

'It was crumpled when we found it, Inspector.'

Dania brought the bag to her face. 'It looks clean. But the fact that it was crumpled suggests it's been used.'

'Exactly. And we may get DNA from it.'

'Hold on, there's something embroidered in the corner. Is that a letter?'

'Yes, white on white is never a good look. I think it's the letter F.'

'I'm inclined to agree. But there's something underneath. I can't make it out.'

'We'll put it under different wavelengths of light. But I want to concentrate on extracting the DNA first. I think it might tell us what we need to know.'

Dania studied him. 'If this belongs to someone whose name begins with F, then it could give us a lead. The problem is that it can't be our prime suspect, or, rather, *my* prime suspect. His name begins with L. Maybe he has a middle name, which he uses formally.'

'If this is Luca Terranova, then it's highly unlikely. As a rule, Italians don't have middle names.'

'It might be Arron McGarry, then. We can easily check.'

'Or it could be someone completely different. A visitor to the Maze?'

'It's possible,' Dania said, thinking of all the other items SOCO had found there. The visitors had been remarkably careless.

'Anyway, I thought you should see it.'

'Would you say this is a man's or a woman's hankie, Cosmo?'

'I'd say either. It's neither too large nor too small. And these days, anything goes.'

'On the subject of going, I need to run. Thanks, Cosmo.'

He smiled, bowing slightly. 'Glad to be of service.'

Dania returned to West Bell Street, and headed straight for the incident room. She filled the team in on her conversation with Cosmo.

'The handkerchief found near the toolbox has the letter F in the corner.' She paused. 'I know we've released Luca Terranova, but can someone check whether he has a middle name beginning with F?'

To their credit, none of the officers raised an objection.

'I can look on his passport,' someone said. 'Just a moment.' He tapped away. 'Nah, just Luca Terranova. No middle name.'

'And what about the background on Arron McGarry?' Dania asked. 'Did anything turn up? I know you've not had long.'

'Nothing so far,' an officer said. 'The guy seemed to have been well behaved. Even when cheering on Dundee United,' he added, with a grin.

'I'm seeing his mother shortly. She might give us something.'

Dania caught their looks. Dealing with the bereaved wasn't something these officers had to do, and their expressions made it clear they were grateful it was left to the higher echelons. Sometimes rank didn't always have its privileges.

Glenna would be at the Manor. There was no time like the present. She left them to it.

But as she hurried out of the main entrance, she saw Glenna stepping out of a light-blue BMW. She waited until the woman had locked the car. 'Mrs McGarry,' she called.

Glenna turned, and walked stiffly towards her. She was wearing baggy black trousers and a loose navy shirt. Her hair, usually elegantly styled, was uncombed and greasy. But it was her expression that made Dania draw in her breath. The haggard face could have been the result of jet lag, but Dania suspected the woman was trying to conceal her grief. Her eyes were brimming with unshed tears.

'Inspector, could we speak?' she said, in a voice full of restrained emotion.

'Of course. I was actually on my way to Alderwood Manor to see you.' She paused as Glenna wiped her eyes. 'Shall we go inside, Mrs McGarry?'

The woman nodded, keeping her gaze on the ground.

Inside the station, Dania arranged for coffee, then showed Glenna into one of the more comfortable rooms. It was the same room where they'd heard Hayley reveal the details of the tiger kidnapping.

Glenna dropped her handbag on the floor, and took a seat on the sofa.

'Mrs McGarry, let me say first how sorry—'

Glenna held up a hand. 'Please let's not waste time on preliminaries, Inspector.' She took a deep breath. 'I want you to tell me how my son died. DCI Ireland said only that he'd been murdered.'

'He was shot through the heart. Death would have been almost instantaneous.'

The emotions came and went on Glenna's face. Relief, perhaps that her son hadn't been knifed or bludgeoned to death, shock that someone had shot him. And finally, curiosity.

'Was it with a shotgun?' she said.

'It was a Beretta.'

'Not a make I'm familiar with,' she said slowly. 'The DCI told me that he was found in the Maze.'

'That's right. We had to close it off while our Forensics team were working there. They've finished now.'

Before she could continue, Glenna said, 'The Maze and all the other attractions at Alderwood will be closed until further notice.'

Dania leant forward. 'Mrs McGarry, to find your son's murderer, we need to establish the motive. Is there anything you can tell me about Arron that might help us?'

'You mean did he have any enemies?'

'Exactly.'

The coffee arrived before Glenna could reply. Dania could see her mulling over the question as she lifted the cup to her lips.

'Inspector,' she said finally, 'for many years I've worked closely with my son on our business ventures. I've got to know the people he's had dealings with. I can't think of a single person who would want to kill him.'

'Was there no one he crossed? Or turned away, leaving them disappointed?'

'No one I can think of.'

'What about his private life? Did he have many friends?'

'Quite a few. They were mainly people who shared his love of football. He'd often have them round for drinks and so on.' Glenna shook her head. 'I'm not being much help, am I?'

Dania smiled. 'On the contrary. It means we won't have to waste our time on fruitless lines of enquiry. There is one other thing I'd like to ask. Does Arron have a middle name?'

'Yes, it's Fergus. After his grandfather. They were devoted to each other. Why do you ask?'

'We found a handkerchief with the letter F. It was in the Maze. Did Arron have one of his grandfather's handkerchiefs as a keepsake, perhaps?'

'He might well have.' Glenna drew her brows together. 'Inspector, I have a question for *you*. I understand that Hayley is staying in a hotel with a police officer. I'd like to have her home with me.'

'I understand, but it's not possible just yet.' Dania set down her cup. 'You see, whoever killed Arron may now intend to target Hayley.'

Glenna froze. 'But why?'

'Until we have a better idea of why Arron was killed, we have to assume that Hayley might also be in the killer's sights.'

The colour drained from Glenna's face. 'I don't understand.'

'It would be best if Hayley continues to stay where she is. She's well protected there.' Dania considered telling Glenna about the tiger kidnapping, but decided this wasn't the time. The woman seemed only just to be holding it together.

'And when will my son's body be released?'

'Not until we apprehend his killer.'

'And will you find his killer, Inspector?' Glenna said quietly.

'I'll do everything in my power. And if you think of anything that could help me, anything at all, then please phone me directly.' She pushed across her card.

Glenna took the card, and slowly got to her feet. She looked like a woman twice her age. And nothing like the woman Dania had first met at Alderwood Manor.

CHAPTER 36

Dania and Honor were in the canteen, finishing their sandwiches. 'So, what did I miss at your briefing?' Honor said, pushing the plate away.

'The handkerchief that SOCO found in the Maze? Cosmo's going to see if he can extract DNA. What's interesting is that there's the letter F in the corner. When I met with Glenna McGarry, she told me that Arron's middle name was Fergus.'

'If the DNA turns out to be Arron's, we're no further forward.'

'It's now down to Marek,' Dania said.

As if on cue, her phone rang. 'It's my brother,' she mouthed to Honor. 'I'll put him on speaker. Hi, Marek. Honor's listening in with me,' she said, in English.

'I'm glad I've caught you ladies. I'll get straight to it. Bruno and I have been continuing making enquiries, and we've come up with something. I don't know how relevant it is to your investigation, but it's to do with Riccardo's trips to Sicily. Now, here's something interesting. From time to time, he didn't return alone. He brought a woman back with him.'

Dania caught Honor's raised eyebrows. 'What did his wife have to say about that?'

'It was after she'd died.'

'He didn't remarry, did he?'

'He didn't.'

'And do we know who this woman was?'

'Yes, her name was Anna Girifalco. She was English, actually. Married Aldo Girifalco and helped him run the wine business in Trapani.'

'I remember now. There was a photo of her in your folder. So, did Aldo ever accompany her?'

'Occasionally. And they brought their young daughter along. They'd all stay at Riccardo's villa.'

'Were the Girifalcos the only people Riccardo went into business with?' Dania said, thinking that if Riccardo had swindled someone, it might have ultimately led to Piero's murder. As a theory, it was a long shot, but she was running out of them.

'As far as I know, he didn't form a company with anyone else. The other thing we picked up was some gossip that Riccardo and Anna's relationship wasn't strictly business.'

'Ah, they were indulging in a bit of hochmagandy, were they?' Honor said.

'That's one way of putting it. But they kept it more or less secret.'

'More or less?' Dania asked.

'More when Anna's husband was with them. Less when he wasn't.'

'What do we know about the husband? Is he still alive?'

'I've no idea.' A pause. 'What are you thinking, Danka? He found out about the affair and is taking his revenge only now? By having one of Riccardo's sons killed?'

'Anything's possible with jealous husbands,' Honor interjected.

'Riccardo was something of a national treasure in Montepulciano,' Marek said. 'Apart from being one of the major employers, he looked after his workers when they retired. There was a generous pension scheme. Bruno said it was to ensure that the next generation would become Terranova employees in the fullness of time.'

'That's a cynical comment,' Dania said.

'All investigators are cynical, Danka. You have to question everything. I'm sure detectives are the same.'

'Look, Marek, any chance you can take yourself off to Sicily, and see what you can find out about the Girifalcos?'

'Great minds think alike. Bruno's offered to drive. In fact, we're about to head off. I'll phone you when we get there.'

'Thanks,' she said, ending the call.

Honor played with her mug. 'You think this affair of Riccardo's has a bearing on the case, boss?'

'Maybe Aldo got wind of what was going on, and decided to take matters into his own hands. Maybe Riccardo's death had nothing to do with his heart. Maybe Anna also died in mysterious circumstances, and Riccardo's sons were next in Aldo's sights.' She smiled. 'Maybe, maybe, maybe.'

'How realistic is it that Aldo would have waited till now to take his revenge by targeting Piero and Luca, though?'

'Wounds can fester for a long time, Honor. And it could have taken Aldo ages to track them down. Perhaps Piero's newfound fame brought him to the man's attention.'

'Yet don't you think that, for a Sicilian, a tiger kidnapping is over the top? Wouldn't Aldo have simply hired a thug to shoot Piero in the street? And what about Piero shouting at someone in the Maze? Where does that come in?'

'We have more questions than answers, I'm afraid.'

They finished their coffee in silence.

★ ★ ★

On Monday morning, a call came in from Cosmo. 'Inspector?' The urgency in his voice made Dania sit up. 'Are you free to come over just now?' he asked.

'Have you got something?' she said, grabbing her bag.

'I think so.'

'I'm on my way.'

A quarter of an hour later, she was sitting beside him, staring into a large computer screen.

'I managed to extract DNA from that handkerchief, the one found in the Maze,' he said.

'And was it Arron's? We learnt that his middle name was Fergus.'

'It's not Arron's, Inspector. The DNA is from a woman.'

Dania stared at him. This was the last thing she'd expected.

'I couldn't find the DNA in the National Database,' Cosmo went on, 'but I compared it to the DNA we've collected so far. What I found was a familial link.'

'To Arron McGarry?' she said, thinking of the letter F on the handkerchief.

'To Luca and Piero Terranova. Whoever deposited that DNA is their half-sister.' Cosmo put his face close to hers, frowning. 'Are you all right? You've got a strange look in your eyes.'

'That's the look I have when I'm thinking,' Dania said mechanically. So, Luca and Piero had a half-sister. 'Is this on the father's side, or the mother's?'

'The father's. Riccardo had a daughter by another woman. Did he marry again?'

'Not to my knowledge. But there were rumours that he'd had an affair.'

She thought back to her last conversation with Marek. The girl that Anna Girifalco occasionally brought to Montepulciano, could that child have been Riccardo's?

265

Cosmo was gazing at her. 'Oh, I nearly forgot,' he said suddenly. 'I managed to get somewhere with the embroidery under the letter F.'

He played with the controls, and a greatly enlarged photo of the corner of the handkerchief appeared.

'I've outlined the details in black to get a better image.'

Although the stitching was coming apart, there was no mistaking it. It was a bird holding a branch in its claw.

'I've seen this before,' Dania said, her voice tailing away. 'It was on a bottle of Marsala. The brand that's produced by the Girifalco family.'

She got slowly to her feet and walked around the lab, running her hands through her hair.

'What are you thinking, Inspector?' Cosmo said, an amused look on his face.

'The owner of this handkerchief is Riccardo Terranova's child with Anna Girifalco. I saw a photo of the girl in Marek's folder. It was taken in Sicily.'

Sicily. Where Marek and Bruno were headed.

'Cosmo, I have to dash. This has been enormously helpful. I can't thank you enough.' She gazed at him, feeling the urge to hug him.

'All part of the service,' he said, with a nod of acknowledgement.

'Marek, can you hear me?' Dania said. She was about to leave for West Bell Street, but decided to try her brother first.

'Only just, Danka. The reception here isn't too good. We're south of Naples. The scenery is spectacular, by the way.'

'Look, can you do something for me? Anna Girifalco had a daughter. She's in one of the photos in your folder. Can you find out what her name was? Forget vital records. The people in the area are sure to know. And see if you can discover what happened to her. Did she leave Sicily, for example, and if so where did she go? And can you ring me as soon as you know?'

'Okay. It'll be tomorrow before we get to Trapani. We're staying over in Agrigento tonight. You really have to visit this country, Danka. It's superb.'

'Just don't get into trouble with the locals.' She had a vision of the men from Agrigento in hats and shabby suits, and wearing pistols in their shoulder holsters. 'I'm sure they all carry guns.'

'You watch too many Hollywood movies. Everyone we've met is super friendly.'

Dania finished the call, and hurried to the station.

The team was waiting in the incident room. Was it her imagination, or was the mood more buoyant than usual?

As quickly as she could, Dania summarised everything she'd learnt, going right back to the beginning. It was a tactic she'd seen work at the Met when she'd been a junior officer. It served to concentrate minds, and highlight the gaps in their knowledge.

'So, we're just waiting on a call from Marek,' she finished.

'There's something we could do in the meantime, boss,' Honor said. 'Didn't Marek say that Anna and her daughter came to Montepulciano and stayed at Riccardo's? Well, Luca is bound to know the name of this girl.'

Dania hesitated. 'I did think about asking him, but I still believe he's involved in some way. Okay, maybe he didn't kill Arron, but I remember how he dodged my questions. And if he's up to something, I don't want to alert him.'

'Do you think this daughter – F – shot Arron in the Maze?' someone said.

'It's possible.'

'And she set up the tiger kidnapping?'

267

'That's more problematic. Hayley and Arron said it was a man with a deep voice.'

'Maybe she had an accomplice,' Honor said. 'A lover. Or a husband.'

Dania nodded. 'I'm more inclined to go with that.'

'It has to be someone who knows the area. Maybe they came over and had a good scout around.'

'On the other hand, F may have had nothing to do with the tiger kidnapping. She might have come to Dundee to meet with Luca. And dropped her handkerchief in the Maze. Although it begs the question: what was she doing there when it was closed?'

'She could have visited on another occasion,' someone said, 'and dropped it then. Should we see if any Italians came over from Sicily in the past few months?'

'That's worth a try. I'd start with the hotels and rentals. You could search for the name Girifalco, although F's surname might be different now.'

Dania was surprised by the alacrity with which they got down to work. She left them to it, although she couldn't help feeling that it was a wasted effort. There was one piece of the puzzle, which, if she could find it, would make everything fall into place. Her problem was that she had no idea where to look.

Dania was at her computer when Marek rang. She'd just finished working through the reports from her team. There was nothing to move the case forward: no Italians had arrived from Sicily in the previous months, and there was no one by the name Girifalco in any of the hotels and rentals. Although this was the outcome she'd expected, she still felt that slump of disappointment at a negative result.

'Danka?' Marek sounded excited. 'I've got that information you were after.'

'Go on,' she urged.

'The name of Anna's daughter. It's a double-barrelled name. Franca-Chiara.'

'Great. How did you discover that?'

'We're in Trapani. There's some sort of wine festival on at the moment. Bruno got talking to the people here. It's amazing how they open up after a few glasses of Marsala.'

'That doesn't surprise me. I know what you're like after a few glasses of vodka.'

'Do you want to hear the rest, or don't you?'

'So what happened to Franca?'

'She worked in the family business for a while. Handled the money side of things, which she was remarkably good at. Interestingly, she divided her time between Trapani and Montepulciano. She left Italy in 2017. Opinion's divided as to where she went.'

'Are there any photos of her?'

'We're working on that. There's a museum here, which has loads of local history. Given that the Girifalcos were huge in Trapani, there are bound to be photos of them, including Franca.'

'And you haven't been in?' Dania said impatiently.

'It's closed for renovation. But Bruno thinks that if we slip a few euros into the curator's hand, we'll get a private, guided tour. The curator's here, actually, and we're about to get him another drink.'

'Good luck.'

As she disconnected, Dania wondered whether Marek's museum tour would throw up anything useful. She rummaged in the desk drawer for the folder, and flicked to the back. There was the photo of Anna and Aldo Girifalco with the girl whom Dania now knew was Franca-Chiara. What would she look like now? Was she in Dundee at this very moment? Could Dania have seen her, spoken to her, even? The thought was tantalising . . .

The call came in while Dania was brushing her teeth after her shower.

'It's me, Marek. I've got some news.' There was a strange note in his voice. Dania couldn't decide if it was disbelief, or despair.

'What is it?' she said quickly.

'Bruno and I are in the museum. I can't believe what I'm seeing. There are photos of her everywhere.'

'Franca-Chiara?'

'I should have suspected when I heard the name.'

'Franca?'

'No, Chiara. It's another word for Clara. Clare. The woman I'm looking at in the photo is unmistakable. She might have dark hair, but it's her, no question.'

'What are you talking about, Marek?' Dania said, trying to curb her impatience.

'Franca-Chiara is none other than Clare Conlee!'

Dania sank on to the edge of the bath, her mind reeling.

'I'll take some photos and send them on,' Marek said. 'Look, I have to go. Bruno's calling me over. I'll be in touch later.'

As Dania waited for the photos to arrive, she tried to remember her single encounter with Clare Conlee. It had been the time she'd gone to Alderwood Manor to collect the hard drive. But was she really Luca's half-sister? Could Marek be mistaken?

The first photo arrived. It was of a girl in her late teens. She was holding up a bottle of Marsala wine with the now-familiar Girifalco label. More photos landed in Dania's mailbox, one showing the older Franca-Chiara with her hair up, leaving more of her face exposed. Dania felt a rush of blood to her head. She saw immediately what Marek had seen. The woman might have dyed her hair blonde, but there was no doubt that she was Clare Conlee.

So, what could this mean? Marek had told her that Clare had married and then divorced soon after, so Conlee would likely be her married name. But Piero's exhibition had been in Dundee since the start of June. Not only that, but Luca had been on local television making an appeal on behalf of his brother. Clare must have been aware of this. And yet she'd said nothing – not even to Marek – about being these men's half-sister.

As Dania gazed at the photo, Piero's words flew into her head: *Don't walk away from me. You won't escape the consequences of your actions. Do you hear me? You won't get away with this.*

He'd been shouting in Italian, and the police had assumed it could only have been to Luca. But what if Clare had also been in the Maze? She could have seen Piero arriving, and slipped in through one of the side entrances, perhaps intending to speak to him. And of course her name hadn't appeared on the list of credit-card transactions because she wouldn't have bought a ticket. Could she be the person Piero had been railing at? If so, what were these 'actions' he'd been referring to?

There was only one way to find out.

Luca Terranova was sitting in the lounge at the Hampton, turning the coffee cup in his hands. He was still smarting from his treatment at the hands of the police. When they'd released him, he hadn't known whether to be relieved or angry. He'd gone to the station in good faith, so that he could set the record straight about what had happened in the Maze. And they'd treated him like a common criminal, accusing him of shooting Arron McGarry.

Not only that, they'd kept him in a cell overnight, the bastards. Mind you, had he been in the inspector's shoes, he'd probably have done the same. But a second shooting? That had rattled him. Especially as it meant that he was now unlikely to discover what exactly Arron had wanted to speak to him about. All he knew was that it had something to do with Piero. Thinking about his brother reminded Luca that there was still the unfinished business the two of them had started. And it was now down to him alone to bring it to completion. The problem was that with things the way they were, he'd had to go back to the beginning and try to come up with an entirely new plan.

Although they'd known Franca's name – Clare Conlee – and where she worked, Piero had failed to establish her address. He'd spent the little time he'd had before being murdered in trying to find it. He'd even attempted to follow her home, but she always managed to lose him. And when Piero had recounted how he'd seen her in the Maze, and shouted at her, Luca knew that she'd have taken even more care not to be tailed.

While he sat cradling the coffee cup, an idea came to him. There *was* one way he could proceed, although it might backfire. But he'd wasted enough time. He swallowed the remains of the coffee, and left the lounge.

CHAPTER 37

As Dania took the road north to Alderwood Manor Lodge, she mentally went through what she would do. Her original plan of challenging Clare Conlee at the East Dock Street premises had been shelved as soon as she'd formulated it. She had no evidence against her, and if the woman was guilty of anything, having the police barging in would serve only to give her the opportunity of destroying the evidence before they could find it. No, Dania intended to sneak into the Lodge and look around while Clare was at work. Colouring outside the lines was something she'd done before, having taken her cue from Marek, who did it regularly. If she found anything remotely suspicious, she would apply for a warrant, and all sins would be forgiven. Perhaps. But Jackie Ireland had always been tolerant of Dania's peccadillos. As an officer whose career had started in the military, she was fond of quoting that all's fair in love and war . . .

Dania turned off the Strathmartine Road on to the A90 and, after a short while, reached the ornamental gate on Emmock Road. She slowed to a crawl, looking out for the Lodge. To her relief, the silver Hyundai was absent. She pulled up in front of the stone building, which she only now appreciated was a mini version of the Manor. At the side was a path wide enough to accommodate a car. Given that Glenna might be out and due to return soon, and would see the Fiat, Dania thought it best to park at the back. She inched along the path and turned right into a small paved courtyard. What she was about to do would, hopefully, not take too long.

She left the car, and pulled on her gloves. The sturdy wooden door was locked but, to her surprise, the diamond-paned casement window was open. It must have slipped Clare's mind, since she would likely leave by the front door. Easily done. Dania lifted the casement stay, pushed the window wide and climbed inside.

The living-cum-dining room had been painted a creamy yellow colour, and was small but comfortably furnished. A tall bookcase stood against one wall, and newspapers littered the dining table, half concealing a laptop. Tempted though she was to fire it up, Dania decided that it would be better left to Tech.

The narrow corridor led to a kitchen, which was clean but contained little to indicate that the occupant was interested in cooking. But then, Dania's was much the same. She looked quickly through the cabinets, finding nothing of interest. Back in the corridor, she was about to climb up to the first floor when she spotted the understairs cupboard. She opened it carefully in case things tumbled out. In the gloom, she made out a vacuum cleaner, and a bowl containing dusters and bottles of cleaning fluid. And a small blue wheelie.

She pulled out the suitcase, and set it on its side. Kneeling, she unzipped it quickly. Inside lay a pair of blue overalls. What had Hayley said about her kidnapper? That he'd been wearing blue workmen's overalls . . .

Her heart thudding in her chest, Dania lifted out the clothes. Underneath was a black balaclava. As she picked it up, she felt something hard inside. It was a small cylindrical device, which she recognised immediately as a voice changer. A test would confirm that the DNA on it was Clare's. But the wheelie had another surprise for her. At the bottom were several cardboard boxes, so old that the writing was faded and almost impossible to read. Only one box had lettering that was clear – *Cartucce Glisenti*. So these must be the 9mm Glisenti cartridges, one of which had killed Arron. A GSR test of her clothes would reveal what Clare had been wearing when she shot him.

Dania sat back on her heels, imagining the scenario: Clare Conlee in the workmen's overalls, kidnapping Hayley, her voice lowered in pitch to make her sound like a man. And handing Arron a Beretta with which to kill Piero. And then killing Arron with another Beretta. So, where was it? Not in the wheelie. Perhaps Clare kept it upstairs. Dania pushed everything back into the case, zipped it up and replaced it in the cupboard.

The first floor consisted of two rooms, a bathroom and a large bedroom. Dania tried the bathroom first, but there were only toiletries in the small cupboard. She lifted the lid of the WC, and looked inside in case the firearm was taped there. It wasn't. She gazed through the round window, wondering if this was the time to leave and apply for a warrant. But she was here, so she might as well continue.

In the bedroom, she slid back the doors of the built-in wardrobe, intending to search the shelves, when she heard the sudden sound of a car engine. She peered through the window, seeing Clare, dressed casually in jeans and a red hoodie, climbing out of the Hyundai. Dania felt the tightness rise in her chest. In a second, Clare would be inside the Lodge. If she went into the living room, she couldn't fail to see the open window and the Fiat in the courtyard. For a split second, Dania considered brazening it out. But a voice inside her told her that, if this was the woman who'd been responsible for the murder of two people, she wouldn't stop at murdering a third.

Dania was out of options. Suddenly, she heard footsteps on the stairs. They were slow and measured, suggesting that Clare was coming up without first going into the living room or kitchen. That gave Dania a chance. She would hide behind the bedroom door, and as soon as the woman entered, make a dash for it. Clare strolled into the bathroom. Even better. But as Dania slipped out into the corridor, the bathroom door flew open and the woman appeared. Too late, Dania remembered that the Fiat was also visible from the round window.

Clare glared defiantly, her mouth twisting in anger. Then, slowly, she lifted the bag off her shoulder and slipped her hand inside. In that instant, Dania knew what her intentions were. She pushed Clare so violently that she lost her footing and fell backwards into the bathroom. Dania slammed the door shut, then raced down the stairs, pulled open the front door and rushed out. There was no time to make it to her car. She ran through the hedges, ducking in and out as she raced towards the Manor. Behind her, she heard running footsteps. Then they stopped, and a second later, something whistled past her head. If this was from the Beretta that had killed Arron, Clare had now fired three shots. So, how many did a Beretta magazine hold? Six? Seven? Dania couldn't remember. Where was Cosmo when she needed him?

She ran like a person demented. Ahead was Alderwood Manor, its front door firmly shut. To the right were lawns and the visitors' car park. But to the left was the opening to the Maze. Her best option was to get as far into the Maze as possible, then try to climb through the hedging. Or, better still, climb over. She rushed in just as another shot rang out. Did that mean there were four bullets left? Or only three?

Dania tried to remember which route she and Honor had taken. She passed the Minotaur, glancing up to see the axe restored to its left hand. She was unsure which turning to take next, but it hardly mattered. The main thing was not to slow down. She struggled through the Maze, and was beginning to think she might find a way out into the woodland when the hedge in front of her moved sharply, barring her way. Clare was in the control room. She could see all Dania's movements. And block them.

But maybe there was a way to outfox her. If Dania made to move one way, then changed direction faster than Clare could manipulate the hedging, she might work her way through the Maze and find an exit. She tried this with a degree of success, but Clare must have seen through the tactic because Dania suddenly found herself crashing into moving hedging. Time to try something else. When the hedge in front of her moved, she turned abruptly and ran back in the direction of the main entrance. This time, the hedging remained stationary, making her suspect that Clare had left the control room and intended to confront her as she left the Maze. But that meant she'd no longer know exactly where Dania was.

She reached the statue of William Wallace and started to climb up, intending to leap over the hedge and on to the path. As she was balancing on the edge of the shield, hoisting herself on to the Wallace's shoulder, she heard the loud cry. It was followed by the sounds of a scuffle. There was a shot, and a moment later a high-pitched scream. Then silence.

Dania jumped down and hurried through the Maze, cursing whenever she had to backtrack, and finally came upon Luca standing beside an unconscious Clare. He was bleeding profusely from his shoulder, the blood soaking the front of his white jacket. In his hand was the Minotaur's axe. He dragged his gaze to

Dania's, then tottered and leant against the hedge, breathing heavily. She knelt beside Clare. The woman's face and head were unmarked, suggesting that Luca had hit her with the flat of the blade. Dania leant over her, feeling the faint warmth of her breath. The woman was alive, but only just.

As Dania gazed at Clare lying where they'd found Arron, and at Luca gripping the axe, then at the Minotaur, again missing the axe from its left hand, she had a strange sense of déjà vu.

CHAPTER 38

'Thank you for coming to see me, Inspector,' Luca said.

He'd been at Ninewells for five days, recovering from the operation to remove the bullet from his shoulder. Painful though the wound must have been, Dania knew that it could have been worse.

She was sitting studying him. 'How are you feeling?'

'Better than I felt yesterday.'

'So, Mr Terranova, are you now prepared to disclose what you've been keeping from us?'

He held her gaze briefly, then looked away.

'Nothing to say?' she went on. 'Then let me say it for you. You and Piero hatched a plot to kill Clare Conlee, your half-sister. In Italy, she was known as Franca-Chiara. Her name before she was married was Girifalco.'

She had his attention. He drew his dark brows together, but continued to say nothing.

'Your father Riccardo died an unbelievably wealthy man, having sold his vineyards and wine business. He left his money equally to his children. To *all* his children. But neither you nor Piero got a penny. All you received were the proceeds of the sale of his Montepulciano apartment.' She paused. 'How am I doing

279

so far?' When he didn't reply, she continued, 'Here's what I think happened. After your father's death, Franca-Chiara found a way to embezzle the money. She vanished without trace. That was several years ago. But you and Piero discovered her new name – Clare Conlee – and that she was working in Dundee. Is that why Piero arranged for his exhibition to come to the V&A?'

Luca gazed at her, his expression suggesting that he was starting to rethink maintaining his silence.

'You planned to kill her,' Dania said. 'The cottage that Piero rented in the middle of nowhere, is that where you were going to do it? Ah, but what about the inheritance? You needed Clare to tell you where she'd hidden the money. And how to access it.'

Luca smoothed back his hair, frowning.

'Mr Terranova, you won't be charged with murder, since your plan failed. But there are other charges we could bring. It's in your interest to tell us the truth.'

He looked at her for a long moment. 'Franca didn't embezzle the funds after our father's death, Inspector. She began the process shortly before he died. We all knew he didn't have long. After his death, when we saw how little we'd inherited, Piero and I started to track down the money. We discovered that Franca had transferred it to her account. And then it had disappeared.'

'What do you think happened?'

'My guess is that the funds have been deposited – well laundered – in one or more banks.' He took a slow breath. 'We were going to extract the account numbers from her.'

'Extract them how?'

'By threatening to kill her. Piero had taken one of the Berettas from our father's collection. But Franca murdered him before we could carry out the plan.'

Dania hesitated. But she'd already told Glenna, and it would soon be in the papers. 'Actually, Mr Terranova, Franca didn't kill Piero. She arranged it so that someone else did.' She went through the main points of the tiger kidnapping.

'So that's what Arron McGarry wanted to tell me,' Luca said, looking dazed.

'But Franca got to him first.'

He shook his head in apparent disbelief.

'To get back to your own kidnap plan,' Dania said, 'once Franca had told you how to access your inheritance, what did you and Piero intend to do?'

'We would each take our share, and leave her the rest.'

'Really? You were just going to let her go?'

'We discovered that she'd also embezzled her parents' money. After discussing it, Piero and I decided she could keep that, too.'

Dania studied him, thinking again of the remoteness of the rented cottage, how a shot from a Beretta was unlikely to be heard, or if it was, it would be assumed that a farmer was out with his shotgun. And how easy it would be to take the body deep into woodland, and bury it somewhere so remote that by the time it was discovered – assuming it ever was – the brothers would be long gone to who-knows-where, having changed their identities several times. But there was little Dania could do. She had no proof that Luca and Piero had intended to kill Franca.

'There's one thing that puzzles me,' she said. 'What Franca did by embezzling the money was illegal. Why didn't you and Piero hire a lawyer to get it back?'

Luca shook his head in apparent disbelief. 'Inspector, have you any idea how long it takes to chase big money?' Without waiting for a reply, he added, 'It can take years, possibly decades. There have been cases where people have died of old age before getting their settlement. And others where everything goes on lawyers' fees, and they run out of money before anything is resolved. It isn't even clear where my father's money is. No, Inspector, Piero and I had neither the time to wait nor the resources to engage a lawyer, always assuming the outcome would be successful. Remember that I'm a freelancer. Sometimes work doesn't come in. As for Piero, many people think that all fashion designers are supremely wealthy, but that's not the case. I've already told you that my brother is still starting out, and needing bank loans.' Luca looked away. 'Threatening Franca was really the only course of action open to us.'

'How much was Riccardo worth on his death, Mr Terranova? Do you have a figure?'

It was several moments before he spoke. 'About one hundred million.'

Dania drew in her breath. She didn't bother asking if this was euros, pounds or dollars. 'Why do you think Franca had Piero killed?' she asked. She knew the answer, but needed Luca to confirm it.

'He saw her in the Maze. He told me afterwards that he should have kept quiet, but something inside him snapped and he shouted abuse and threatened her.'

'She must have suspected that he'd expose her. And if he did, she'd be ruined.' Dania inclined her head respectfully. 'You didn't see her there yourself, by any chance?'

Luca's expression darkened. 'If I had, I'd have . . .' He took a deep breath. 'I had to return to London. Piero said he was looking at places to rent as he'd be in Dundee for a couple of months, and he'd keep trying to find where Franca was living. She must have been keeping a low profile after seeing him in the Maze.' He paused. 'We had several phone conversations about the next steps.

He assured me that he had the matter in hand, and we needed to be patient. He said he'd be in touch as soon as he had Franca's address. A couple of days later, we texted, and that was the last time I heard from him. Eventually, I hired your brother to try and find him. I had no idea he was already dead.'

'Franca could have found Piero's rental by following him from the V&A. And then set up the tiger kidnapping.'

They gazed at one another. Dania wondered what, if anything, she could charge him with. Culpable and reckless conduct was out, since no one had actually kidnapped Franca. Attempt to commit an offence was stronger. Conspiracy to murder was more difficult, as Luca flatly refused to admit that that had been the intention. And they lacked the evidence. And the unlicensed Beretta had been found in Piero's cottage, not in Luca's room at the Hampton.

'What do you intend to do now, Mr Terranova? Continue searching for your inheritance?' Which would be a hugely larger sum than before, since Piero was now dead.

'Of course.'

'We checked Franca's phone and personal laptop,' Dania said. 'And also the one she used at *Dundee Today*. There was nothing to indicate where the money is banked. Our finance department did a thorough check. They found no lists of account numbers. Could she have hidden that information in Sicily or Montepulciano, perhaps?'

'It's possible.'

'Will you go there and look?'

Luca smiled. 'Perhaps your brother would be prepared to help me.'

Dania returned the smile. 'Actually, he knows someone in Italy, a man called Bruno, who is more than capable. I'm sure Marek could pass on his contact details.' She hesitated. 'Or you could wait for Franca to come out of her coma.'

'The doctors tell me it's unlikely to be any time soon, if it happens at all.'

After a pause, Dania got to her feet. 'I need to be going, Mr Terranova.'

'Goodbye, Inspector.' He held out his hand. 'Perhaps, before I leave Dundee, we can go to the Overgate and you can accompany me once more on the piano?' he said, with a question in his voice.

'So, how did Luca finally find Clare's address, Danka?'

Dania, Marek and Honor were sitting on the steps in the Overgate not far from Mick's mobile coffee van, and enjoying his complimentary coffees.

'I discovered that he did it by impersonating a police officer,' Dania said. 'He rang the *Dundee Today* office, saying he was from West Bell Street. They needed to speak to Clare, and could she come to the station straight away? His plan was to confront her as she left the building. But he was told by the secretary that Clare was at home that day. The man gave Luca her Alderwood Manor Lodge address.'

'Surely, impersonating a police officer is a chargeable office.'

'It is. But I'm not sure I want to do anything about it. By driving to Alderwood to find Clare, then seeing her enter the Maze and going in after her, he probably saved my life.'

'It was bad luck that she took the day off,' Honor said. 'Do you think she wanted to know where Hayley was? And was hoping to worm it out of Glenna?'

'Possibly.'

'What I can't understand is why Clare wasn't living it up somewhere. She had all that dosh.'

'I think the job at *Dundee Today* was simply her cover. I'm guessing she was lying low so she wouldn't come to the attention of her brothers. Eventually, she'd give up work, change her identity again and live in luxury somewhere. It's what I'd do.'

'Ah, but I'd find you, Danka. No question.'

'Where do you think the money is, boss?' Honor said.

'Probably in a Swiss bank,' Dania said. 'They have a long history of keeping client information secret, and not even confirming that those clients bank with them. Admittedly this is slowly changing, but it would still take years, and more money than Luca and Piero had, to get their hands on their inheritance.'

'Yep. And greed is a powerful emotion. Even if the brothers were comfortably off, I think that being cheated out of their share of a fortune might well make them think up a plan to get their hands on it. Clare must have known they'd come after her.'

Marek sipped his coffee. 'You know, she certainly fooled me with that perfect, accentless English. She must have learnt the language from her mother.'

'Don't forget also that she'd dyed her hair,' Dania said. 'It made her look less like her brothers.'

'Did I tell you that we finally found her in the Maze?' Honor said. 'That day Piero was shouting in Italian? She was wearing a pink-and-white-striped bucket hat. We discovered it in the Lodge. Otherwise we'd never have known it was her on that recording. It was just a tiny bit of footage.'

'She knew where the cameras are, so she could avoid them. Assuming she wanted to. But I think she went into the Maze for a look around, perhaps to check that everything was working properly, and it was her bad luck that Piero happened to be there at the same time. As for killing Arron, I learnt from Hayley that Clare was present when Arron confessed. She would have concluded that she had little time in which to act. She'd have seen Hayley drive past the Lodge on her way to Edinburgh and realised that Arron was on his own. Then she'd have taken her Beretta and gone to the Maze to wait for him.'

It wasn't difficult to imagine how the scene would have played out. Clare knew the base state, so waited somewhere beyond the hedging where the birds were. When Arron arrived with the ladder, her first shot missed him. He rushed away and grabbed the Minotaur's axe. She followed him, and shot him dead. She drove off just before Luca arrived.

Marek was gazing into his coffee. 'I've been thinking a lot about this. When Piero's fashion show came to the V&A, Clare didn't interview him. She sent someone else. And I was the one she asked to attend the opening reception.' He shook his head. 'She must have thought that Piero didn't know her married name and, if she stayed out of sight, she'd be okay. The fashion show would end, and he would leave eventually. But running into him at the Maze changed all that. I should have guessed that something wasn't right when she saw Luca on television. She sort of froze.'

'You really liked her, didn't you?' Dania said softly.

'I did. She was a great boss.'

He said it with such feeling that Dania decided he needed cheering up. She handed Honor her cup, and got to her feet. 'What shall I play, Marek?'

He looked at her in surprise. 'Well . . .' he said, scratching his ear.

CHAPTER 39

Glenna McGarry entered the building on East Dock Street, and made for what had once been Clare Conlee's office. She was aware that the staff, some standing, some sitting at their desks, would be wondering what was to happen to their jobs now that – if the rumour was true – Alderwood Manor Maze and the other attractions were to close. Would Glenna be leaving Dundee, as they feared? And what did that mean for *Dundee Today*? Did she intend to sell it? She was about to put their minds at rest.

'Marek, could you come into my office, please?' she said.

As he closed the door behind him, she heard the chatter start up among the staff.

'Take a seat,' she said.

He lowered himself into the chair. He was dressed smartly in a dark-blue suit, and his expression was less one of hope and more one of curiosity. Given his reputation, he would be snapped up by the other Dundee newspapers, assuming that was what he wanted. Or he could devote all his time to freelance work, at which he excelled.

Glenna clasped her hands together. 'Marek, I'd like you to run *Dundee Today*.'

The look of amazement on his face told her that this wasn't what he'd expected.

'I don't intend to make anyone redundant,' she went on. 'I want you to continue to make a success of the newspaper. You'll be given a free hand to make any changes you see fit. From time to time, you and I will meet and you can brief me on developments. Other than that, you're unlikely to see much of me. If you run the place efficiently, you'll have the time to continue with your freelance investigative work, which I would urge you to do.' She paused. 'Do you have any questions?'

'I don't think I do,' he said slowly.

'Then, do you accept?' When he hesitated, she added, 'I will, of course, give you time to think about it.'

'I don't need time, Glenna. I accept. But I do have one question. Why don't you want to run the paper yourself?'

'I intend to devote myself to looking after Hayley and her child, when he's born. Hayley needs me now more than ever. She's in a fragile condition.'

'I understand. And the Maze and the various attractions? Who will run those?'

'I've decided to close everything down.' She got to her feet, and indicated the room with a sweep of her arm. 'The office is yours, Mr Gorski. I'll leave you to inform your staff.' With a brief smile, she headed for the door.

Partway along the corridor, she heard the cheering and whooping behind her. It seemed that the staff of *Dundee Today* were just as excited at Marek's promotion as she was.

In the car park, Glenna sat in the BMW and stared straight ahead, her hands resting lightly on the wheel. The last time she'd met with Inspector Gorska, the detective had told her what Hayley hadn't. It had come as a shock to discover that her daughter-in-law had been kidnapped, and Arron forced to murder someone to have her released. Doubtless the details would come out at Clare's trial, always assuming she came out of the coma. Glenna had thought long and hard about how she would feel if Clare were to spend the rest of her life behind bars. But wouldn't she get herself a top lawyer and make a successful plea for a reduced sentence? The thought that she might one day be walking the streets as a free woman was too much for Glenna. She knew one of the doctors at Ninewells, and knew also that he was hugely indebted to her family for the charitable donation that had put him through medical school. He would know how to make it look as though Clare's death had been inevitable.

Glenna took out her phone, and called Milo Slaughter.

The staff at the V&A were taking down the mannequins, and carefully unpinning Piero's creations. Luca Terranova had asked them to pack the clothes ready for shipping to London, where he would sell them at auction. They were coming to the end, with only one or two mannequins left. Sylvia pushed back her hair, and unzipped a dove-grey chiffon gown with a long train. What she loved about it was that the colour deepened the further along the train you went. She was sorely tempted to sneak into the ladies and try it on, but it was impossible under the supervisor's steely gaze.

She had lifted the mannequin away, and was gathering up the dress when she spotted something lying underneath. It looked like a mobile. She turned it over, seeing a red case decorated with dragonflies. It was Piero's phone, no question. Those dragonflies were unmistakable. And his name was inscribed on the case. So, what was it doing here? It could only be that he'd dropped it.

Turning away from the supervisor, she switched it on, only to find that the battery was dead. She wondered if she could slip off the case and keep it for herself, but the supervisor had seen her, and was marching over. Bummer!

'Let me have that,' he said, in a voice that brooked no argument. He held out his hand.

'I think it's Piero's phone. I found it under the gown.'

He was frowning. 'We need to give this to the polis.'

'Not to his brother?'

'The man was murdered, ken. This could be part of the evidence.'

'It's lost its charge.'

'And you know this how?'

'I tried to switch it on.'

'Why?'

'To see whose it was.'

The supervisor looked at her in a way that made her feel uncomfortable. He turned the phone over. 'The name's on the case.'

'Oh, I didn't see that. Shall I take it to the police?'

'I'll do that. You need to finish up here.'

Sylvia watched him stroll out of the display area towards the front door. She was the last one there, all the others having left for their break. She picked up the grey gown and folded it quickly. Being chiffon, she was able to get it down to a surprisingly small size.

She gazed at it for a long moment. Then, after a furtive glance around, she stuffed it inside her hoodie.

Dania was in the incident room when the call came in from reception.

'Inspector, something's been handed in. I've taken the man's details. He works at the V&A.'

'What is it?'

'A mobile phone. It has the name Piero Terranova inscribed on the case.'

'I'm on my way.'

She hurried to the reception desk. The duty sergeant held up the phone. The red case was covered with dragonflies.

'They were taking the display down, and found it under one of the dresses, ma'am,' the sergeant said. 'The man who handed it in said it needs charging. Good luck with that,' he added cynically.

'Thanks.'

On her way to Tech, Dania ran into Honor. 'Piero's phone has finally turned up at the V&A,' she said.

'Don't tell me, boss. It's completely dead.'

'I seem to remember that the last time there was a signal logged was in June.'

'It happened to mine once. It'll take ages to charge.'

'I'm sure Tech can replace the battery.'

'Can I come along?' Honor licked her lips. 'Who knows what we'll find?'

A couple of minutes later, they were watching one of the techies, a young woman with a pixie haircut, replacing the battery. She switched on the mobile. It fired up without requesting a PIN.

'Can I leave you to it?' she said. 'If you have any problems, give me a shout.'

Back in the incident room, they sat at Dania's desk, huddling over the phone.

'So, what have we got, boss?'

'All the usual apps. Here's the one he uses for payments.'

'Try the text messages.'

'Ah, there are several between him and Luca.' Dania scrolled through. 'He says he's booked in at the Hampton, another one to say his exhibition is starting soon and there's loads of work setting it up. That's on June the fourth. Then one saying that he's found a suitable place to rent. And he's hiring a car.'

'We've seen these texts on Luca's phone, boss. Try going back a bit.'

'No, nothing relevant. I think anything important was said rather than sent as a message.' She paused. 'Hold on, he'd installed a voice recorder. There's only one recording. It's dated April the second.'

'This year, boss?'

'Yes. Where was Piero then? New York?'

'I guess so.'

Dania tapped the icon.

Two men were talking. One spoke with an English accent, the other sounded American.

'*Here's the cash, Rocco. You'd better count it.*' A pause. '*And you're sure the cartridges will fit the Beretta? It's an M1923.*'

'*I know my Berettas. And, yeah, the cartridges will fit the M1923. So, you a collector, or what?*'

'*Me? No. I design women's clothes.*'

'*Jeez, really? Say, you gonna be using your Beretta back in England? I hear firearms aren't allowed across the Pond. Guess you don't have a Second Amendment like we do, huh?*'

'*When can I expect to get the cartridges?*'

'*Tomorrow. Same time.*'

'*Here?*'

'*Sure. Why not? It's nice and quiet.*' A pause. '*Anyways, what are you planning on doing with the Beretta?*'

'That's my business.'

'I'm just curious, pal. I mean, we're not going to be seeing each other after tomorrow, is all.'

'How do I know you'll show up?'

'Ask around. Anyone will tell you Rocco keeps his word. And you've only given me half the money. But I'd still like to know what your plans are. I mean, if they go to shit, I'd hate to think your English cops would come looking for me.'

'Why would they?'

'Okay, just tell me what you're planning. You don't have to say who the mark is.'

A pause. 'Someone swindled me and my brother out of our inheritance. We intend to get our money back.'

'And then you're going to blow this person away?' A longer pause. 'Still not saying? Well, let me tell you something, pal. You wanna threaten someone, you can do it with an unloaded piece. You only buy cartridges if you intend to use them. See you tomorrow.'

A loud creaking, followed by footsteps, which grew fainter. Then the sound of a door closing.

Dania and Honor gazed at one another.

'That's the first time I've heard Piero's voice,' Dania said softly.

'Why do you think he made the recording?'

'No idea.'

'Insurance?'

'Seems pointless. I mean, if this Rocco had decided not to show up with the ammunition, there's not a lot Piero could have done about it. What was he thinking? Find Rocco and play him the recording, threatening to go to the police because he hadn't got his ammo?' Dania shrugged. 'Perhaps that was Piero's intention.'

'Rocco obviously delivered the goods, so why didn't Piero delete the recording? You think he simply forgot?'

'He must have.' Dania nodded at the phone. 'It's interesting what Rocco says. You only buy cartridges if you intend to use them.'

'In the US, for sure,' Honor sneered.

'But maybe Piero only wanted to *show* Clare the cartridges. Possibly even load the Beretta in front of her. That would scare me into giving up information. There's nothing on the recording to say that he and Luca actually intended to kill Clare once they'd got the bank account numbers.'

'Luca will never set the story straight, will he?' Honor shook her head. 'You know, boss,' she added wistfully, 'policing used to be so much more straightforward.'

CHAPTER 40

Chloe was sitting under a tree watching the workmen in the Maze. The guys had been at it all morning, removing the statues and smashing them, and uprooting the hedges. They threw everything into the back of a huge lorry and, as soon as it was full, drove off, returning some time later with the lorry empty, ready for the next load. Having learnt about the tunnels, Chloe knew that someone would have had to release the hedges and statues from the mechanism underneath before the men could lift them off the tracks.

'How long do you think this is going to take?' Ailsa said, lying back and staring at the sky.

'I've no idea.'

Chloe picked up a blade of grass and chewed it. The leaves were changing as summer turned to autumn, the heat of the previous weeks all but evaporated. The cool breeze rustling the branches was much more to her liking. As she gazed at the workmen, her regret that the Maze competition hadn't gone ahead turned to frustration. The good citizens of Dundee had read about what had gone on there, and a few weeks earlier, not only had Glenna McGarry cancelled the competition, she'd announced that the Maze would not be reopening.

What rankled with Chloe was that the prize money – one thousand quid – should have been theirs, and no mistake. All that work they'd put in gone to waste. And with the Maze dismantled, they'd never have another chance. She threw the stalk away, thinking of what that money could have bought them. A metal detector would have been top of the list. It meant they wouldn't have to keep pinching their dad's.

She got to her feet, and brushed the leaves off the backs of her legs. 'Well, are we giving it another go, or what?'

'I suppose so, now we're here. Do you want to do it, eh?'

Chloe pulled on the headphones, adjusting them, and picked up the metal detector. 'Where shall we try first?'

Ailsa looked around thoughtfully. 'That guy at school said those Roman coins were buried here in this woodland.' She smiled slyly. 'I reckon that means they're somewhere completely different.'

'Then let's go further over. There. Beyond those fields.'

'Okay.'

Ten minutes later, they'd reached the trees. Chloe switched on the detector, and swung the search coil rhythmically.

She hadn't gone far when she heard the squeal. It was much louder than when they'd found the buried man with the pistol. She tore off the headphones, and stared at Ailsa. Her sister's breath was coming in short, ragged bursts. Then her face softened into a smile. She lifted the spade.

'So, which one of us is doing the digging, eh?'

Elspeth let herself into Alderwood Manor Lodge. Glenna McGarry had engaged her to clear the house, and given strict instructions as to how to do it. It would take possibly one more trip but she was nearing the end, having already packed up the clothes and toiletries. The polis had been in first and removed some items, according to Mrs McGarry, but it hadn't taken them long to conduct their business.

The cardboard boxes were stacked up in each room. Today, it was the turn of the living room and kitchen. She was to pack everything carefully, binning anything that obviously didn't need to be kept, such as opened packets of food – she'd been advised that she was welcome to take for herself any food that was unopened – but items such as newspapers and flyers were to be given the boot. Elspeth had done this many times before and knew the drill. She'd come armed with a number of large bin bags for the purpose.

The kitchen would be cleared first, she decided. She worked quickly and efficiently, wrapping the crockery before stacking it in the boxes. As she wrapped and packed, she wondered why Mrs McGarry was disposing of everything, given that this lodge was always rented fully furnished. There'd been a rumour that the previous tenant had blotted her copybook in some way, which would explain why the polis had been here, but more than that she didn't know. It would likely be on the news before too long.

The packing finished, Elspeth strolled into the living room. This was a much nicer space than the cramped kitchen, with views out over the lawns and statues. She gathered up the old newspapers scattered over the dining table. There were copies of the *Courier* and the *Tele*, but most were *Dundee Today*, a paper she hadn't tried. She glanced through the one on top, then folded it into her handbag to read later. The other papers went into the bin bag. The trinkets on the sideboard and the contents of the drawers – mostly fancy cutlery – were next. Which left only the books on the shelves. She was about to light a fag when she noticed the smoke detector. Maybe not, she decided, putting the packet away.

Elspeth ambled over to the bookcase. Whoever had lived here was something of a reader. There were books of every kind, from chic lit to hardback tomes on military history. They must have come with the house, as many looked old and smelt musty. During her training, she'd been told to shake each book before packing it away, something she was tempted to ignore as time was moving on. But she'd once found a twenty-pound note inside a biography of Che Guevara. Mind you, between the pages of a crime novel she'd also found an old bacon rind used as a bookmark. The book and rind had gone straight into the bin. She'd kept the twenty-pound note . . .

She set about shaking and packing, starting at the top and working her way down. As expected, a few things fell out: bookmarks, cuttings from newspapers, scraps of paper with scribbled poems or shopping lists. Into the black bag.

Elspeth had reached the bottom shelf, which was full of books in Italian, and was shaking one called *I Promessi Sposi* when a sheet fell out. The paper was good quality. She unfolded it and scanned the contents. At the top were the letters BCGE. Beneath were several rows of long numbers, each starting with the letters CH.

She crumpled up the paper, and dropped it into the bag.

ACKNOWLEDGEMENTS

Heartfelt thanks go to my agent, Jenny Brown, and publisher, Krystyna Green, for their ongoing support, and for suggesting ways in which this novel could be improved. I am also deeply grateful to Howard Watson for doing such a magnificent job of editing. My thanks extend to PC Mark for his helpful advice on police procedure, and to Amanda Keats and the team at Little, Brown for their hard work in getting the novel to publication.